Born in Southern United States, the author has traveled extensively and has lived in Italy, Spain, and Canada. Among her works are *Happy Hour at Midnight* and *Treasures of War.* She now lives with her husband in British Columbia, Canada, collecting experiences for a new novel.

To Bill, my brother and best friend.

Diana Reed Morris

FLOWER OF THE SOUTH

From the Politically Incorrect Diaries
of Lucinda Lee Alexander

AUSTIN MACAULEY PUBLISHERS™

LONDON * CAMBRIDGE * NEW YORK * SHARJAH

Ordering Information
Quantity sales: Special discounts are available on quantity purchases by corporations, associations, and others. For details, contact the publisher at the address below.

Publisher's Cataloging-in-Publication data
Morris, Diana Reed
Flower of the South

ISBN 9781647504953 (Paperback)
ISBN 9781647504946 (Hardback)
ISBN 9781647504960 (ePub e-book)

Library of Congress Control Number: 2021908316

www.austinmacauley.com/us

First Published (2021)
Austin Macauley Publishers LLC
40 Wall Street, 33rd Floor, Suite 3302
New York, NY 10005
USA

mail-usa@austinmacauley.com
+1 (646) 5125767

It has been said that a work of fiction is one-third the author's life, one-third other people's stories, and one-third imagination. A part of me is written into this book and as I re-read the pages, I often visualize moments in my past. I am a Southerner by heritage and have ancestors who are considered "old South" as well as "hillbilly". The tapestry that is my life is the result of the intermingling of these two cultures.

Regarding the ghosts, I often imagine the words of my ancestors but am well aware that they do not truly exist as entities in life. I wish I had opportunity to hear their stories from their own lips, but I have done my best to create their personalities and points of view.

While I take responsibility for errors of content, I gladly give praise to those who graciously served as personal readers and critics. I give thanks to, Alberta Woodworth, Donya Greenwell, and Lois Anderson for their generosity of time and for their comments and support.

Special thanks are due to my brother, Bill Reed, to whom this book is dedicated.

To my husband, I give thanks for his patience, encouragement, and sense of humor.

Preface

Few of us are fortunate enough to know the purpose of our lives but I knew early on that my talent was empathy. My raison d'être was to recognize the reality of other people's experiences, to find ways to lend credence to their truths. It has been my own salvation as well, giving me identity and satisfaction.

I am old but not quite as aged as my friend Lucinda, Lucinda Lee Alexander. How we met is not as important as the fact of our acquaintanceship. She was born immediately after the end of World War II, and I about ten years later. We met as adults, both of us members of the Society of Descendants of the South, an organization the membership of which must prove genealogical relationship to a participant in the War Between the States, also referred to in our circles as the Civil War, or the War of Northern Aggression.

While I was married and had immediate family duties and obligations, Lucinda Lee was single, and when I knew her, a flower in its fullness. At first I knew her as Miss Alexander, an educated, articulate and refined lady whose opinions were always expressed as stories. It seems every woman, we were all women in our organization, had a story to tell, some had many stories, sprinkling them at our feet like flower girls at a wedding.

We were Southern women, different in our characters from California girls or New York socialites or prairie women. We knew inherently, in our blood, the power of violence and outrage, the value of the gentle word, the manners of the drawing room. We knew the rules of behavior well enough to break them occasionally without fear. We were tethered to our history, aware of the burdens and the blessings we shared. True, we were all white. We knew we carried privilege, and we had expectations of respect. We never pretended otherwise. We were not dainty, obedient, repressed, or helpless. We were socially prepared.

I admit I told stories myself, especially those related to me by my paternal grandmother. Now I fear my stories seem to meld with those of Lucinda Lee's and those of other earnest, historically-minded pale women with blue-green-gray eyes whose great-grandparents had buried silver in the yard to avoid losing it all to General Sherman.

Everyone had a version of that story, though I sincerely doubt they were all truthful testaments, in the sense of actual historical happenings. But, never mind, truth can be set on the back stoop while we ladies luncheon and protect ourselves from the sun.

Each of us in the descendants chose a flower as our personal badge. With many beautiful Southern flowers to choose from, I selected the hydrangea because we had beautiful snowballs in the front of our house when I was growing up. Lucinda Lee chose magnolia, that beautiful large blossom with large shiny leaves. She said she lived when she was a child on Magnolia Street, and there wasn't a magnolia in sight.

In order to learn the realities of the lives of others, one must gain trust. Trust was never a problem for me. Lucinda Lee recognized her words to me would be respected, that I would listen attentively and would understand the nuanced significance of the culture and times and honor behind the words themselves. I know this to be true because Lucinda Lee told me herself. She would say, "This story is just between us." I understood that to mean that she did not want the content to return to her as gossip. I kept those words to myself.

My dear husband especially liked Lucinda Lee, and as the years progressed we included her in our family occasions. In my memory are pictures of the two of them sitting comfortably in our then-paneled den, drinking Scotch whiskey and talking vigorously about all manner of subjects, but mostly politics. The two of them continue to inhabit my memory although neither is now amongst those of us who have survived the pains and joys of life.

The Descendants thrived in the Southern states and had branches in other parts of the US. Our branch met in Chicago where a sufficient number of Southerners were dispersed among the Northern Blue Coats. Because some of the ladies worked, Lucinda Lee was an attorney, two ladies were physicians, and several were connected in other ways with health care or government, we varied our meeting times, sometimes during luncheon, sometimes cocktails, occasionally dinner. We always had a program and food. Not everyone attended every meeting. In truth, none of us was poor. We were a prosperous bunch but then prosperity is relative, isn't it?

Initially I thought my jottings, my notes, were a secret. Who would suspect that I came home from the meetings and luncheons and recorded what I could remember of the various offerings? They were offerings as sure as we put envelopes in the church collection plate, these words spoken among ourselves, were offerings to me. Grist for my mill, a northerner might say. I prefer cotton for my gin, patches for my quilt. I became skilled in my note-taking and could write verbatim those words spoken hours earlier. I tried to hide my notes, but eventually found hiding them impossible as notebooks piled up in a plastic carton under our bed. Something sensual occurs for me when I place a pen on paper and watch the words spill out before me like candy in the making, hot in the boiling pot, dripping in a slow thread from the back of a spoon. Perhaps if I were learning to write today, I would experience that same emotion using Microsoft. Something about forming the letters in longhand marked the passage of time, the flow of blood through veins, the spaces between events, the crossing out of crises, the full stops of respite.

From these stored notebooks, I have managed to revive Lucinda Lee Alexander. She met her end on foreign soil having late in life married an Englishman unknown to the rest of us. Her nieces cleared her apartment and offered me a gift in value beyond any other: Lucinda Lee's diaries. She wrote as she talked; as I read I heard her voice, much like mine I suppose, each word drawn out to expand a two-syllable word to three, a three to four or even five, the flat soft "i," the slowness of it all. "Divine fried pies." Those are my favorite words of hers. "I remember those divine fried peach pies of summer." I can hear her say these words. I can taste the juicy peaches, chopped into uniform pieces, surrounded by sweet nectar, encased in pastry soft but flaky, sprinkled generously with confectioner's sugar. These she described to me, to us, as a memory of her childhood. Perhaps some lovely lady in her childhood was the cook who produced fried peach pies. Perhaps it was her maid Maggie, loyal to a fault, each to the other. I rather suspect though that it was Mrs. Watson, Sarah's mother. Unless she mentioned this detail in her diaries, we will never know, but it is enough to savor the words stored in my memory.

About those diaries, there were six, one for each decade of Lucinda Lee's life. The first, clearly the first, was covered in a fleshy pink vinyl, the lock intact, the little key tethered to the back tab by a thin, worn, threadlike ribbon.

11

The last two diaries were larger in size, the covers beautiful Florentine marbleized designs with gilt-edged paper. She probably bought these in Florence, one of her favorite cities. The three in the middle, for middle years, were each covered in dark leather, one blue, one deep red, and one black. Inside the back cover of the blue one was a sticker with the logo of the club we belonged to, the Society of the Descendants of the South.

When I received the diaries and after a marathon of pouring through her words, I began to dream about putting pen to paper. I retrieved the clear plastic box under the bed and dumped on the floor my many notebooks filled with truths, perceived truths and downright lies. Themes emerged in my mind, and I began fulfilling my dream of preserving the past. Most of what follows belongs to Lucinda Lee. Here and there I have introduced the tales of other flowers, woven in to form the daisy chain that emerged. I beg the indulgences of my friend's nieces and hope they understand the tales within are not all about their aunt. I refer particularly to the embarrassing ones.

I have occasionally presented Lucinda Lee's diary word for word as it was written. I imagine, like most diarists, she wrote after the fact, not every day but often enough to record her experiences and feelings. She did not always date her entries.

Who can say what gave her the idea to include the thoughts of her ancestors? I merely acted as a scribe when I came across words. I don't know if Lucinda Lee was playing a game with herself or not. If so, the game went on for many years. It seems to me that she really did hear the words of her forebears, although not in the schizophrenic sense. I think the ancestors were always with her as they are always with Southerners. Their lives have meaning to us. We do what we want to do, but we are aware of their points of view.

Lucinda made visits almost annually to Zona although I did not record each visit as she always praised her Aunt Lillian's homemade bread, more praise than we as readers would find interesting. As with those trips, I frequently merged several entries into one, creating a story, told by Lucinda Lee, the clay molded by my own hands.

"To be forewarned is to be forearmed," was one of Lucinda Lee's favorite adages. To the reader of the recollections: caution. Some of the stories are not pretty, behavior and attitudes the result of a culture passed over by law, justice, and simply the passage of time. No apologies are to be found here, just a recording about people who existed in a place at a given time. To those desirous of a world built on egalitarian values, free of prejudice, free of distinctions of class, race, free of division between the privileged and the unjustly trampled upon, where all parents are kind and all children are good, Lucinda Lee Alexander will prove both an advocate and a detractor. Duplicity is the nature of life as a Southerner. Even the enlightened, I count myself among them, are deeply branded by the past. I ask not for forgiveness or pity. I stand tall in pride. We were who we were. I do not ask for judgment but accept that my forebears and I may be judged, even harshly. On Lucinda Lee's behalf, I ask you to be open-minded, but I recognize you will form your own opinions. As a Southerner, I pay homage to my ancestry, to their failures and their accomplishments, and I pay homage to my friend, Lucinda Lee Alexander.

Diana Reed Morris.

Diaries One and Two
1945–1963
Birth – High School

Child of the Neighborhood: A Memoir

In moments of clarity, memories flood the mind in a series of black and white vignettes. The earliest surface as events in this or that room with persons present or in isolation. They are not dreams. They are real experiences, irreproducible and unverifiable. No one exists to refute what is mine. These memories float in unexpected order, needing no sorting as intrinsically they belong to a sequence that is a life lived or being lived.

The flood includes the moment, many moments when we, an unknown we, but undoubtedly not I alone, were together in Bill's or John's or Flo's car excitedly facing William Faulkner's house, disappointed that he wasn't sitting on the porch but exhilarated at our bravery, at our desire to encounter greatness even if, maybe because of, the risk. It is the emotion that is memorable, one of joy, of discovery, of potential.

The flood also includes memories early in the evolution of personhood, as vignettes of early life, of wanting cookies from a box in an upper kitchen cabinet. Looking up at the counter top, puzzling how to extract the goodies so highly placed out of reach until the solution occurs, feeling myself drag a chair, a heavy chair, from the dining room, watching myself climb its heights to stand in victory. The images become a series of slides projected one at a time until a flowing coherent story can be visualized.

There was a time when, as children, unformed, we were not concerned with memory. We were concerned with cartwheels, fireflies, homemade ice cream and whether there were snakes in the empty lot on the corner. Passion, sex, adultery, war, politics and prejudice did not exist. Friendship, loyalty, learning, green grass and good weather for swimming: as children we didn't think about what was important, we knew.

In the family album is a black and white photo of me taken when I was about ten or eleven years old. I am bright, well-scrubbed, wearing a starched cotton dress and saddle shoes. Schoolbooks are under my arm and I have the face of an angel, a dark-haired angel with pale eyes and a broad smile. Visible in the background are three very large houses, the homes of my three neighborhood friends: Sarah, Silva Ann, and Patty. My memories of that time are those of the little girl in the photo. Temptation exists to manipulate events and feelings to fit today's sense of self but to do so negates the reality of the earlier effort to absorb the world and all that it offered.

Our house was the smallest but we had a huge yard and a driveway that went from Magnolia Street to the alley. We were the first on the block to have a television and an air conditioning unit. My parents were the youngest, and I was the youngest girl child.

Mother and Dad were constantly challenging each other, testing the limits of patience and endurance and although a state of peace and love always resulted, it was attained through trouble and strife. To avoid the skirmishes I sought refuge in the homes of neighbors.

The house across the street and at the far end of the block belonged to Sarah's family. Her full name was Marian Sarah Watson. She had red hair which she wore in braids. She also had a piano and a quiet house because her father worked for the railroad, odd hours that meant he often slept during the day.

Sarah's mother, Cora was her first name but I never called her that, had grey hair, pulled back to the nape of her neck. She had three much older children, a daughter married to a professional baseball player (Sarah and I sometimes listened to the games on the radio), and two sons. I loved Billy who was gentle, handsome, and deaf. He lived at the School for the Deaf and came home on holidays. David was a Marine and went away to war in Korea. I thought of him as sharp, perhaps because he had a chiseled profile or perhaps it was the seam in the front of his uniform trousers. He had beautiful white teeth. Billy didn't have angles. Best of all he looked at us when we spoke. He taught Sarah and me how to spell out words in sign language. It became our secret way of communicating. P-I-A-N-O, I would spell out and Sarah would give me a piano lesson. We played hymns from the old Methodist hymnal. The most appealing were the ones with the fewest sharps and flats.

I found the sheet music for Tchaikovsky's Concerto in B-Flat Minor and spent months to perfect my finger work. Although my timing was undoubtedly hideous and I knew nothing about the pedals, I was proud of my efforts.

I always thought Sarah was very lucky. She had her own playhouse in the back yard, a badminton set, and space on the side of the house to play croquet. The little house had a front porch and screens on the windows which we particularly appreciated during mosquito season.

When Sarah's father was sleeping, we lounged about in the playhouse taking turns reading stories we wrote, always about children and their accomplishments. We had the expectation of performance, high academic grades and high praise. Even in summer when the temperatures were too high for mid-day outdoor activity, we amused ourselves with word games, board games, made-up stories. My favorite was about the little Chinese Boy Fu-Yu who cooked rice for his mother when she returned from her day toiling in the rice paddies. I think I had just read Pearl Buck's *The Good Earth* imagining my life as I would live it in China.

On very hot days Sarah's mother brought lemonade out to us. In early autumn we did homework in the little house, each of us pouring over our school assignments with the intensity and fervor of religious converts. Because the little house had no electricity, as darkness fell around six o'clock, we had to abandon this childhood retreat.

Sarah was a year older than me. Patty was two years older and Silva Ann was three years older. Patty was interested in boys and had a swing on her front porch where she entertained her friends. I was not always asked to visit, but when I dared cross the street, it was like graduating from cotton socks to silk stockings. I sat on the Hall's porch steps watching Patty flirt, watching the boys try to get her attention.

The Halls lived directly across the street from us. Their house looked large from the outside but inside it had lots of small rooms. The back yard rivalled ours, but was filled with the kennels for their hunting dogs, usually hounds that frequently disturbed the quiet summer nights and made my father angry.

Mother told me that Patty's father Bernie was kin to my father but never to mention it. The two men did not speak to each other, and Mother barely acknowledged Ruby, Patty's mother. Ruby wore generously-applied Merle Norman cosmetics and very tight dresses made of large floral-patterned fabrics. My mother was very stylish. She earmarked pages in fashion magazines and was particularly fond of the New Look. She had a small waist and wore suits with peplums. She said less is more when it comes to make-up and advised me always to under-dress for special occasions.

Silva Ann's house, the Kirby house, was the largest on the block and stood in the middle, between the Watson's and the Hall's houses. It had an iron post fence around it and a gate at center front. The house was clapboard, painted a deep red, raised with a lower lattice design, no porch but a grand front door with etched glass panels on either side. Bay windows decorated each side of the broad entry. Once inside, the house seemed split in two. To the left of the entry hall was the home of Silva Ann and her mother Lottie. To the right were the rooms devoted to Silva Ann's aunt and grandfather. Each side had a kitchen and bathroom, large parlor and bedrooms. Across the back of the house was a sleeping porch. I loved this house primarily because Aunt Faye enjoyed my company and welcomed me. We played Scrabble, tackled crossword puzzles together, and talked about my schoolwork. She helped me learn geography and state capitols.

Beyond the back garden, separating all that belonged to the Kirby property was a tall fence covered with honeysuckle. As a child, I thought the alley was an unsafe place, honeysuckle or not, a place for tramps although I kept alert and never saw one. I think maybe the larger dangers were bees and insect bites although my brother Sam said snakes could live in that alley.

Lottie made it clear that her daughter was special. In their parlor was a framed photograph of Silva Ann's father. He was killed in the Second World War. Silva Ann was the only one of us on the block who did not have a father. Lottie closely supervised Silva Ann. Maybe she felt the need to be both mother and father. She styled Silva Ann's hair in vertical curls like those worn by Scarlett O'Hara. My mother styled my hair, too, using bobby pins although there never were enough, most of them having gone to bobby pin heaven along with disappearing socks.

One never just showed up at the Kirby house; one was invited, and then graciously received by Silva Ann and her mother. I grew to believe Silva Ann would be Miss America one day. I think Silva Ann thought so too.

The Kirby's had a yardman who was instructed to keep the lawn on the west side of the house dense with tall bushes and flowering shrubs. This was the side of the house shared with the Hall's property. The Halls kept their shades drawn on the east side of their house and neither Patty nor Silva Ann dared walk on the sidewalk in front of either house. Even I realized the importance of keeping separate my friendships on the block.

While Ruby and Lottie never spoke to or of one another, my father never spoke to Bernie. I thought it was because Bernie drove a bus and my father preferred his own peppy red convertible. Bernie wore a grey uniform and my father wore suits and neckties. None of the women worked outside their homes, but none had time to socialize. Mother thought Cora Watson was old and never cared to speak to her. Mr. Watson didn't seem to like anybody. At dinner one Sunday when David was home after military training, Mr. Watson reprimanded him for coming home late the night before. Mr. Watson said he wouldn't have that kind of behavior in his house. Quite soon after, David left for Korea.

According to Patty, whispered to me in secrecy, Ruby knew that Bernie was "seeing" Silva Ann's mother, Lottie. It was puzzling to me because I didn't know what "seeing" meant. Patty knew about things that were unknown to me. She was the first on the block to get breasts, and she wore sweaters. One afternoon she climbed onto a motorcycle, wrapped her arms around the boy-driver and rode off. I avoided her house for a week because Ruby yelled so loudly at Patty that even across the street in innocence, I suffered pangs of guilt.

Patty's family did not go to church and neither did the Kirby's. Only the Watsons and my mother and I dressed up on Sunday mornings and traveled to our respective churches for Sunday school and 11:00 service. Sarah and I read Bible stories when we ran out of library books. I particularly enjoyed biographies and fantasized about life as Florence Nightingale, Amelia Earhart or Madame Curie. My limited interest in chemistry cast doubt on my winning a Nobel Prize in that field, but I thought I had a chance as a teacher or a nurse or maybe as President of the United States.

Among the girls, I was the common denominator. I was friend to each but none of them were friends. Once Silva Ann told me her mother called me a dog. "She's like a dog. She goes where they feed and pet her." This hurt my feelings, and I rarely went to Silva Ann's home again except to visit Aunt Faye, not really my aunt, but I loved her. She was old, a retired teacher, and the caregiver of her father. I remember him in a bed placed in the bay window alcove. The day Grandpa Kirby died our street was blocked by parked cars. I was considered too young to attend the funeral but sneaked over after all the guests disappeared to tell Aunt Faye how sad I felt and how worried I was that she would be lonely.

21

In my thirteenth year, we moved to a modern house on Hillside Drive, overlooking the old neighborhood. Mother and Dad continued their War between the North and the South, Mother born in the Northern State of Illinois, an intruder, almost as bad as the carpetbaggers. There was no real neighborhood on the Hill, the houses being on large plots of land separated by double garages and swimming pools.

When Sarah was 18 years old, she married an evangelist, but I don't know what happened to Patty and Silva Ann.

Claudette and Clark

In the part of the world that claims me, my family is considered "Old South," basically meaning existing since before the tyranny of King George caused us all to rise up and establish our right to live as we pleased. And, my "Old South" family did just that, lived as they pleased, that is.

In a world of ins and outs, my father's family was so "in" that rules did not apply, or so they thought. My mother's family was not "in" and didn't know which rules applied or were breakable. I don't think they even knew society had rules. They had their own.

Mother's maternal family was mountain people, choosing for generations to live in remote rocky terrain away from imposing and impinging society. Mother's mother made the mistake of leaving the mountain. She followed her heart to marry a Scots-Irish man who sold bottled water that he claimed had medicinal value. Their questionable adventure led them away from Grannie Reenie's Highland roots, to a small Northern town where they produced ten children of varying qualities, some committed, and some who should have been committed.

Mother was the first girl child, born to dream. Escape clearly at the core of her motivations, she saw herself in Veronica Lake, Jane Wyman, and Deanna Durban. World War II provided her with the opportunity to debut on a broad stage where she hoped her talents would be recognized and admired.

Her road to freedom was over a thousand miles long. She traversed by train excitedly reaching San Diego, California, a hub of shipyard war effort. She easily found work utilizing her typing and shorthand skills, and moved into a miniscule apartment shared with two teachers. She took a public bus to and from her job. The only secretary in an elementary school filled with military children, she was valued, praised, and important to a mission. She soon expanded her wardrobe and her admirers, one of whom eyed her with interest every morning as they traveled to their separate jobs. He had red hair and freckles and a patch on his jacket that read "Engineering Corps." She noticed him noticing her. She gave him the eye, a direct gaze followed by a flutter. He responded with the same smile he gave his mother, she being the only other familiar woman in his life. This ritual occurred on Monday, Tuesday, and Wednesday. On Thursday, he made his move.

When the bus reached Mother's stop that morning, he jumped to action, zipping speedily down the aisle to the opened door, took the stairs in two brisk moves and waited in position to help Mother maneuver the dangers of bus egress. This allowed him to hold her hand for several seconds, an obvious thrill to both of them, a symbol for their current desire and future coupling.

Mother was impressed by my father's courtly behavior but impatient at his lack of speed in carrying the relationship further. Taking matters into her own hands, she asked him if he liked the "pictures." She enjoyed going to the pictures on a Saturday night, she revealed. It seemed he too enjoyed the pictures or so he said and she suggested they meet at the Rialto at a given time for the latest Van Johnson-June Allison romantic comedy.

My father reserved seating in the loge section of the Rialto theatre, hoping to impress further the flirtatious girl with the dark long tresses and communicative green eyes, not to mention the shapely figure which actually both frightened and drew him to her.

Despite his lack of experience with women, he was well-versed in the gentlemanly arts. His southern accent and his attentiveness to detail, his snappy appearance – he always wore tailored suits – and his lovely red hair and freckles charmed her. She described him to her roommates as fun and handsome, and she thought he was smart. When he proposed after only a month, she accepted.

He required parental consent for marriage. He was old enough for the Engineering Corps but not of age for marriage. Although she was a year younger than he, the legal age for women was younger. A Justice of the Peace married them on Thanksgiving Day, assuring them a long-weekend honeymoon which they spent dawn to dusk, then dusk to dawn in their new apartment, one all-purpose room with an attached bathroom. They enjoyed running water, both hot and cold, and a hot-plate and new small sized-to-fit refrigerator. These life luxuries and the possibility of happy-ever-after served as foundations to the first six or seven weeks of realized bliss.

Mother spoke about their sex life as though it was associated with Paris. "Oo-la-la," she said when I asked her years later about sex. I suspect she was not virginal when she married and that perhaps my father's long-lived anger expressed in heated arguments and accusation-filled bouts of battle were somehow related to disappointment. I saw Mother in action in later years, flirting with men much younger than I. She always captured them, and then flung them away in irritation at their assumptions. I never acquired the knack, didn't really want it. If placed under hypnosis, I could probably recall the exact words of those accusations, spoken loudly and frighteningly to my young ears, but I would rather not remember.

When the war ended, they purchased a Ford automobile and drove across country to central Arkansas, to the home of my family, to Argenta, home of Alexander's since 1852. Tires were the most troublesome problem of their travels, rubber being unavailable. As I recall, my father said he had to patch the tires repeatedly because no new ones could be found for sale.

Not one to be left a passenger in life, my mother announced on Day 2 of their journey that she would like to drive. Dad pulled off the hard-top road, Mother got behind the gigantic wheel, put her foot on a pedal and promptly found herself and my father rolling rapidly down a grassy hillside. Mother described this as humorous. I never learned my father's reaction. I envision their journey like the movie "It Happened One Night," but I could be wrong.

When, after numerous days driving and nights spent in motor courts, they reached Quapaw County, Dad's territory. They drove through farmland once owned by Alexander's, some acreage still under family control, although the Depression had done much to limit family holdings. Eager to show off his attractive new bride, my father headed for Uncle Fred and Aunt Lena's General Store about ten miles out of town on the highway. Uncle Fred had been in the First World War, returning proudly from France. He was a businessman and a man of the world, although he had never been out of Quapaw County before the war, and now that he was resettled in his home, he intended never to leave the county again. Aunt Lena's people were all buried in the cemetery out by the big oak tree alongside Alexander's dating back to the years early in Arkansas's statehood.

My father introduced Mother to them. "Where are you from?" they asked.

"Up North," said my mother.

"North, like where?" they pressed.

"Northern Illinois," Mother replied. Big mistake.

Why didn't she say, "My people were mountain people, originally from the Highlands. They came across the ocean, fought in the Revolution, then traveled west in covered wagons, just like you Alexander's. Mother's people settled first in the mountains of Tennessee then in the mountains in Arkansas. My father's people left Virginia for a more northerly destination."

She could have boasted, "The first white baby born in, what is now, Tennessee was my ancestor."

No, my mother said, "My people are from Illinois and Indiana."

This doomed her. She was forevermore a Yankee on Southern land, an interloper, and whether or not my father loved her or tried to protect her, it was of no consequence. She never found her footing.

Confusion

My father has a devil inside him. That's what they taught us in Sunday school, that the devil can sit on the shoulder of the person who doesn't believe and eventually he slides inside the body and makes the person do bad things. When I look at my father at the breakfast table, he looks regular, like a regular person. He talks with me and asks about my schoolwork, what I am studying, what I am reading. He tells me he wants me to be a lawyer because they make decisions and earn a lot of money. He also tells me that tomatoes are fruit, and I know that is true. Maybe I will be a lawyer. I think most Presidents are lawyers, and I might want to be President. I am not certain. I would have to be the first woman President. I am not sure about that.

What is confusing to me is that I think Mother and Father are not my real parents. I think it is possible someone switched babies at the hospital and that I belong to another family. I am a good person. I get good grades in school, and I am nice to people. I love my brother Sam even though he has a bicycle, and I do not. He is a boy and does what boys do. If I were switched at birth, maybe he was also because I think he is my real brother.

Mother is home all the time although I cannot say what she does between 7:45 in the morning when we leave the house to walk to school and 3:30 when we get home in the afternoon. I think she cooks and cleans and wears aprons because that is what she does in the summer when we are not in school. It used to be very hot in our house during the summer. Mother wore pedal pushers and sleeveless blouses and didn't want to cook in the oven. It is not as hot since my father installed a window-unit air conditioner. It almost cools the entire house. It is easier to sleep at night, and there are fewer mosquitoes to bother us.

Mother is a great cook and we eat corn on the cob, and fried chicken, and roast beef, and filet mignon, and Cornish game hens, and spaghetti with Italian sauce, and home-made yeast rolls that make the house smell good. Mother hangs washing on the line in the back yard, and she irons sitting down. She complains that my hair is straight and gives me permanents. She is always busy. Mother goes to the library for music and checks out records with music that has no words. She does all these things when my father is out of town as he is most of the time. He is an engineer and works on projects which means he leaves our town and goes somewhere else for days at a time. I am sad to say it, but these are peaceful times. When he returns, he is loud and yells at Mother and she cries and yells back. The nights are bad. But, the days are good. I find this very confusing.

Most confusing is whether or not we are rich. My father wears shoes that he has made just for him. He has more than one black suit, a dark blue suit and jackets made of soft fabrics, white shirts that he wears with cufflinks. His favorite are jade Buddha's. Mother has a new mink stole.

He says we are rich. When we eat lobster that he brings home from a restaurant, he wonders what the poor people are eating. But, there is no money for me to take piano lessons, no money to buy a piano, and I had to wear the white formal twice to parties because we couldn't afford to buy a new dress for me. Mother helped me out with a great idea. She bought a long piece of wide pink grosgrain ribbon and made a belt that I wrapped around the waistline of the white gown. It felt like a new dress.

So, what are we? Rich or poor? Not normal, I think. Other fathers and mothers seem to like each other all the time. Mine only like each other at breakfast. They kiss each other in the mornings. I find this very confusing. What makes them so angry at night and loving on each other in the mornings? When I asked Mother about this, she says my father was spoiled by his mother. I may only be a child, but this makes no sense to me. My world is a seesaw. Are we happy? Are we sad? Are we like everyone else? Are we rich? Are we poor? Are these really my parents? It is hot outside, but cold inside. We rent our house. Don't rich people own their homes? According to my father, we're going to move to the Hillside. I think only rich and happy people live there.

My father is supposed to come home tonight. Sam has already taken off on his bicycle. I'm going to go the library, and afterward will spend the night at the Watson's. It is nicer there.

Angry Voices

At ten years of age, I know the feeling of relief that I am in Argenta in the sixth grade and not starting ninth grade in Little Rock. The *Arkansas Gazette* covers the story of those Black students trying to enter Central High School. My family does not subscribe to the *Gazette* because they say it is too liberal, but I see the front page and the pictures at the newsstand across the street from my elementary school.

We have Black people in Argenta, but it is beyond my imagination to consider our being in the same classroom. I cannot repeat the words I have heard, not even in my diary, words that are filled with anger. I hear these words everywhere there are adults.

When I was born, Mother and Dad lived in an apartment over Chronister's Grocery Store. The store is still there, next to Argenta High School. Across the street is a large open field owned by Mr. Chronister. He also owns the house next to the field, a one-story brick house where his son Tuck and Tuck's wife Lilly live. Tuck and Lilly and my parents have been friends for a little more than the length of my life.

Today is Monday. I don't know what will happen. Yesterday, I played at the piano while Mother, Dad, Tuck and Lilly sat around the kitchen table at the Chronister's house. I usually like these visits because no one bothers me while I practice playing from sheet music stored in the piano bench.

Tuck and Lilly are a twosome. No one ever speaks of Tuck without also mentioning Lilly. "Tuck and Lilly worked in the store today," or "after you were born, Tuck and Lilly came over with presents," or "Tuck and Lilly babysat while we went to the movies." Always sentences about Tuck are sentences about Lilly.

They always seemed nice, nice to my parents and to me, but now I do not want ever to return to their home.

I am afraid of Tuck.

I probably wasn't supposed to be listening to the adults talking, but I could only play the piano so loud, not loud enough to muffle Tuck's voice.

In fairness, I am not exactly sure what he meant, but he was talking about taking a gun over to Little Rock and shooting someone. I think my father was trying to convince him not to do it.

Tuck was burning with anger because even when we left and good-byes were being said, he was red with rage. I asked Mother and Dad to explain Tuck's anger to me, whether he would hurt someone. I got no reassurances.

I intend to avoid Tuck forever in the future. I witness enough anger in my own home; I do not need more from Tuck Chronister who is really only on the periphery of my life.

Mother and Dad are Democrats. Dad is very vocal about disapproval of President Eisenhower, a Republican. Secretly Mother tells me whenever she and Dad vote, she usually cancels his vote. I think perhaps she is not always a Democrat, but we do not discuss this.

At school there are thirty children in my sixth-grade classroom. Mother does not like the teacher, and the feeling is mutual. I could have predicted this clash because Mother was rude and broke the rules of social behavior. I know these rules better than Mother because Grandmother Alexander is always eager to teach me, and I am eager to learn. Mother telephoned my teacher to correct her pronunciation of a very difficult word, one I cannot spell. How did Mrs. Barton react? I think she considered Mother's behavior a direct confrontation. We Southern females do not confront directly, says Grandmother, but if someone confronts us, we smile and say something like, "I am sure you mean well, bless your heart" and if we are old enough we add, "dear" or some such endearment. I am not old enough to do that part of it. I do expect Mrs. Barton to retaliate, not against me, but against Mother, but I am not sure Mother will know that she has been retaliated against, because Mother does not know the rules.

I ask Mrs. Barton, "How do I know if I am a Democrat or a Republican?"

She does not respond immediately, then says, "You are a member of the party of your parents."

I disagree with this but do not say so. I think it probable that I will decide for myself what party I belong to. For certain, I will not choose to join a party of angry, raised, threatening voices. I wish to be ladylike, kind, and to follow the Golden Rule.

On the Surface

Clarence Monroe Harwell, II, was a victim of his name, betrayed by his parents at the onset. With no possibility of a diminutive nickname, not Jimmie, or Johnnie, or Joey, he became and was, through his earliest school years, Clarence II. His father, Clarence Monroe Harwell, I, was well-known to us children because he worked for J.C. Penny, in the shoe department. Every Easter and every August we rushed to buy shoes, and we encountered Mr. Harwell, I. He was short in stature and precise, having us stand in our anklets, to enable him to determine with accuracy this year's shoe size.

Clarence II, resembled his father. From six years old onward, he stood with military posture, his hair buzz cut, his clear blue eyes revealing his honesty and rectitude. On school tests, his scores always landed mid-range. He never quite made it beyond average. With Charles II it was the effort that mattered.

He was first a Cub Scout, then a Boy Scout and without doubt he was on course to reach the pinnacle, especially after his picture appeared on the front page of the Argenta Dispatch being given a certificate of recognition by the Governor himself. This governor was a bigot and a blowhard, eventually laughed out of office, but in that memorable photograph, he was recognizing our very own mediocre Clarence II whose humble face revealed the seriousness of the event.

I was there at the time, in the school gymnasium cum auditorium, Clarence II on stage, wearing his safety-patrol-boy regalia, a white belt and silver badge, the governor rushing in surrounded by photographers and other important people. On patrol, stationed at the nearby train tracks, Clarence II rescued a child from near-death. The child had dropped her book on the railroad tracks just as a switch engine was approaching. Clarence II left his post and ran over to shove her aside as the engine sped by. A motorist waiting at the crossing reported the event to the school principal who then contacted the school board and the rest was recorded in that photograph. The wayward child whose life was endangered was not identified, the crown being placed on the head of the hero, Clarence II. For days, weeks even, Clarence II served as hallway monitor, free to direct us as we marched to cafeteria or to the front or back playground. Our lines were straight, if not our backs, but somehow Clarence II's presence raised us all.

Two years later his father died in hospital of some rare or at least unknown disease and Clarence number 2 became Clarence number 1. At the end of the school year he and his mother moved from our town but I am sure he was a rock for her and later in life produced his own IIs who have IIIs by now.

On the other side of the railroad tracks, at about 14th Street, a block off Main, was Darktown. I never saw the homes or met any of the children who lived there. It was the era of separate but equal, but like the exaltation of Clarence II or the exhortations of the governor, what was on the surface was not the entirety of the story. Personal presentation was not the self. The mediocre boy was at core a brave hero while the smiling congratulatory gold standard was more enthralled with the gold than the standard.

Zona

July, 1956. Since Mother likes to get an early start, we have already laid out our clothes for the day, actually two days because we are going to spend the night at Aunt Lillian and Uncle Jack's cabin. We were there last year for the reunion but didn't stay the night. I'm glad to be leaving and hope Dad does not wake up to see us off.

He was a monster last night; I am unsure if Mother got any sleep. I was awake through most of it. Sam and I hid in the closet when our father started throwing dishes on the floor of the kitchen. He scares me.

I find if I press a finger against each ear and hum, I can block out some of the noise, but I cannot hold this position for long. Sam wanted to climb out the window on his side of the room but we could not get the screen unlatched. I was afraid of the drop to the ground but Sam was not.

When I couldn't wait any longer, I opened the closet door as quietly as possible and crept through the bedroom. I placed my hand on the bedroom door knob and as slowly as I possibly could, I rotated it slightly to the right, listening for the click and hoping the door wouldn't squeak as it opened. I sucked in my breath trying to make myself less heavy and braved the first step into the hallway. Only three steps to the bathroom. Vivid now were the sounds from the kitchen, Dad's gravelly, dusty sing-song, attacking, blaming, the spaces between the words as frightening as the words, Mother gasping, saying his name over and over, pleading.

I was afraid to flush the toilet but did so out of habit, and ran quickly back to the bedroom. I prayed I had attracted no attention.

Sam was waiting for me, a sentry standing guard. He nodded toward the window and on this attempt, we succeeded in opening the latch but couldn't push the screen loose. Hearing footsteps in the hall, we scrambled back into the closet, sitting on the floor behind clothes and suitcases. I grabbed Sam's arm.

The legs were Mother's as was the voice that said, "What are you doing in here? Get into your beds."

Neither of us spoke.

"Where is Dad?" I whispered.

"He's in bed."

We felt safe enough to emerge from the closet, both Sam and I, he in his cowboy pajamas, I in my second-best Baby Dolls, because I had packed the newer ones and my cotton robe in a bag for our sleepover in the mountains.

"Stay out of the closet," Mother said looking in the mirror hanging over our chest of drawers.

Sam, in his youth bed, turned to the wall. Mother leaned over to kiss him good night.

"How many more hours before we leave?" I asked her, keeping my voice as quiet as possible because I didn't want Sam to stir and I certainly didn't want my father to hear me. I wanted him to be sleeping soundly, dead to the world.

"Go to sleep," Mother said and climbed into bed with me.

"Mother, why don't you leave Dad?" I whispered.

"Because he would follow me. Besides I have no money. And, I love him."

****

We have two cars. Dad drives the red Pontiac, and Mother drives a Plymouth. Sam is very interested in cars and on the road to the mountains, we complete in a "First to see a Studebaker" game. Sam always wins, but I always win in the "Spot an out-of-state license plate" game. There aren't very many of these allowing us to keep the list of the ones we have seen in our heads.

Sam and I know the way to Zona as we have been going to the reunion every summer since we were quite small. Mother is a watchful driver and we are attentive passengers. We all notice when a familiar gas station or cafe is now closed or when the road detours due to new construction. We know the way and we know the little spot on the mountain road, Zona it says on the sign above the post office. The post office is always on the left side of the road across from the general store-cafe with the two gas pumps out front. Before we get to Zona we have to complete the flat part of the trip, Argenta to Clayville. The road is hardtop all the way, mostly two-way. Mother is good at passing, and Sam and I help her make sure that no cars are in the way. We smile and wave at drivers we pass. We do it the same way every year.

At Clayville we turn right at the little store where I lost my pink necklace. We think it just fell off when I leaned over to get a grape Nehi out of the cooler. When we turn right, the road begins immediately to climb into the Ozarks. It is early enough in the day for this side of the mountain to be in the shade. In summer the colors are dull gray and brown. The trees, the land, even the few people we see are parched and droop downward. On this lower level there are no fir trees. We see those later up top.

On our right, the mountain slopes upward, on our left, increasingly as we wind upward, stone barriers, perhaps three feet by two feet, protect us from sure death. These were built so long ago that many are deteriorated at the edges. The worst part of the journey is ahead, the part that always scares Mother. It bears the name "hairpin curve" and connects two sections of mountain. Someone placed a huge sign on the side of the road immediately before entering the curve.

"Which will it be, Heaven or Hell?"

The sign always freaks us out, and when we were younger, Sam and I hid on the floor of the back seat.

"Get out of there. Sit and be quiet." We were always admonished but early on I concluded Mother was scared. I think she didn't want us to add to her problems.

Today, Sam sits next to her in the front, and I sit in the back, biting my lip but saying nothing. Sam probably chose the front seat because the long drop down, down to tree tops and gray boulders, is on the driver's side. Both terrified and thrilled, I am sitting directly behind Mother, and, holding my breath, I look out the window. We seem to be inches from the edge and the distance down is great. I hope no vehicle approaches us. If it does, one of us has to back up. Please, no tractors. A horse would be okay, but please, no trucks.

"It wasn't that bad," says Mother.

"I think it was terrifying. We could have fallen over the edge. We could have somersaulted and ended up on those rocks."

"Every year you kids get scared and every year I get us through. You are being very silly."

As soon as she can, she pulls the car to the side of the road. I notice a slight tremor as she wipes first her left hand, then her right hand on a Kleenex. She reaches into her pocketbook for a powder compact and daubs a puff at her shiny nose. Lastly, she replaces her lipstick. I want to climb out of the car but am concerned about ticks. Sam throws me a piece of chocolate, has one himself. I eat mine, looking out the window on Sam's side. I think I see movement in the forest, probably squirrels, deer, or maybe wild pigs. This is the home of the Razorback, a majestic hog, but not one I would like us to encounter.

"How much longer?" I ask, but I know. Forty-five minutes if the road is good.

"Forty-five minutes if the road is still good," Mother says. "Do you remember the time we stopped at the general store to get directions to Low Glen?"

This is a familiar story. We tell it each time we go to the reunion. Of course we remember. I don't know which I remember seeing first, the gas pumps or G.W. We tell it again.

****

As we approach Zona, the hardtop road flattens. On the right is our first destination, always exciting because it reminds Sam and me of pioneer days. Sam is definitely a fan of Daniel Boone and Davy Crockett and imagines himself as an explorer, a hunter, a man who lives off the land trailing wild animals and eating over an open fire. I have no such imaginings but find the general store quaint, interesting, although I deplore the dust outside.

The sign says "Gas" and it is correct. Pulling off the road onto the forecourt covers the car in fine, red dust. I never seem to roll the window up in time to prevent this spray in my face. Two pumps provide us with an option, ESSO regular or ESSO diesel. I pay no attention because I want to get inside the store. Two large crates serve as steps up to the screen door. The building is a simple rectangle, mostly made of wood but sheets of corrugated tin are bent over the corners. We do not have buildings like this in Argenta. Beyond that screen door are treasures, candies in glass cases, pickles in barrels, cold drinks in coolers and best of all, a collection of stuffed animals – always a challenge to identify – mounted and hanging across the back wall.

I wander around feeling the warm smile of the woman behind the cash register. She has a much-lined face and thin lips. She has been in the sun too often without the protection of suntan lotion. Grandmother Alexander says dark skin is a sign of the lower classes who have to work in the fields. Grandmother's skin is alabaster, because she never picked cotton. This lady behind the cash register has not picked cotton either because they don't grow it here on top of the mountains. Maybe she has picked beans, or tomatoes, or pulled a mule-plow. I'm not going to ask her because she seems nice and I don't want to insult her or pry.

I put a quarter on the counter and buy several pieces of orange jellies. These always stick to the teeth and last a long time. I would prefer chocolate but as hot as it is outdoors, even on top of the mountain, chocolate would melt. I want to leave room in my stomach for the food at the reunion. It is the best food in the world, especially Aunt Lillian's homemade bread. I cross my fingers and hope she has made bread again this year.

I leave Sam in the store and walk out the screen door, listening to it slam behind me. Screen doors slamming make a particular recognizable noise, one that I like, but slamming is only allowed one time going in and one time going out.

Mother is standing by the ESSO regular pump, under the canopy, talking to a thin man with no front teeth. He couldn't eat orange jellies. He has very pale blue eyes directed at Mother. She is actually happy, smiling and looking back at this man with an intensity I have not seen before in her. I am surprised, more curious than stunned. The man has red hair with a few wisps of yellow gray. He holds the gas pump with one hand, the other seems limp at his side.

When he has finished filling the tank, he washes the windscreen which desperately needs it. The procedure takes a few minutes as water and dust combine for a muddy mixture that requires two or three applications and swipes.

Toothless man, I hate calling him that even in retrospect, as it is disrespectful, the man-with-the-red-hair and Mother enter the store together, passing me, still talking and paying no heed to my presence. I walk to the car, enjoy an orange jelly, am joined a few minutes later by Sam and Mother.

"That was your cousin," Mother said.

I am in shock because he does not look like our Alexander cousins.

"He is my second cousin, your third cousin."

This takes a minute to absorb. Sam is looking out the window paying no attention to the conversation. He is no help in figuring this out.

"We're related to Uncle Jack. He's your Mother's brother."

"Lucinda Lee, this is pretty complicated. Do you really want to know?"

"Try," I persist. No wonder Mother gets annoyed with me. Sometimes I should just leave well enough alone.

"Uncle Jack and my mother Irene – that's your Grandmother Reenie – are Tilsons, brother and sister. They married a McKay brother and sister. G.W. is a McKay. Just let it go at that."

It is obvious that I am causing a problem by asking so many questions but I cannot help myself, "What does G.W. stand for?"

"George Washington. George Washington McKay. He was a soldier in the Second World War."

This was another shocking fact. Zona seemed so far off the track, away from civilization. It was a revelation that the Army could find him, all this far from the real world as I know it.

"You mean men from here fought in the war?"

"Of course." Sitting in the back seat, I could feel Mother's scowl of disapproval. "Ask Uncle Jack about the war and how many men fought. He is older than my mother. She was born in 1901. Yes, Uncle Jack would have fought in World War 1."

"As did Dad's Uncle Fred." I added this to show off. "What's wrong with G.W.?"

"The war."

"Did he give you directions to Low Glen?"

Sam perked up. Directions were usually his business.

"He said to turn left past the post office, before the garage."

Mother starts the car, pulls around the pump onto the main, the only, road, and stops after a few yards. There is no traffic, no one to prevent us stopping in the roadway. We see the post office on the left and the garage, both hard to miss. In between is a dirt road, the ruts and rocks visible even from a distance.

"That's it?" I am incredulous. Sam's eyes are wide, but his mouth is shut.

"G.W. says the school bus makes it down the road, so can we." She turns left, and we bobble up and down all the way to Aunt Lillian's and Uncle Jack's.

I think of the little engine that could. We are the little car that could.

Mother tells Dad this story when we return home. He does not laugh.

Joy of Christmas

December 20, 1960. The Christmas tree is trimmed with colorful balls and tinsel. On the floor adjacent to the tree is a multicolored disc that rotates and makes the tree appear red or green or blue. When I stand out on the driveway and Mother opens the drapes, at night the tree looks very grand.

We decided to open presents on Christmas Eve and have placed candles on the sideboard. The room will look special by candlelight.

We will go to Grandmother Alexander's house for Christmas Day dinner as is our tradition. The women bring food and finish the cooking in Grandmother's kitchen. At fifteen years of age, I am considered a child and am expected to stay out of the way. Besides, I have no clue how to cook. I am never allowed in the kitchen at home. Mother always says I get in her way, and I do.

Mother is preparing a Jello-carrot salad and ambrosia. Dad is expected to prepare the cornbread. It is his usual job. He makes it two days before Christmas, dries it out on the countertop, crumbles it and takes it to Granny for use in making sage and cornbread dressing.

I love Christmas, but doesn't everyone? I love the carols, the Christmas story at church, the decorations, the lights. Maybe tonight we will drive around our neighborhood, perhaps even downtown, to see how the homes and streets are lit up. It is always festive and makes me feel warmth and happiness.

I earn money now as a tutor and babysitting. Several families call on me as my reputation has spread in the neighborhood. I babysit for two children belonging to a physician and his wife, two children, one a baby, for a pharmacist (not our pharmacist, but the doctor's wife recommended me), three children of our associate pastor. I adore all the children and look forward to the weekends. Tutoring is a new activity for me. I have two students, one a young boy I am helping with math and history, another who is younger and needs encouragement with reading.

When I am asked what I want to be when I grow up, I say "a lawyer" because Dad thinks that is best. I do love these children, and I love tutoring. Perhaps I will be a teacher.

The money I earn is mine. Mother says I am to buy my clothing from now on. I have bought clothes, but saved enough to buy Christmas presents, a few. I bought individual crystal fruit bowls for Mother, a tie for Dad, and for Sam, I got something special, a horn that he can attach to his bicycle. Everything is wrapped and under the tree.

December 24, 1960. Once again the Christmas ghost visited our house. Mother, Sam, and I waited until nine o'clock Christmas Eve for Dad to arrive home. We were very tense as the hours passed because we knew what was coming, literally and figuratively. Mother closed the drapes at ten o'clock, and we went to our separate bedrooms to try to sleep. I was successful but during the night I was awakened by loud sounds in the house. I knew those sounds. It was my father, throwing things, stumbling over the presents. I only hoped he wouldn't crush the gift I had bought and wrapped for Sam. Why did I buy glass for Mother?

December 25, 1960. Dear Diary, I write this at night because the day that was supposed to be a celebration didn't exactly turn out to be pleasant.

Dad wasn't awake early enough for us to open presents with breakfast. Sam and I ate in silence, dressed in our jammies and robes. We hoped to be able to open presents before we had to leave for Grandmother Alexander's house at noon. Christmas dinner is always served at two o'clock.

Mother was awake before Sam and me. She had already rearranged the living room. The color rotating disc was gone and the candles were not on the sideboard, but everything else looked generally like it had been the night before. I peered into the refrigerator, checking to see if Dad had thrown out either the Jello salad or the ambrosia. That's the kind of thing he usually did, but luck was with us this time.

He finally woke up around eleven, dressed and joined us in the kitchen. By this time, Sam and I were dressed as well in our Sunday clothes, prepared to leave for Grandmother's house as soon as Dad finished his breakfast. Mother had escaped to ready herself. I thought we would just forget about the presents until another time.

"Merry Christmas! Has Santa been here?" His eyes were red but he had completed his usual toilette and smelled like a million dollars. I think his aftershave is the same as the one used by the newly-elected president, John F. Kennedy, who is Catholic. There was no discussion about him at the Christmas dinner table. Just after the new President was elected, Dad said the President's father was a whisky drummer, something Dad should know about.

As if there had been no disappointment the previous night, we four organized ourselves in the living room, Dad handing out presents one at a time, each person opening a gift, expressing maximum surprise and pleasure.

This is our way. No one ever admits to disappointment, anger, or fear. Dad is the only one who gets to express these negative emotions, and then they are out of control. Mother says he has "fits."

After the opening of the gifts, we loaded the car with a few more presents and Mother's salad and ambrosia. We drove through Argenta out onto the pike where Grandmother lives. Her house is red brick, set back from the road. Already there were three cars parked on the driveway and one pulled into the front yard. Grandmother does not like that, but I guess one of the men did it, and she said nothing. Everything was beautiful at Grandmother Alexander's house. We were all well-mannered in her presence.

Soft Kisses

Summer, 1962. The contrast between last night and today is enormous. The blow-up at home, another fit, Mother would call it, made leaving today for the mountain reunion all the sweeter. My thoughts toward my father are unkind but hardly match in ugliness the words he spoke last night. He directs his anger toward Mother but Sam and I are in the house. We hear everything. I cannot repeat, even in writing in my diary, the horrible words and phrases he uses.

When finally he goes to bed, he snores heavily and loudly, but it is a relief to Sam and me. I fall asleep eager for the dawn because we will get in the car, Mother, Sam, and I and drive to Zona. Is it possible to love a place because it is your escape destination? It represents for me kindness and calm. Dangers exist on the mountain, but for me it is a refuge from the dangers in Argenta.

We drive past the filling station, turn off the main road past the post office and the Wardlaw garage onto the rutted road to Low Glen. We are slightly late today because we stopped along the way for a Continental breakfast which is Mother's term for coffee and a sweet roll. We didn't eat much because the reunion is all about food and conversation, a great deal of food and actually a great deal of conversation.

Parking the car is difficult because the road is narrow, wide enough for the mules or one car, and has deep gullies on both sides that serve to drain water during heavy rains. Uncle Jack tells us to park past the pavilion, just a matter of driving uphill a few yards. It is okay to park there in the road because no traffic will be coming down. Everyone who lives up on that road is already at the reunion.

Uncle Jack follows us on foot. He helps Mother out of the car, kisses us all, and carries a food basket that we have brought with us. He makes all these motions with little effort although I hear creaks in his knees and notice for the first time that the joints in his fingers are swollen. This is a man of the land. I imagine those hands holding onto the plow. I have seen him in the fields and know his work is laborious and must be hard on the body.

I do not notice the crowd in the pavilion because the Wardlaw boys are walking toward us. Sam rushes ahead to join them. The Wardlaws have been on the mountain almost as long as my family. Wardlaw Settlement was named for their great-grandfather. They were strict Evangelical Believers but not today. If they are anything, they are Presbyterian like everyone else in this part of the mountain.

The oldest of the three boys is Stoke who is about three years older than me. That would make him about twenty years old. Chance Wardlaw, the really cute one, is my age, and Cyril is two years younger. They are great fellows, a little wild but always fun.

R.E.L. Wardlaw is their father. He opened up the garage in 1921 according to the metal sign over the door. Someone recently tacked to the side of the door a post with the words "and Sons" burned into the wood. R.E.L. doesn't always attend the reunion. The Wardlaws are not direct kin, unless we are connected somewhere back in time.

Aunt Lillian usually tells the Wardlaws when Sam and I are coming and the boys show up to see us. When we were younger, they showed up to see Sam. I don't remember ever spending much time with them. I don't know what they did when they were together, but the Wardlaw boys had shotguns and enthralled my brother with their expertise looking for animals and the like. I was always afraid of snakes and creepy crawly things and stayed with the women and old people in the pavilion.

This year the ladies have been cooking for days and the trestle table is groaning with food. Mother has brought a cake. When Dad wasn't home last night by eight o'clock, she assumed he would come home in a fit, and she hid the cake. I don't know where. Otherwise it might have ended up on the kitchen wall.

Aunt Lillian apologizes to me because she has forgotten to bring her homemade bread. Overhearing her, Stoke Wardlaw volunteered to walk the mile and a half to her house. "I'll get it for you, Ms. Lillian. It wouldn't be a reunion without your bread. Maybe Lucinda Lee would like to walk with me." No doubt his words were meant to be an invitation, but what I heard was "Lucinda Lee will walk with me." I was willing to accept the order.

"Off with you," Aunt Lillian said, "but don't dally."

I study Stoke as we walked. His long hair blazes red in the strong summer sun. He parts it on the side and a stray piece flops over his right eye. His features are pleasing, but he is not exactly handsome. I think his shoulders are round because he is tall and has to lean forward to converse with those of us who are shorter.

I don't know how I appear to Stoke. My tanned legs are visible below the hem of the beige Bermuda shorts. Likewise my arms and face are tanned, a series of freckles that merge in the summer. My hair is deep auburn in color, my eyes are pale grey or green depending on the color of my clothes or the light. Despite the hours spent in classrooms, I am fairly muscular, probably from swimming. My greatest asset and my most embarrassing feature is my full chest. I would like smaller breasts.

The sky is a shade of periwinkle, pale, heart-breaking in its beauty, contrasting with the salmon pink color of the dusty roadway. Stoke tells me the names of the plants alongside the road, mostly weeds, dandelions and the like. Fence comprised of wire attached to vertical posts runs the length of the fields. Where the fields have not been cleared, rocks scattered about make the landscape look rugged and difficult to farm, but the occasional cow seems happy enough.

On our left the land belongs to Uncle Jack. On the right are the tumbled down remains of my great-grandmother's house, where Uncle Jack and my mother's mother were raised. G.W. owns the property now.

Stoke and I are in the moment. We do not talk about the past. We are more involved in today. We talk about university. He brags about the University of Arkansas; tells me he is particularly interested in automotive science. He is home for the summer but returns in a few weeks to classes and campus life. He does not mention a girlfriend.

I tell him I am entering senior year in high school and will apply to several colleges. My first choice is Emory University in Atlanta. "My father wants me to study law," I tell him. "Law appeals to me as well."

"You'll be good. You're smart," he replies. "Maybe you can get my brothers out of jail someday."

"No way, I'm going to study corporate law. You don't think your brothers will get into trouble, do you? I thought you boys were 'by the book'."

"Wardlaws have never been 'by the book'."

"I thought your great-granddaddy was a big-time preacher."

"Oh that. That went by the wayside during the Depression and Prohibition."

Our conversation ends as we reach Aunt Lillian's house. No one locks doors on the mountain. We just walk through the side screen door, near the well and breathe in the amorous odor of the bread.

"I would really like to kiss you right now," Stoke says.

"That would be okay with me," I reply lowering my head, adopting the demure attitude I want to project. I do not want Stoke to think I am easy, but I am dying for the kiss.

I think Stoke is more experienced than I probably due to his being at university. His being more experienced is fitting according to the teen magazines I read. A girl wants a boy who knows what he is doing.

I am determined that kissing is as far as I will go, and keep to plan, with some effort.

We walk back to the pavilion, remembering the bread. I am slightly worried everyone will look at us and know we have been kissing. The disappointing truth is that no one even noticed we were gone.

I join the women at the trestle table and fuss with arranging napkins and plates already in place. Aunt Lillian slices the bread, and goes about the business of shooing flies away.

Only two people at this gathering know the real truth. I wonder when I will see Stoke again.

Houses and Water

Old people like Uncle Jack and Aunt Lillian take careful listening to if you want to understand what they are saying. Young people on the mountain are easy enough to talk with but the old people require time and patience and figuring out.

Their verbs are all wrong. They don't use the correct verbs for plural subjects. They drop the sound of the "g" at the end of "ing."

I am Southern and have read that Northerners think we talk slowly and sound funny. Uncle Jack does not sound like Sam or me, but he is Southern too. I'm thinking there are different Southern dialects or maybe different sounds that fall into the larger category of "Southern" speech. Argenta is near Memphis, just across the river from Mississippi. I think my accent is more like Mississippi.

Without hard study I would say Uncle Jack (and Aunt Lillian and all the rest of the old people) talk even slower than I do. To me the sound is very musical. Back in the city, people would say they sound like hillbillies, because they are, but they are my hillbillies, and are far from ignorant like the stereotype.

I am thinking about this because after the reunion, Mother said we would spend the night on the mountain. To my knowledge we had not planned to stay but Mother produced a small suitcase from the trunk of the car. I guess she had been planning on it before we left home, probably because Dad had acted so badly. When he is mean, we all want to leave home.

Mother did not pack all my necessities, no hair curlers, no robe or gown. I will have to make do. I do have clean undies and an outfit for tomorrow. Mother says I'll manage.

****

I am fascinated by Aunt Lillian's house. In the city we do not have houses like hers. We would call it a log cabin. Out of respect for her, I will call it a house. Probably Uncle Jack split the logs and built it himself.

The simplicity of it allows me to use my algebra skills. The house is basically a square with four quadrants: living room, kitchen, two bedrooms. A long-covered porch crosses the front of the house and a screened door off the kitchen opens out to the well and a path to the privy. The triangular structure that comprises the roof gives the house a loft, accessible by a ladder.

Mother and I will sleep on cots in the front bedroom. Sam is delighted to sleep in the loft.

After nibbling on reunion leftovers, Mother and I wash up at the kitchen sink using the hand pump to deliver water to a basin, cold water. Aunt Lillian is proud of the pump, telling us it saves her from having to walk outside to the well when she has to do laundry. For our bathing, she boils water in a kettle to take the sting out of the cold. Sam is already up in the loft. He will take a shower in the morning, outside at the well. That sounds even colder to me, but Sam makes his own decisions.

Although we were sweaty and hot all afternoon, as the sun goes down we feel the cool of the mountain. The quiet is startling. I hear only a few strange sounds never heard in the city. I sleep well under one of Aunt Lillian's quilts.

****

Uncle Jack and Aunt Lillian put us to shame for our city ways. We apparently waste away most of the morning. I have no idea what time I awoke, but when I went into the kitchen, Aunt Lillian had already made two loaves of bread, both sitting proudly on the kitchen table. Uncle Jack, having taken the day off yesterday for the reunion, is already out in the field. Aunt Lillian says she has already fed the chickens and milked the cow. This pleases me as I am terrified of chickens and cannot imagine doing whatever is required of a milkmaid. Bless Aunt Lillian.

Mother wants to do two things before we leave the mountain. She wants to cross the road and explore the run-down remains of the Tilson house, the house of her grandparents, where her mother and Uncle Jack were raised. Even though I walked the road yesterday, I do not recall seeing this house, but Mother says it is a distance back from the road. It is good that I am wearing walking shoes, but I only have Bermuda shorts and do not want to scratch my legs. Aunt Lillian says she will loan me a pair of long pants.

Mother also wants to visit G.W. who has especially invited us. He owns the old Tilson place and all the land on that side of the road, from Uncle Jack's house to the pavilion. He may also own the springs but this is unclear. We are to meet him at the pavilion.

Aunt Lillian reaches into a cupboard and produces a light blue tinted bottle labelled Zona Spring Water, Fresh, Clean, Healthy. She says that G.W. is having success bottling and selling Low Glen spring water to stores in the valley.

To Mother she says, "Your daddy sold bottled water down in Clayville before you were born. He said it was from the springs, but it weren't. He just filled bottles with Clayville city water, right from a tap. I guess no one knew the difference."

I guess Mother's father was a con artist.

Aunt Lillian informs us that G.W. is doing the business "honest."

She says, "Go see for yourself. He'll make somethin' out of it."

****

Mother and I, afraid of snakes, ticks, mosquitoes, and practically all other wild beasties, walk slowly carrying large sticks. Fearless Sam bounds ahead. The path to the old Tilson place is somewhat cleared, at least we can detect it below our feet as we trample onward pushing blackberry bushes and brambles aside.

Mother yells at Sam to be careful. "The well is somewhere in front of the house. Don't fall in. We couldn't get you out." She is serious, but Sam is not. He is excited and impervious to danger. He makes a mission of searching for the well but never finds it. This keeps him busy while Mother and I climb into what remains of the house. Two or three wooden steps at the door are strong enough to hold our weight but we do not trust the stairs up to the second floor. It was a big house.

Surprisingly Mother finds a framed picture on the wall. It is a portrait of a blond child adorned with an oversized pink bow in her hair. The hand-written name "Mattie" is visible through the dirty glass that remains intact. How did this picture survive? Mother carefully removes it from the nail that has held it in place for over fifty years, holds it to her breast and says, "Mattie was my grandmother."

I feel a deep connection to this house, maybe because my mother's attitude is reverential. Isn't it funny how the feeling of life lingers even in a run-down shambles of an old log house?

****

We meet G.W. at the pavilion just before midday. I am still trying to work out my relation to him. Mother said third cousin.

Her mood is good. Mine is souring. I don't mind seeing the pavilion again, but I am not sure about the water bottling operation. Sam is eager to learn about G.W.'s business. He wants to know if G.W. uses a generator, whether he bottles here or somewhere else, how does he accumulate the water, does he divert the stream? Sam is very chatty. I am sullen.

Mother tells me, "Stay in the car if you want. Read a book."

I ask her how long before we leave. She doesn't know. I don't want to leave the mountain. Nothing feels right for me at the moment. I don't want to go back to Dad's fits. I have to return to school if I want to go to Emory University. Stoke is here in Zona, but not for long. He'll be going to Fayetteville in a couple of weeks. I can't plan my life around him. I'm only sixteen, seventeen this year. Life sucks.

I read in the car while Mother and Sam talk with G.W. They are very animated and even at a distance I hear them laughing. I can't stand not knowing what they are talking about.

When I approach them in the pavilion, they are leaning over the railing and talking about the water. The talking doesn't stop for me, but G.W. smiles in my direction allowing me to see that he now has teeth. He has a narrow face, and his hair is cut like he was still in the army. His lips are thin but he has deep laugh lines at the corners of his mouth. His voice is recognizable, the same slow broad sound of all my people on the mountain. I feel his warmth.

"Next time you come up here, you'll find things changed. Not the pavilion. It will always be here. I have plans for Zona Water. How does this sound: Tastes like the Highlands, Made in the Ozarks, USA?"

Mother loves it. She is flirting!

We do not visit G.W.'s house. He says he has a small place where he does the bottling in the back. Sam asks him about McKay Mash. I've never heard of it, but he and Sam have a real laugh over it. I guess it is a "guy thing."

I don't want to stay, but I don't want to leave.

History

When Grandmother Alexander decided it was time for me to learn about family history, there was no denying her. She meant, of course, the Alexander side of the family. I think there may be something funny about her side of the family, the Clarks and the McClellans. I dare not ask her. For the record, Granny's name is Pauline Clark Alexander. Her father was a Clark and her mother was a McClellan. I think if I dig deeply enough – which I will not – I will find that somewhere in her McClellan past is a Yankee or a Yankee sympathizer. We will not speak of it.

Her efforts to acquire my interest didn't turn out to be difficult, not least because I have already become a provisional member of the Descendants under Granny's membership number. My full investiture will occur when I reach the adult age of twenty-one.

I attended several meetings in Argenta along with Grandmother, enjoying topics like "American Indians in the War of Northern Aggression," "The Plantation Mistress as Physician," and "House Servants prior to 1860." I found all these topics fascinating but was annoyed that I was excused from school for the two hours' monthly meeting. Although I was given this permission due to my high class standing, it was always an effort to catch up with the material I missed. Not that big an effort, if I am honest with myself, but I do enjoy school classes as much as I enjoy these monthly outings with Grandmother.

It is a pain in the neck though that on Descendants' days, I have to change clothes in Granny's car. My school clothes are not "nice" enough for the meeting. I have it figured out. I wear a knife-pleated light wool glen plaid skirt to school with a twin-set and my saddle shoes. In the car, I slip off the shoes and change to my Sunday heels. I have to wear awful footies because there is no way I can put on a garter belt and hosiery in the car. I replace the cardigan with the glen plaid boxy suit jacket. Woe is me, though, because I have to reverse this process in the car after the meeting. Granny will not hear any complaints from me. She says it is not easy to be a woman.

****

The worry about university is over. I applied to three schools and was accepted by all. The choice was painful, but I selected Emory University in Atlanta. A girl who graduated last year from my high school chose Emory and she's given me encouragement, says campus life is great, that I will love the dorms and my classmates. She promises parties, boys and friends. I am looking forward to leaving home. Atlanta is far away from Argenta. I am sorry to be leaving Grandmother Alexander and Sam, but we have had many conversations about my future, and everyone agrees I should go, except Mother, who says I would be better off nearer home. I don't know why she would say that. I am eager to leave, ready to leave as soon as this term and summer are over.

I spend as much of my time as possible with Sam. Once he finishes high school, he will follow me, maybe not to the same university but definitely out of state. Sam apologizes for the obstacles parents put in my way and says he admires me. He says I am his role model. I am a female Moses parting the Red Sea to enable both of us to escape tyranny.

"Tyranny" is an important concept in my American history class. I owe Mr. Bragg credit for use of this word as we learn in greater depth than earlier years about the tyranny of King George III. I ache to travel to England, to see for myself the roots of this tyranny. For now books and lectures will have to suffice.

Mr. Bragg also is responsible for guiding us through the War Between the States. His stories are similar to those told by Grandmother Alexander. The Braggs fought in Mississippi and at Shiloh while my Alexanders fought from Arkansas, Alabama, South Carolina, and Virginia. I think my great-grandfather Samuel Jefferson Alexander fought in Mississippi so maybe they all knew each other.

Mr. Bragg teaches us about secession, political compromises, Northern industrialization, and Southern economics. The war was fought for the rights of states to determine their own destinies and for economic reasons. Our entire economic system was crushed by the Northern invaders. After the war our civilization, our genteel culture was demolished by carpetbaggers and Northern businessmen who wanted our property. According to Mr. Bragg, we won the war primarily because our Southern boys and men were honorable and Christian. They knew how to shoot straight and they fought courageously and skillfully, protecting our land.

About our land, on Sunday afternoons, after Mother, Sam, and I return from church, after Sunday dinner and clean-up, Dad says he wants to take us out for a drive. We know this is required. He is sober on Sunday afternoons and is usually in good humor. The Sunday drive route takes us through the industrial part of Argenta with Dad carefully pointing out any new business development. Next is the turn-off to the Pike, past Grandmother Alexander's house, twenty miles on the old highway to the Alexander farm, or, what was the Alexander farm until the end of the 1930s.

Dad says as we pass a certain fence, "This land all belonged to Grandpa Alexander. The house set back up in those trees." He is speaking about Samuel Jefferson Alexander, my great-grandfather.

Dad points to his left. I see the house in my mind because Granny has shown me a photograph of Samuel Jefferson's wife Georgia, Georgia's sister Ida and a hired man standing in the yard with the frame house in the background. Granny has described the interior of the house, and I know it had a front parlor and a large room in the back of the house where cotton was carded for quilt batting. In the picture are other buildings, all part of the farm, one for the horses, one for farm machinery and wagons, one for cold storage, and others I am uncertain about. I'm sure they had pigs, but they would not have been kept near the house.

My great-grandmother Georgia is pretty. Both she and her sister are wearing long dark-colored dresses and have their hair wound up off their necks. Ida is wearing an apron. She is always called "the spinster." Because she never married, she shuttled between the homes of relatives, dependent for food and shelter. In return she helped birth the babies and tend the sick. My father calls them "Grandmother" and "Aunt" and it is too cumbersome for me always to identify them except by their first names.

"On the right," Dad continues, as always, "were the pear trees. Prettiest white blossoms." He pulls off the road and parks. There is no traffic.

"This is where Grandpa was run down." Dad always pauses here for a moment of silence out of respect for his Grandpa, Samuel Jefferson Alexander.

"Tiny Grant, big fellow, ran over him. 1935. Tiny bought a new car, and this was one of the only roads in the county, used mainly by farm equipment, mules and the like. We transported cotton in a large truck from our place to the gin. Drove it down this road."

Dad was just a boy then, but I can imagine what it was like. He probably sat up front with his grandfather, but maybe he sat on top of the cotton. I have been behind cotton trucks before, have watched wispy white bolls escape from under the tarpaulin. I love cotton.

"This county road cut across our farm. We fought it, but it was progress. Grandpa was 85 years old. He came out of the house and decided to walk over to the pear orchard. He got half-way or so across the road when Tiny Grant, a bad one that Tiny, a Grant, what would you expect, Tiny Grant came over the hill in his new car and ran right over Grandpa. Cut him down in his prime."

To comment at this moment would interrupt Dad's moment of grief. I always felt sad for Georgia, but I know from other stories that she lived well in widowhood and was much loved. Before restarting our Sunday drive, Dad adds, "This road was filled with mourners after Grandpa's death. He was a great man."

We proceed to the Alexander family cemetery. It is now part of a larger cemetery that is an historic site. The sign at its entrance notes its beginnings in 1854, the year the Alexanders, Douglases, the Wilsons and the Woods arrived here in covered wagons having traveled across unsettled lands and up the Mississippi River just past Natchez to found Argenta. I guess some people must have made it all that distance only to die after reaching their destination.

We park and walk to our section. I know where every Alexander is buried. I know who they are. The cemetery is laid out on a hill gently sloping down to a stream that the Indians called Shona. Over the years we (by "we," I mean our family back at least two or three generations) have formed the habit of calling the cemetery Bayou Shona, and our section is closest to the stream where the land was first used as a burial site.

I always start my tour in the oldest part where small stone tablets mark the graves of my great-great grandparents, Andrew Jefferson Alexander and his wife Margaret Wright Alexander. He was born in South Carolina in 1825, and he and Margaret were in the first wagon train to arrive in what became Argenta.

I also visit the graves of my Alexander great-grandparents, Samuel Jefferson Alexander and his Alabama-born wife Georgia Hayfield. Great-

Grandmother Georgia shares a headstone, an obelisk, with her sister Ida and one other sister I know nothing about. Supposedly, her "house servant" is buried near her, but I doubt it. I doubt there are any black people buried in this cemetery. Why would a "house servant" (I am sure this is a euphemism) want to be buried near her mistress (her white mistress)?

Nearby, under the landmark, comforting, oak tree, is the grave of Samuel Jefferson Alexander, my father's grandfather, killed by Tiny Grant. Samuel Jefferson fought in the last year of the war, aged fifteen he was, and he survived. On his tombstone are an embossed Confederate flag and the words "An Honorable Man." It is because of him (and all the others) that I exist, and it is because of him that I qualify as a provisional member of the Descendants. I am absolutely certain no Grants are buried in this cemetery.

****

After Grandmother Alexander tells me I need to learn more about my ancestors, I tell her I already know about the Alexanders because of my visits to Bayou Shona. She tells me I need to learn about the people who came before the Alexanders who are buried in Bayou Shona. I need to know the ancestors who fought in the Revolutionary War. "Ours is an old family. Knowing your past won't make you a better person," she says, "but it will help you know who you are."

I protest. "Granny, I'm a senior in high school and have to keep my grades up. I am babysitting and tutoring to earn money to take to university. And church, I am program chairman for Wednesday night fellowship. I'm busy."

"You won't have me forever and I won't have my memory forever." Granny is thinking about the past. I'm thinking about getting away from my parents, about my future.

"We have cousins in Memphis. I'm going to write to them today, a letter to introduce you. I want you to meet with them next summer before you go to Atlanta. They might let you make copies of some of their documents. Of course, they are also in the Descendants. Perhaps they would invite you to attend a meeting with them."

I stop protesting. It is hopeless. Other people direct my life, even though some of them are dead.

I believe it was at this moment that I became aware that my future would be influenced by the lives and thoughts of my ancestors.

Diaries Three and Four

1963–1995

High School Graduation – Retirement

Unbelievable

November 22, 1963. President John F. Kennedy was shot and killed in Dallas today. I was in World Civilization class, attended by all freshmen. Professor Evans stopped lecturing to read a message passed to him from the Teaching Assistant. The professor actually wobbled slightly. He looked down on all of us sitting in pews in the assembly hall, the only room on campus large enough for my class. The message was devastating.

As I walked from class to the dorm, I think I looked my usual paragon of proper decorum, but my inner voice was frantic, actively communicating conflicting messages. I had grown accustomed to the voices of the ancestors but often, particularly concerning politics, I found their thoughts unsettling.

Great Grandfather Alexander: What has the country come to that we kill our President? Of course he wasn't the first one. I wasn't old enough to vote for Lincoln but I fought in the war that he and his kind started. That doesn't mean I wanted him dead. No, that's not true. I wanted anything to happen that would make the war end. Maybe I was wrong because death in that way made Lincoln a martyr. After he was killed, my daddy and mother went to church and prayed for his soul. You should go to church and pray for the soul of John F. Kennedy and for the future of this country. Myself, I always liked William Jennings Bryan, a man who understood money and farmers. William Jennings Bryan, you should learn more about him.

Along with about fifty other girls, I am sitting on the floor watching television in one of the dorm lounges. I don't think I will move from this spot. We are all crying and watching Jackie Kennedy. What will happen to our country?

Granny Alexander: The world will go on. Your grandfather has been clearing his garden and we've been enjoying the food I canned during the summer, food you like, plum jam (We had good plums this year.) I put up twenty quarts of tomatoes and almost as many pole beans. When are you coming to visit? I had my Sunday School class over last Wednesday. I made two cakes, a coconut cake and your favorite carrot cake. We had a real nice time. When are you coming to visit? Don't watch too much television. I read that it can ruin your eyes.

Mother: What is Jackie wearing?

I Can Pour!

My brother is brilliant. The little chubby fellow who hid with me in the closet, the one who wanted a sober father to play ball with him, the very one who rode his bicycle every day to God-knows-where just to avoid having to return home, that fellow, my brother Sam. He has won a full merit scholarship to Georgia Tech. Please God, don't let Mother and Dad decide to move to Atlanta, ever.

Hallelujah! We have made it, out of that demeaning, humiliating, hateful, terrifying house. But I worry about Mother. She telephones every Sunday, not to ask about me or my friends, or my problems, or grades, or any of the things she could ask me about. I noticed she can talk with me for half an hour and never ask a question.

One week she cries and wants to leave Dad but cannot because she has no money and no way to earn a living. Another week she tells me about her new Tahitian Pearl ring or her mink jacket.

"Should I have gotten a coat?" she asks.

I am totally independent of these people, at least financially. I applied for and received federal loans. With a Descendants' scholarship and my work tutoring and babysitting, I am making it on my own. Thankfully, I learned to type in high school. I watch the help-wanted bulletin boards on campus. When a professor has a large grant proposal or report to prepare, more work than his secretary can handle, I am able to earn good money. I have also typed several Ph.D. theses and have a reputation that wins me more business. If only I had more hours in a day.

Mother: You'll have to support yourself. We don't have enough money to pay for you to be a student all your life.

Dad: I work for you. All the money we have will be yours one day.

Grandmother McKay: What for do you need all that education? You used to stub your toe. You come to visit in the summers and you always stubbed your toe. That's who you are, the little girl who stubbed her toe. Why do you need all that education from such a fancy school? Get married and settle down. My mother had eight children and wanted more. I birthed twelve children. Look at my life. It ain't so bad.

Grandmother McKay, I cannot explain to you the value of education, but I am happy you feel your life was good. I speak these thoughts aloud and hope no one around me thinks I am crazy.

My goal remains law school. Grades are important to me. Freshman year was tough. Which was harder – classes and competition, or life in the dorm? The only competition I had in high school was from the boys in Advanced Placement classes, about a dozen of them who always scored higher than I did, but I always was the highest scoring girl. Here there are many more than a dozen boys smarter and more aggressive than I am. I am keenly aware that these are the types of men who will be my adversaries in the law.

Great-Grandmother Georgia Alexander: I don't know much about being a lawyer. They called my father Doc because he was good at healing people who were sick. We lived on a farm outside Opelika, no certified doctors there. I was proud of my father. When he was soldiering in the War, about 1865, he saw terrible things, men who lost their arms or legs. When he came home and began doctoring, he said he would never cut off any limb but he could give out medicines. He had a knack. I think he was helped by Mother's medicine chest. He could use those medicines and heal fever and summer complaint. I wish I had Mother's medicine chest. It was old, probably came with her when they crossed the mountains, might have belonged to her mother. Women have a soft, healing touch. Maybe you should be a nurse.

Much of my life has been spent hiding in the closet, smiling in public, and performing in school. In university, there is no hiding. I went to a fraternity beer-and-band party with a boy from my calculus class. We danced for hours and had a great time. After our second date, he said he had never met a girl so remote. Hurt my feelings, but I guess I have to work on being less remote. First, I have to figure out what it means. Inside I feel engaged in life but I am aware that I am different. I experience anxiety when I am called upon to speak in class. I try to cover up my shakiness but am not always successful. I am different from the girls from happy families. I don't know if I am different-good or different-bad. When the butterflies and fears float in my insides, I know I am different-bad.

My dormitory roommate is a debutante from Memphis. We are a great match. She comes from a happy family and tells me stories about her childhood. I tell her about my cousins in Memphis. Jennifer's mother knows them from the Descendants' meetings.

Great-Great Aunt Ida Hayfield: Foolishness, a bunch of foolishness. All that bowing and scraping and dressing up for balls. My sister Georgia and I were from solid stock. We didn't need any debutante foolishness. We spent our time on the farm, helping out in the house and schooling with the preacher when he had time for us. We never worked in the fields. My skin was pure white because I never got sun on me. We had pretty things and our own buggy. The only things we had time for was church, not some fool-heartedness over being a debutante. Those people may be fine people, but who came before them? We've been here since before this country was a country. You don't owe anything to anyone called a debutante.

When the weather turned cold in November, she received a gift from home, not the usual Constant Comment and homemade cookies. Even Jennifer was surprised by the gorgeous sheared beaver jacket that fit her perfectly. It fit me, too, and I am sure she would let me wear it if I wanted.

Great-Grandmother Mattie Bain: Girl, I coulda given you my fur coat. Daddy made it for me out of rabbit skins. Acourse I had to skin some of them rabbits. Bet yer friend's Daddy didn't kill them beavers.

Jennifer is popular and has the maximum number of dates allowed per week. It is a crazy system. We are allowed two dates per week. A date is defined as any night out of the dorm past 10 p.m. The absolute deadline for return to the dorm without expulsion is 11:00 p.m. Sunday through Thursday, midnight Friday night and 1:00 a.m. Saturday night. Most girls do not waste their two allowed dates on Sunday through Thursday.

I have double-dated with Jennifer and one or another of her admirers. My most unusual request for a date was from the German post-doc who is my instructor in German Language 103. I couldn't believe he asked me out. He is too aggressive for me. I told him we weren't allowed to date our teachers, which is true. He must have learned his lesson because I never heard about any other coed being asked out by him. It was awkward, though, in his class. I made A's in German, but I believe I deserved the grade.

Dad, Grandfather Alexander, Great Grandfather Alexander: It is good to learn other languages. It is important to see the world. You are in University, the first in our family. Your life will be better than ours. That is the American way. The Germans murdered our boys in two World Wars. You do not want to be too friendly with the Germans. You did the right thing when you told him you weren't allowed to date teachers. He made a mistake asking you to step out with him because he is your teacher. You do not know what other mistakes he has made or will make. He would not fit into our family.

Grandmother McKay: Do you think you are better than him? He is a professor. There are plenty of Germans living in this country who are good people. I know a German man who lives outside town and is well-fixed. Yes, I went to dinner with him. If he is good enough for me, the German professor is good enough for you. I imagine your Alexander relatives are too good for the German. You do what you want and ignore them. Just don't stub your toes!

Last Sunday I poured at an Open House at the home of another of my dorm friends. Cynthia's father has a successful construction business and he and Cynthia's mother love to entertain. I met the governor and the mayor as well as several local celebrities. Cynthia's mother complimented my pouring.

She said, "We'll have Lucinda Lee over again. She pours well."

Of course, my name was in the Society section of the *Atlanta Constitution*. Being an Alexander is sometimes a plus. When people ask me where I am from, I do not say Argenta, I say, "My people are from South Carolina, before it was a state."

Granny Alexander: The Alexanders and the Clarks are from York District, South Carolina. We don't call it York County because we were there before it was a county. We lived on the Catawba River. Our family were people of stature. Our Alexander forebear fought in the American Revolution and his wife was a heroine in that war. Many boys in our family fought in the Civil

War. We are Old South. It is common to have your name in the newspaper. My Mother told me you only have your name in a newspaper when you are born and when you die. Was it in the Society section?

Apology

Dear Diary,

We know that I am writing to myself. What is the purpose of a diary? Samuel Pepys provided us with a view of life during the Plague and the Great Fire in London. Samuel Johnson wrote about his friend Boswell (I have to work mentally to get this straight: Johnson about Boswell, not Boswell about Johnson.) Anne Frank gave us an understanding and insight into the terrors of her time and taught us how a person could not only cope but could find joy in the worst of circumstances. My favorite diarist is Anais Nin. *Henry and June.* But not the parts about her father.

Again, I ask, what is the purpose of a diary?

1. To allow the diarist a means of regurgitating all that has been ingested.
2. To serve as a keeper of data so that later in life the diarist can review, absorb, understand those factors that have contributed to his personhood (word from Psychology 101).
3. To enable biographers to write an accurate story of the diarist's life.
4. To aid in personal growth.
5. To paint a picture of the times.
6. To remind the diarist of all his/her triumphs and mistakes.
7. To serve as data for an autobiography.
8. To prove that a person lived, not just existed, but lived.
9. To provide an activity for people who have nothing else to do with their lives.

Maybe there are more reasons, but I am particularly concerned about #6 and #8. Do I need to remind myself of my mistakes? Would I want some descendant of mine to read these pages? Would that descendant want to know about me? If I go back to my pink diary and read what I wrote as a child, I am sad and embarrassed. What good is that? By writing, I am pretending that I am talking to a friend, a dear friend. But who exactly is this "diary" person? No one, an inanimate object. Am I such a loser that I have to write to this inanimate object because I have nothing better to do?

The world is a happening. We are making history. My generation is making history. We are baby-boomers, the largest generation in history. We can change the world. We can conquer space. We can live as one people and not fear each other. We can create racial harmony. We can do something for our country. The times are changing, and I do not need to write to an inanimate object to give me something to do.

I promise myself that I will keep these diaries, just in case someone wants to write my autobiography, but for now I will go on sabbatical. I will absorb all that is happening in the world around me. I will devote myself to learning and to people and to preparing myself for the future. I might even be able to help the world to change.

****

I am in the dorm now and the girl in the room next door has her stereo speakers hung on the wall. She plays Barbra Streisand's *People* constantly. Personally, I have become a huge fan of Delta blues.

****

That's it for now, diary. I have made my decision.

No Longer an Undergrad

I am standing on Michigan Avenue, in the midst of the Magnificent Mile, looking up at skyscrapers and trying to look like I fit in. Across the street is the John Hancock Center, all aluminum and glass with large X-structures that make an amazing design. On this avenue are the venerable Drake Hotel, not so exciting from the outside but probably elegant inside, the historic Water Tower, the Wrigley Building. I see Saks Fifth Avenue, boutiques everywhere, and stylish people on the sidewalk, as well as families who are obviously tourists.

Why are buildings making me cry? I stand here and tears are in my eyes. It must be the wind.

If I have time before classes begin, I want to take the Frank Lloyd Wright tour. I must find the Chicago Art Institute and the History Museum. I expect these to be the places that provide me with release from the stress of law school. Who am I kidding? Maybe there will be no time for relief of stress. Stress may be the norm for the three years ahead of me, awful thought.

There is a reason it is called the Windy City. Even in September, I feel the wind, warm wind, but who cares about the weather? I am in Chicago, one of the greatest powerhouse cities in the world. I dry my tears. I don't want anyone to think I am a child or a hick in the big city.

I arrived a week before the Democrat National Convention, just in time to avoid the masses of arrivals. Dad refused to pay airfare for me. He volunteered that information. I never asked. He all too often has expressed his opinion about my going to a "pinko Northern school." I posted an ad in student unions at Emory and Georgia Tech and was able to hitch a ride with a couple who were headed to Chicago to join the protestors. If Dad knew that, he would really spring a leak or burst a gasket or whatever men do when they explode with anger. The important point is that I made it, stayed in a hostel for two nights until I was able to find an apartment, a super cheap third-floor walk-up, furnished, but with no air conditioning. I cannot believe I have space to myself, my own bedroom, living room, kitchen and bathroom, all mine. The apartment has a desk and a bookcase which I cannot yet fill as I sold all my textbooks to the Emory bookstore for spendable cash.

From my bedroom I overlook another brick building. I must hang a sheet or something over the bedroom window or I will become much too familiar with the person across the way.

Granny Alexander: What you really mean is that you need to hang that sheet over the window to keep your neighbor from seeing you. But never mind how you said it. Modesty is a virtue. It says so in the Bible.

The living room provides two windows with shades, overlooking the front sidewalk. I feel very adult but will have to watch my funds closely. Three more years loom ahead of me before I can earn serious money, the proviso being I must survive, graduate, and get a job. It is painful to read that sentence. On the one hand three years seem like a brief interlude but on the other I know it will be very challenging, that day by day the time may pass more slowly. I know this because the years I lived in Argenta went by very slowly – and painfully – while the five years at Emory went by very quickly. I am not the physicist that Sam is becoming, but I understand that time is variable and requires a frame of reference. I often wonder what is my frame of reference. I know about myself that I am persistent, that I can endure, that I can make goals and reach for them. I know I have fears but I can push them into the depths, stomp on them, and belch them up, pass them out as gas. No, I cannot say those things. I cannot even think those things. I am a flower. I am a flower. I am a flower.

****

Today the pull of the protests was strong. I fought my desire to be in the middle of the action because I was afraid. I could have been hit over the head. I was afraid of being caught in the violence and afraid of getting arrested (what a way that would be to start my career in law school). In the midst of violence, even on its periphery, I feel my heart racing, my lips quiver, something inside me screams, but I don't think it is visible or audible. On the outside I am always an Alexander not like my father, more like my granny.

Granny Alexander: Remember to sit with your knees together and your ankles crossed.

As soon as my telephone was installed, Dad called to tell me to stay off the streets. He thinks the Chicago police are corrupt but have every right to remove the protesters who in his mind are all unwashed hippies with long hair. He does not realize they are not just being removed. They are being beaten and arrested. He probably doesn't care. I do not try to convince him about the righteousness of their protests, but I do say truthfully that I will avoid danger.

It is odd that my father would telephone to express concern about my safety when he isn't concerned enough about me to help with my education. If he had helped pay for my undergraduate years, I could have finished with my class – in four years. I had to work and earn tuition and room and board. Five years it took me, but I did it. I am not a psychology major, but I think my father's attitude has something to do with control. He thinks he has control over me. At this point in my life, I really do not care what he thinks about me. Is it melodramatic to say I have suffered because of him? I am struggling with unkind thoughts toward him. I feel the tension of conflicting ideas. Should I love my father no matter what or wish him dead? Maybe it would be less drastic to wish him out of my life. I cannot forget the fear and anxiety of his fits, the ugly words, the food thrown against the wall, the cruelty of it all.

I set these thoughts aside. I am eager to meet the other students in my building but doubt I will have much time to party. The boys downstairs had a big bash last night, and I dropped in to dance and have one drink. A group huddled in the kitchen was smoking pot and one of the bedroom doors was closed. One of the hosts told me they were all undergraduates, and he was expecting to be called up by the draft any day. He said, "I'll be a second lieutenant leading men into battle. First one in." He was matter of fact about it all, but the poignancy of the moment stayed with me for the rest of the evening.

Sam is enrolled in ROTC. He is anti-Vietnam War but refuses to escape to Canada. He is hopeful he can fulfill his obligation in the US. Sam is starting his third year at Georgia Tech and even though we rarely saw each other when I was at Emory, knowing that we were in the same city was a comfort. I have invited him to Chicago but doubt he will have enough money or time to come during the school year. He used Grandmother Alexander's house as his address and spends holidays with her. I don't know where I will spend my holidays. I am basically on my own. I don't mind being alone. I feel free. I am accustomed to making my own decisions.

I walk around campus, finding the main library used by undergrads, the administration building, the dorms, and various buildings devoted to different disciplines. It is a clear day, and I am not alone. Freshmen who arrive early are excitedly rushing around from one quadrangle to another, enjoying their freedom, not yet burdened by classes, competition and assignments. Same is true for me.

My academic life will be centered in the building that houses only the law school, its classrooms, offices and fabulous library. I have toured the building once before, during my application interview, but now, as I stroll through the corridors, the reality of my life is sinking in. I feel both apprehension and confidence, breathing in ever-expanding assurance and breathing out in fits and starts.

Matriculation is both organized and confusing. Someone has done the organization and knows how I am supposed to proceed, but I find it a bit of a struggle. Two hundred of us are in the lobby, one hundred ninety-eight boys and two girls. I spot the other girl and run to her to introduce myself, to establish a link, to connect to someone hopefully like me. Talking in the crowd is impossible. We agree to meet for coffee in the basement. I have already figured out that is where students load up on caffeine.

I am registered for my courses, have my schedule in hand, and must face the bookstore which is packed with boys grabbing heavy books. One of the boys assumes I work in the store and asks me for help finding a certain text. He is annoyed when I try to tell him I am his classmate. He has no time to listen.

Coffee. I meet Sylvia and am perhaps more thrilled than she is. She has difficulty understanding my Southern accent. I don't want to make a premature judgment, but I think she hears my accent and stereotypes me as a hillbilly. Maybe I should tell her about my hillbilly Ozark relatives. That would give her a shock. Truth is, her accent isn't that easy to follow. She speaks very rapidly and swallows her words. I don't want to judge her by her speech. We are the only girls in the class. We need to support each other. Does she understand the importance of cooperation and support? Time will tell.

Great-Great Grandfather John Henry McKay: We chose to be what you call hillbillies. My father and his father and his father before him all the way back to the Highlands understood fighting for our land and for our rights to live as we pleased. My Pap was a born explorer, and when it was my turn, I followed the sun through the mountains and ended up west of the Mississippi River in country never seen by white men before me. I would rather be clearing my own land and breathing free than coming up again' the snakes in Philadelphia and Washington and all those big cities in the east. We work hard and keep to ourselves. You would do well to do the same.

Sylvia tells me, "It is every woman for herself." I draw my own conclusion.

Grandmother Alexander: Adjust your expectations. You are living in the North now. She may have no manners but you do.

Classes begin tomorrow. Tonight I am tucking in. Maybe I should be reading Homer or Shakespeare or Marcus Aurelius, but I think I will relax with Agatha Christie.

****

Yes, I am writing again in my diary. I never promised myself never to write. As anyone can see from what I have written above, I have a great deal to say, and like it or not, it seems the one who must listen to what I say is you, Dear Diary.

Adult Now

June 18, 1969. I am old enough now to eschew writing in a diary. I think I pushed "Dear Diary" as far as possible given my age. This begins a proper adult journal. I have completed two years of law school in Chicago and my father is dead. Disparate facts, but both contribute to my adulthood.

I know the Argenta police have incorrectly recorded his death as a suicide. It is actually more complicated because the death certificate says, and I have seen it myself, that he died of burns. That is true.

Several people had sufficient motive to kill my father, including me, and I had the strength and determination to do the deed, but I did not. My brother? Sam, my intelligent, wonderful, all-boy brother? I was always the family's designated smart person, but Sam is working toward his Ph.D. in Physics. He knows things of which I have no understanding. Sam would protect our mother, but he has not the heart or the stomach of a murderer.

No one will be charged, but I will know before I die who did the deed. Without knowing, I am incomplete and driven to resolve the unknown.

My father was a monster but like every child of abuse, I found in my abuser some admirable qualities. Such irony both to love and hate, and I have felt both, at times simultaneously. When I examine the book of accounts, the negatives are writ large and numerous. At the top of the list of positives would be his value of education. Without education I would have no options. Except for the one time he threw me to ground breaking my eyeglasses, he never harmed me physically. His method of damage was emotional. The moments he valued my intellect do not balance the moments of terror and demeaning accusations.

Also on the asset side of the sheet is the value for financial independence. Linked in general to an independence of total existence that has made me a puppet to no one. I am grateful for my independence, both of spirit and finance but the ultimate gratitude is to myself for endurance and forbearance and effort.

Do other belles know their own worth as I do? I think yes. Do other belles make up stories to hide the truth, to disguise the ugliness, to create a favorable impression in the listener's mind? I am sure of it.

To the matter of my father's death, these are the details I choose to tell today.

From Argenta, I received a telephone call, the type no person usually wants but expects to occur at some time always in the future.

"Come home, Sis, our father is in the hospital," Sam's voice was strong and certain.

"Immediately? Are you okay?"

"I am okay. It is our father. He is near death, unconscious and in the hospital."

"And mother?"

"Here with me."

"What happened? You can tell me now. I can't bear not knowing."

"He is in the Burn Unit."

"Oh, my God." I sounded sufficiently startled and agonized.

"He tried to kill himself."

Questions flooded my brain. Our father would not commit suicide. He might kill someone. Suicide by fire, no, too painful. He would use a gun.

"I'll book a flight for tonight. Don't worry about me. Love you."

"Me, too."

Sam picked me up at the airport and on the drive to the hospital he filled me in on events. Apparently the parents had had a particularly horrid week, with Dad locking Mother in her room, with food and dishes thrown, with Mother eventually running from the house to refuge at a neighbor's home. The neighbor summoned the sheriff who took Mother to a shelter.

Mother said she telephoned a taxi and returned to the house a few hours later. There she found Dad in the back yard working on a lawn mower. They argued, he telling her she was worthless and back and forth it went until he poured gasoline over himself and lit a match.

Sam says the ambulance came quickly, and Dad was taken to the hospital. Mother then called Sam.

Dad was in very bad, near death condition, obviously sunk in the stupor of heavy pain medications. Sam and Mother met with the doctors who explained the seriousness of the burns, potential treatment, and probability that Dad would not pull through. They presented Sam and Mother with a legal form for their signature approving a "Do not resuscitate" order. Mother signed with Sam in total agreement.

A few hours later Dad was conscious and requested everything possible be done to support his life.

Sam said this was problematic because Dad now would not speak with Mother or him but did want to see me.

I did not want to see him but always dutiful, that's what we Southerners are, I agreed.

Hospitals are their own universe. I made my way, following signs, to the Burn Unit. First hit with the smell of the corridor, I became nauseated and uncertain I could face Dad in the red and black skinless, powerless agony Sam had described. Like staff I was required to wear a protective gown, mask, gloves and booties – hardly recognizing the yellow canary I had become.

How can one make a burn treatment unit cheerful? It was the gloomy, eerie place I anticipated. I saw a nurse eating her lunch in a room beyond the nursing station. I cannot think how she had learned to accept the work she had to do, to feel enough at ease with it to do something so mundane as to eat her lunch. The word hero came to mind. These doctors and nurses were something special to be able to work every day with people in such pain. Not for me. Give me the law, paper, winning and losing, skillful argument, life and death in the courtroom, not in this place.

Nothing could have prepared me for the scene in my father's room. He may have been conscious but he was already in hell. I looked at him, and he said, "Keep your mother away from me." All the words from his mouth were vicious. There were no good-bye admissions of guilt, no requests for forgiveness, and no pleas to me or to God for atonement, just vile anger.

I said, although he didn't hear me, "I don't understand any of this."

He did not respond, seemed to pass out.

That was my last interaction with the man who was my father, whom I think loved me but could not express it, who caused pain to us all. His mother, dear Grandmother Alexander wrote his obituary, "A son of the South, he was the pride of the family. He will be sorely missed and is now among the angels."

Although I no longer believe in a loving god, I ask, are not Sam and I the source of pride for the family? Where is Dad now but underground in the family cemetery where he belongs? I will reread Dante to learn which stage of Hell is now his home.

Preached to Hell

Granny Alexander now refers to Dad's death as an accident. In the manner of all aggrieved mothers, she tells her friends during condolence calls, that his accident is the trial of her life, that no experience in life is as difficult as the death of a child. No matter that my father was forty-five years old.

My grandmother is magnificent in her grief. She wears black well and has the ability to help stumbling callers express themselves effortlessly.

Mother and I are staying in Granny's home. We are not expected to feel comfort in the Hillside house. Sam is staying with a cousin, third cousin, I think, although my mind cannot focus on subtle questions of family relationships.

I try to project positive thoughts but these are unusual circumstances. My father's death is recorded as a suicide. There are visitors who consider his act a crime. To make matters worse, we are eschewing the standard procedure of visitation, church service, graveside service, and home visitation afterward. Luckily, our family funeral director, Ernest, understands our need.

"Under the circumstances," suggests the well-named Ernest, "perhaps you want only a graveside service."

He came to us. After all, his family has buried our family for generations. We are all on first name basis.

Ernest wears a dark suit and dark tie. I notice red enamel cufflinks in a dog shape, Irish Setters, I think. I imagine this choice as a frivolity, a personal statement of rebellion against the grimness of his vocation.

There is no discussion of cost. We will pay whatever is required. He will not overcharge us as he anticipates future business from our family. Am I mistaken, or is he calculating Granny's age, as we consider answers to his many questions about order of service, seating arrangements, and preferences for flower sprays?

Before leaving, after he has guided us through the maze of potential social and religious error or embarrassment, he hands me a large white envelope containing a book by Elizabeth Kubler-Ross about stages of grief, also several pamphlets with pastel covers, embossed with gold crosses. One is a book of daily devotionals for the family in mourning. I thank him mirroring his solemnity.

The plans are complete. We are proceeding through a process, like a formal meal, starters, salad, entree, dessert, coffee. I would say we have completed the shopping for salad ingredients. I am thinking about food because Granny's kitchen is filled with casseroles and cakes.

After the graveside service (the casket closed, of course), forty or fifty people called at Granny's house. I suppose it was a wake of sorts, but I think of a wake as a rowdy affair, and this one was restrained. We had not wanted this visitation, but it was impossible to turn people away. The women sat inside and the men gathered outside passing a bottle of spirits among them. I did not know, or didn't know that I knew, over half of the attendees. Every woman brought food and every man told us that he was available to help in any way we ladies needed help.

I think Southerners believe that food will resolve every problem. Feed a fever, starve a cold. Definitely feed grief.

The conversation was scripted. Most of our guests avoided mention of my studies in Chicago. Some thought I was living in New York. Some mentioned my life in St. Louis. It seems everyone knew I was in school somewhere but anywhere north of town was foreign. I don't correct any of these geographic errors. What does it matter to my family, whether I am in Chicago? Once I introduced Granny to a college friend of mine who had studied for a year in Japan. Granny said, "How nice. How was the weather?" I am not criticizing Granny, just recognizing her world does not include Japan, or Chicago.

All our guests knew Granny, and she was the center of attention, although Mother ran a close second. An alien would know this by counting people. Granny was always surrounded by people. Mother usually had a maximum of three people attending her. The greater the number of people around you, the more important you are. I usually had one person speaking to me, or none.

One lady, unknown to me, said, "You are (great) Aunt Martha's daughter, right?"

The son of Granny's second husband's daughter embarrassed me with his over-loud comments. "I think Mother has a picture of us at a birthday party. You were in diapers. Did you know you were a plump baby? I think your mother fed you very well."

And my favorite from an old friend of Granny's, certain she had identified me: "You're the one who never married."

"I am only twenty-five," I reply defensively.

"Do you like living up there in Chicago (New York or Boston)?"

"I'm in law school."

"Do you have any marriage prospects? I don't suppose there are many Southern boys up there?"

By dark, everyone had left and, sitting alone in the den, my body heavy against the recliner, it occurred to me that my expertise would be required for the next phase of my father's "after-life." I am not yet an attorney, but I am already good at estates. One thing I learned today is that the event carries a person through.

****

Mother announces she needs to retrieve some personal items, clothes, jewelry, toiletries from the Hillside house. She is anxious fearing her reaction to the scene in the back yard. She wants me to accompany her, to enter the house first and close all the drapes and curtains in the back of the house. I agree to do this small task knowing Mother wants to be protected from the reality of the past, and why not?

The house is locked, but I have Mother's keys. The front of the house appears unchanged but the kitchen is messy. Dad had expelled Mother a few days before the accident, let her in, and expelled her again. He had shown no interest in housekeeping. At first I think "why hasn't the kitchen been cleaned," but who would do the cleaning? I have the same feeling as I look through a kitchen window and take in the near back yard filled with the detritus of emergency services and police.

I spy the darkened, burned lawn beyond the swimming pool. It is the size of a hot tub. Why hasn't grass grown over that dead patch? Because Lucinda Lee, it will take weeks before the yard is normal again.

I quickly close the kitchen curtains, walk slowly into the back bedrooms, shutting out the events of the past few days as I close the various shutters and drapes. I am on a mission and complete my task to enable Mother to complete hers. We each have our role to fulfill. I need to be carried through by the event.

Mother is quick. She knows exactly where to find her suitcases, which drawers and closets to access. I pay no attention to how she packs but follow her directions as she gathers her necessities. Actually not all is necessary but what difference does it make?

Back in the car we laugh and instead of returning immediately to Granny's house, we drive with windows down in the direction opposite from the cemetery, opposite from the Alexander farm. We are in opposition, celebrating release. I feel the elation of a sixteen-year-old with a new driving license. Mother's feelings are always hard to assess because she sometimes says one thing but does something completely antithetical, like saying she loved my father when I am not sure she did. Today, her feelings seem to mirror mine. She seems released, like some internal stricture has been opened, and now she can breathe. That is how I feel.

We become somber again when we return to Granny's house. We find Granny entertaining an old woman with dyed red hair. Granny reminds us the guest is Atha Latta, Carter's sister. I try to remember Carter but cannot. Mrs. Latta is telling a story about yet another unknown but somehow related person whose death must have occurred before I was born. The deeper Mrs. L. delves into the excesses of this man's life, the more stalwart her posture. Finally, she concludes triumphantly, "He was so bad, the pastor preached him to hell."

Granny Alexander is visibly shaken. Her friend Atha cannot stop, "To hell, preached him straight to hell for his sins."

"I don't remember that," Granny whispers.

"No, you were going to the Baptist Church." This seemed to explain all the mysteries to Granny who sat back in her chair and after taking a moment to recognize the gravity of being preached to hell, offered Mrs. Latta a cup of coffee and her choice of dessert.

Atha Latta, had she attended, would have been greatly disappointed in my father's graveside service. Not a religious man, my father had no personal relationship with salvation. The service was gentle, light on theology, and just long enough to satisfy the mourners who cared about the decorous rituals of death.

****

In my weariness I did precisely what I do as a student: I made a to-do list. Lists bring two joys. One feels one can control the set if one can determine everything that goes into the set. I am that one. The reminder of a list is that activity can lead to completion, an end-point once all entries are scratched off the list. Crossing out each completed item reinforces my sense of power. I can do all of this. I feel this power until I write, "Help Mother determine where she will live." I don't even have to write the full sentence to feel anxiety creeping in, "Help Mother" is sufficient to unleash my angst.

Bacon and Business

Two steadfast rules we follow: (1) business is not discussed at table and (2) say nothing that will upset Granny. It is the morning following the funeral. We are fortifying ourselves as a prelude to the next Odyssean obstacle. Polyphemus is dead. What next? Surely we have overcome the worst.

I awoke with worries. I found no answers in Kubler-Ross. The daily devotional did not apply to me. Mother, money, Chicago, Sam's future, Hillside, all appear as detailed entries on the to-do list tucked in my pocket. To my knowledge Dad had managed the financial affairs. I knew very little about their resources. Did Mother even have a chequeing account or credit card? Had she ever been a part of decision-making? Would she allow me to help her? How assertive should I be?

Sam would need to return to Atlanta. Eventually I would need to return to Chicago. My neighbor was accumulating my mail and would keep an eye on my apartment, but I had rent to pay on the first of the month and my summer library job would disappear if I did not report for duty.

I dressed in jeans and a designer pullover given me by Mother for last year's birthday and went into the dining room for breakfast. An old house, the dining room was adjacent to the kitchen, separated by a single swinging door now propped open to reveal Granny Alexander at the stovetop, cooking bacon. The smell was heavenly. Who doesn't like the smell and sound of crisp bacon frying in a cast iron skillet? I gave Granny a good-morning hug and upon learning she had slept well, filled a plate and joined Mother and Sam in the dining room.

"You two have a head start on the day," I said. "After breakfast could we have a little powwow?"

Sam laughed. "That's why I came over early. You're not the only organized, get-down-to-business person in the family."

I grimaced. "I will happily share responsibility."

"Have some grits, Sis. Don't take matters so seriously. We know you're the hotshot lawyer."

"And you're the hotshot what? Physicist? Chemical engineer? When will you decide?" I was on a roll, and I had not even sat down yet. "When are you ever going to stop being a student?"

"About the same time as you," Sam sealed the conversation with a win and a grin.

Granny Alexander emerged from the kitchen and handed the tray of bacon to Sam. She gave him a sweet, loving smile and got a kiss from him as a reward.

Mother picks at her food and cautions me about overeating. She compliments my pullover. I thank her again as she had gifted it to me. She denies remembering. She comments on my hair, suggesting my face would look less round if I parted my hair on the side. She is right. I do not challenge her opinions about clothing or appearance. It is her expertise just as Granny is socially skilled and a great cook. I do not think I have yet established my forte but to everyone else I am the "smart one." I think brains should exclude me from fixation on figure and appearance, but in Mother's presence I am compliant. I leave one slice of bacon on my plate and do not eat toasted bread. Forgive me. I cannot resist the grits.

Granny retires to her kitchen while Mother, Sam, and I settle ourselves with coffee in the living room. It is the first time since the "accident" that we three have been alone. We are of one feeling: relief. The abuser is gone. Among the three of us, the charade of grief is unnecessary. We are well-fed and have motivation to resolve whatever hurdles are ahead.

As I dig into my pocket for my list, Mother opens our meeting, "I am going to Zona, at least for a while."

Sam and I are surprised. When your mother tells you what she is going to do, you do not question her. You are the child. She is the master (in this case, mistress) of her own fate. Sam and I nod and simultaneously say, "Okay." This is the "Jump" command followed by the "how high" response.

She continues, "I talked last night with G.W., and he wants me to recover on the mountain."

"I didn't know G.W. knew about Dad," I said.

"We've talked now and then. He is a very kind man, Aunt Lillian´s nephew, not direct kin to us, but you do remember him, I'm sure."

"If you want to go to Zona, of course we'll help you. Do you want us to drive you up to Zona? I wouldn't mind seeing the old homefolk's territory again," Sam volunteered.

"G.W. has changed a lot since you saw him as children."

"Does he have teeth now?" I want to ask, but do not.

Mother has more to tell us. "G.W. is a man of means now. He owns a business that he runs from Zona. He says he could use a good lawyer, even one trained in Chicago, and he thinks Sam would find his business interesting."

"Tell us, Mother, we are dying to know. What is his business?"

"Do you remember the springs?" We nod. "He is bottling and selling Low Glen Springs water."

Wow. Good old enterprising toothless G.W. I am wondering if he has legal rights to the springs.

"He owns the springs, you know," Mother says as though she is reading my mind. This is why I never think about my boyfriends and sex in her presence. Some things I want to keep private.

"I can't wait." I trail off as Sam picks up the conversation.

"I have news about the house. Uncle Fred's son Oscar wants to buy it. He made an offer while we were talking yesterday after the service. Granted, he had had a little sip of bourbon, but I think he will stand by his offer."

Sam hands Mother a slip of paper. I lean over and see the number written on it. My immediate reaction is positive, but I don't know house and land values in this area. I say, "Selling the house would solve a problem, wouldn't it?" This is a statement, not a question. "I can't imagine your living there again."

"I have no happy memories at Hillside."

This comment pauses our conversation. In unison we reach for our coffee. Finding it cold, Sam goes to the kitchen and returns with the coffee tray. The coffee ritual allows us a moment to shake off the connection to our unhappy memories.

"Do you need time to adjust to what has happened?" I ask Mother. As I write that question, I find it odd. Where did that word "adjust" come from? Did I read it in Kubler-Ross? Of course, Mother needs time to adjust, as do we all. Are we just going to go on as though nothing has happened? None of us looks as though we are in any state of distress. We are eating well. No one looks haggard. No one is complaining of lost sleep. I've just had bacon and grits, and I feel good.

"No. I want the rest of my clothing removed from Hillside, also the photos and maybe one or two other personal items, and then I want to leave. If Oscar wants the contents of the house, so be it. Frankly, your father had broken most of my china and, I don't want to think about it."

I move into gear. I don't want to think about the bad times either. I ask, "Do I have your permission to manage the real estate transaction? And may I remove any business files? I am guessing Dad kept files somewhere in the house."

"Yes. Take care of all of it. He kept his files in a corner of the basement in a little office that he said I couldn't enter. I have no idea what you will find there."

There is a frivolous quality to Mother's attitude. She has divorced herself from the realities concerning money and property. She clearly just wants out. I'm in planning mode, ready to tidy up, to organize, to connect the dots, to take care of business.

Sam asks her, "When do you want to drive up to Zona?" Sam is the more sympathetic of us. He is more generous toward Mother, is protective. This is the role he has wanted to fulfill since childhood. As a boy he needed weapons and the only ones at hand were rocks, useless against the nuclear capacity of his enemy. Now there is no need for weaponry. Sam's love toward Mother is evident, unhindered. He will place her needs as a priority in his life.

He assures her, "I will drive you to Zona whenever you want to go."

"I want to go, too. I want to see old G.W., oops, the new G.W."

We decide to telephone two people today, both cousins: our lawyer and our banker. Sam and I will go to Hillside to retrieve the business files, and while I work this afternoon on finance, Sam will take Mother shopping. She wants walking shoes, boots and other clothes "for the mountain." Only later, I realize we have our roles reversed. In some households, wouldn't I have taken Mother shopping? But, we are not "other households."

The Shock of Road Construction

Events of the outside world have taken a back seat to the must-do tasks confronting me at the moment. Sam has become Mother's support person, and I have become the business manager. The house is being sold to Oscar Alexander, contents and all, as is. Mother has a current account at the bank and has been instructed in the art of writing cheques as well as the importance of keeping a record of those transactions. She has never had an account of her own, but I was proud of her at the bank as she never showed any sign of nerves. She just asked, demurely, I might add, where she was supposed to sign her name.

Granny Alexander: A widow can sign her own name. When my first husband was alive, I signed my name Mrs. Thomas Jefferson Alexander. Never on cheques, I might add, as I never had my own money back then. If he had died, instead of running away, I would have signed my name Mrs. Pauline Clark Alexander. I brought this up because Dorothea can now sign her name Mrs. Dorothea Alexander. Does she know that? Does she know she should keep some extra money stored away, not in the bank?

When the banks closed, I was already married to Thomas and had lost one baby and had another. I wouldn't have known that the banks closed except Thomas came home from somewhere. I think he had been up in Memphis selling vegetables and working out a price for my daddy's cotton. Anyway, he came into the kitchen. I can still remember I was cooking field peas. He said, "Sit down, Pauline." He was serious and I thought something had made him angry. "Sit down, Pauline," and I did, wearing my apron, your Daddy playing on the floor. In those days we didn't have a fancy dining room. We had a wooden table and chairs right in the kitchen where I made my bread and plucked chickens and did just about everything I had to do to keep food in our stomachs. And just when I sat down, I had to get up again because he said,

"Pauline, fetch your egg money." He was so serious that I didn't ask any questions. I got back up and went into our bedroom, opened the top drawer of the chest and got my coin purse. When I returned to the kitchen table, I placed the coin purse between us. Thomas said, "Open it and count it." He just sat there, straight and stiff, but that was his normal self. It was his face that was serious. "One, two, three, seven, seventeen, twenty-two." I was not the best with arithmetic, but I could surely count coins. I finished at $4.62, money I had been saving for Christmas when we always spent extra to buy oranges and walnuts and tinsel. Thomas pulled paper notes from his pants pocket, put them on the table, got up and went into our bedroom, returning with more paper notes which he added to the growing pile. For a moment, I felt like we were richer than I had thought. Thomas counted it all, slowly, as if he were chewing a piece of my Sunday pork roast, savoring every bit of the gravy, but he was careful and intense and not smiling as he would have been chewing on that pork roast. "$57.83. That's all the money we have and all we are going to have. The bank closed today." I didn't understand. Thomas had always handled our money, except my egg money. "Pauline, that is all the money we have now. The bank has no money. We have to make this money last." We made it through. That's another story. I never had a bank account. Banks are hard to understand, but mainly they want to make money, not take care of my money. Always keep a goodly amount of money hidden away at home in case the bank closes.

We haven't yet sorted out the cars, both Cadillacs (his and hers). I cannot take a Cadillac back to Chicago. Where would I park it? It would cost me too much money. Mother doesn't want them either. We'll figure it out.

Mother has applied for widow's benefits. The Social Security worker was very understanding and helpful. Our cousin, the banker, is assisting in transfer of stock ownership to Mother's name. We understand these details require death certificates which Ernest, our funeral director, will acquire on our behalf.

I have had no time alone and miss solitude and personal space. The business of death carries a person through the first days of grief. Kubler-Ross doesn't say anything about all the work that absorbs a grieving person, except, of course, in my position, under these peculiar circumstances, I am not grieving. Or maybe this is denial.

Feeling I deserve time out, I take one of the cars and drive toward our old neighborhood in Argenta. Turning off the highway onto Main Street, I pass the high school, still the same 1920s Art Deco facade. The football field is surrounded by a modern structure for seating and huge lighting poles lean into this Colosseum to the gods of sport.

Further down Main is the junior high set back from the road. It has fallen on bad times. Venetian blinds in the windows parallel to the street are broken and weeds are popping up through cracks in the parking lot. It is June. No classes are in session. No children are in the playground.

I pull into the empty parking lot and envision my classmates gathered in the hallways. I want to remember only good times.

The old neighborhood is only six city blocks away. A city block is about three-hundred feet. Sam and I walked to and from school, not together as I was a girl and walked with my friends, and he was a boy and rode his bicycle.

As I drive on, the landscape changes. Main Street veers off to the right. Ahead of me, where Main Street used to be is now an industrial court comprised of one-story concrete-block buildings. Signs advertise space for rent.

It is not possible to make a left turn. My old neighborhood was on the left. I turn right and at the first opportunity pull to the curb and park. I think I am near the Catholic Church, but I am not sure. We lived on the other side of Main Street. I feel disoriented and walk back to the point where Main Street veered off course. I walk to the corner where a large mulberry tree always made the sidewalk messy.

Where our house was, the unhappy little house with the big back yard, there is now a construction site. The site expands to include the Kirby's grand Victorian house and Sarah's corner house with the lawn for croquet. Gone is the Hall house with the hydrangea bush with the blue and pink snowballs. Gone is the fence on the alley covered in honeysuckle. Gone is the empty lot next door to our house where Sam used to play among the tall weeds. My familiar hideaways are all gone. It looks like they have given way to the progress of new road construction.

Waves of sadness overwhelm me. My knees begin to buckle. I cannot see ahead of me. I only see and feel tears as I am overcome with emotion. I am immersed in sadness and grief. Never again will I have a chance to relive that past, and in the reliving the chance to make it happy and wholesome. It is no more.

The Way to the Top

I joined McTavish and Willis because it was a prestigious firm, and I wouldn't have to try any cases in court. My difficulties with anxiety were abating and new medication had reduced the migraines significantly, but I was smart enough to know court appearances, especially battles against aggressive male attorneys, could trigger a reappearance of my weaknesses. In court weakness is loss.

The firm occupied two lower floors and three upper floors of the Grady Building in the heart of the city. Junior staff members were on floors four and five, senior staff on floor fifteen, partners and their private secretaries and additional personnel were on sixteen. Other support staff were on fourteen and a private members-only club – to which all senior staff and partners belonged – was in the penthouse.

My job interview took place in the club. The partner implied I warranted this treatment because my grades were fabulous, my references top rate. I think the real reason was my gender. They needed a woman to show their progressive, forward thinking and probably to meet new federal requirements for gender opportunity and equality. They wanted to impress me, to make me think my life with their firm would be all about lunch in the penthouse and fawning men.

If I had been Black it would have been better for them, but no Black women graduated that year in my class. Only one other woman received her degree, and she was as white as I. We rarely had time for sisterhood, but I did consider her a soul mate, a partner in crime, and I always felt relief when I saw her in class. If she were to make it, maybe I could as well.

After graduation she joined the US Department of Justice, low-grade but a position with a future. At entry she could count on good money and regular advancement. My salary offer wasn't bad. I started at a level higher than the income of the average family of four.

A few junior staff members had separate offices, but I, being the most junior of the junior and a woman, was given a cubicle adjacent to the other women, secretaries all. Initially I was miffed, but eventually I learned that two or three secretaries knew the law better than the inferior junior staff. I hitched my wagon to the thoroughbred super secretaries, listening eagerly to their chatter about the attorneys, cases, partners, and wives. It seemed I had joined a firm rife with internal intrigue.

Low-status attorney Joe Johnson was sleeping with one of the secretaries. He eagerly leaned over her desk, pushing papers around, and apparently after hours he confided secrets to her. He told her that Mr. Willis and Mr. McTavish had long ago decided which one was the adjudicator and which one the administrator. As a result, Mr. Willis's billings practically supported the firm while Mr. McTavish sat on his ever-expanding bottom and handled dealings with suppliers over the cost of paper and whether or not to change from Coke machine to Pepsi in the fifth-floor lounge. At least that's what secretary Cindy said Joe Johnson said. Mr. Willis was the money-maker and Mr. McTavish was the paper-pusher. This information about the firm's chief partners spread from floor to floor until Mr. McTavish's personal secretary met with Joe Johnson's honey ending the honey's career that very day.

The firm represented corporate clients. I swallowed my rebellious urgings, nodded welcomingly to men-in-suits who passed my cubicle. With no need to know their names, and recognizing those who wished to remain invisible, I usually thought of them as the funeral man, or the agricultural giant, or the airplane people. In the beginning I never got close enough to know or to be known. I was a glorified, well-paid go-fer.

Joe Johnson wasn't the only one sleeping around. The office, at least on the two lower floors, was sex city. It worked to my advantage.

I am not bad-looking myself although Grandmother Alexander would not want me to say so. It is just that I don't want to compromise myself or expose myself to any vulgarisms or acquire a vulgar reputation. After all, I have heard the secretaries' gossip. I don't want to be their subject of conversation. I hope to have a long, profitable, successful career in the law.

I limit my sexual relationships to men in my outside-the-office life, primarily men I meet in my condo building or in the neighborhood. Doctors and scientists seem to be the ones who attract me and who are interested enough in me to crash through my personal barriers. I have been told that I am "commitment averse" but I define myself as "picky," holding out for the totally flawless fellow.

Doctors have demanding schedules, but then, so do I. I am mostly dating medical and surgical residents from the nearby world-class medical center. They are about as willing to commit to a long-term relationship as I am. Sex is sex, an identity. My attitude is not particularly soft and cuddly. I do like to have a male partner who enjoys symphony or the occasional theatre performance, but I can go alone to museums.

I would love a loving relationship but as Granny said, "There is nothing better than a good, mutually-satisfying marriage, but short of that, it is better to be single." I never knew Grandfather Alexander, and I wonder if he and Granny had a mutually-satisfying marriage. I know that he ran off, leaving her with no money and a child to raise alone.

Mother's mother, Reenie Tilson McKay, didn't fare well in the love market. She had twelve children, not all by the same man. And certainly my own Mother did badly, marrying a man capable of monster behaviors.

Grandmother Reenie McKay: Just hold on, girlie. I was not always old and slow. It is true that I have twelve children, of course all of them grew up now. Lee McKay showed up on the mountain looking for water to fill up bottles he could sell down in the valley. He saw me at Low Glen. He could sing, and he could dance a jig, and he begged me to come away with him. I was fifteen. My mother was quiet, and my Pap was strict. They wanted me to stay on the mountain and be a teacher. Mam said I was smart. But Lee could sing, and he could dance, and he wanted me to go with him. "Go where?" I asked him. "Off the mountain," he said, "to the big, wide world." "Who could say no to that?" We had a time, then he took to drink, and I did what any other woman'd do. I found me another man, and when he don't work, I found me another.

My biggest problem at the office is Scott Allen Samuels. He held a private office on my floor, an office with a window. He was a good-looking man, a graduate of a prestigious East Coast school. His father was a senior partner, meaning he had a legacy in the firm. He wore a wedding ring, and the secretaries said his wife was a gorgeous woman who owned an art gallery in one of the up-and-coming trendy areas of town. I never met her, but I noticed Gloria Sawyer, secretary from on-high, the fifteenth floor, frequent Scott's office. The Samuels-Sawyer merger was discussed in the break room, usually in hushed tones feigning excited expectation of disaster.

Samuels and Sawyer must have been oblivious to their surroundings as Mr. Funeral Association arrived for his appointment one Friday afternoon and with his own sense of entitlement walked directly into Scott Samuels's office only to find the two lovers in a deliciously salacious position. The door open for much too long gave us all a bare-bottomed view of at least one of the couple, difficult to say which.

My Grandmother Alexander always said, "What goes on behind closed doors should remain behind closed doors." Personally, I think the Las Vegas tourism board owes her for use of this slogan.

In the ever-extending moments that followed, it became obvious that Samuels and Sawyer were in fact unable to separate, not unwilling, physically unable. Even from a distance, I noted an expression approaching panic on the face of Scott Samuels.

I could not help myself. I jumped into action, pulling the client from his frozen position in Mr. Samuels´ doorway, suggesting we go to the break room or even to the lobby where there is a coffee vendor. The funeral man, I should be an adult and call him by name as he is the President of the state's Funeral Directors Association. Mr. Wintermeyer – why am I thinking "Winterbottom?"– surely had seen a sufficient number of nude bodies, a sufficient number of "moving parts" to be inured to what he witnessed in his attorney´s office.

Unfortunately, maybe truly fortunately for me in the long-run, Mr. Wintermeyer did not want coffee. He insisted on speaking immediately with Mr. McTavish. Thinking briefly of my desire for McTavish and Willis to remain in business, I accompanied Mr. Wintermeyer to the sixteenth floor, rarefied air for me. In my deepest, most charming Southern voice, the one that usually appears only after drinking at least one Scotch on the Rocks, I insisted he relax in one of the low-slung over-pillowed sofas, that he enjoy the panoramic view of our Chi-Town. Surprisingly he complied. I credit myself with skill, with power in semi-social situations. I sat with him and chatted about the skyline, the amazingly beautiful architecture, the loveliness of the traffic, the fortunate quality due to all of us who chose to live in Chicago. He commented on my accent, recognizing that I must be Southern, and that led us to a conversation about his family vacation to New Orleans, his good friend, the Director of the Texas Association of Funeral Directors, his desire to travel more in the South. I agreed with him that the Southern United States have a unique quality of beauty and charm and assured him that he would find any travels in my home neck of the woods to be welcoming and friendly both to himself and his family. I perhaps laid it on too thick but it seemed not to have done harm.

I ended up in the enormous, plantation-sized enormous, office of Mr. McTavish. He seemed to fill the space which I as a Southern woman took in completely in its entirety: Georgian mahogany pedestal desk with tooled leather writing surface, wing-back chairs covered in Jacobean crewelwork depicting exotic plant shapes, a lovely but new Oriental rug in soft pastel colors, floor-to-ceiling windows on two walls, and two landscape paintings to my left that looked vaguely like the Highlands. I stood facing that desk and the impressive personage behind it.

Many people are fooled by my Southern accent. Slow voice means slow mind is assumed. This assumption can lead to a dangerous, oft surprising outcome. In front of Mr. McTavish in surroundings designed to intimidate, I felt perfectly at ease. I was born to flourish in elegance. I am a flower of the South.

I detailed "the situation" to Mr. McTavish. He listened without interrupting me. When I was finished and had explained Mr. Wintermeyer's need for ventilation and reassurance, Mr. McTavish thanked me quite formally, and I all but backed out of the room.

Granny Alexander: I am proud of you. At least you didn't have to curtsey.
Grandmother Reenie McKay: Remember that these are men. Show a little leg or wiggle just a little.

Not forgetting Mr. Wintermeyer, I set aside my knowledge of the funeral industry, recently gleaned from reading Jessica Mitford's *The American Way of Death,* unkind to Mr. Wintermeyer's chosen profession. I joined him in his secluded nook, asked him to identify several Chicago landmarks easily visible through those gigantic windows. It was with relief that I could leave when Mr. Wintermeyer was invited to join Mr. McTavish in the grand office.

I wish I could have been in that office, as a listener, not a participant, but alas, it was by invitation only. Instead I dutifully returned to my low-level home territory. Mr. Scott Allen Samuels was now fully dressed, sans Ms. Sawyer, standing at my cubicle. Pressing me anxiously for information, I told him what I had done with Mr. Wintermeyer. His face reddened, and it was all that I could do to maintain my serious composure as the earlier vision of his face, not really his face but that which I saw through the open doorway, was the real Scott Allen Samuels.

On Monday I was transferred to the sixteenth floor.

Ms. Sawyer was toast and Scott Allen Samuels, being a man, suffered for about two weeks as jokes about his prowess made the rounds.

****

Wasting no time, Mr. McTavish summoned me into his office. His secretary Ava accompanied me, but with a nod of his head, she was dismissed, closing the door behind her. Surprisingly, Mr. McTavish indicated I was to sit. I had no idea what to expect. He had no just cause to fire me.

"I asked you to come in because I have a task that needs doing."

I read the anxiety in his face, somewhere around the edges of his mouth, a slight quiver.

He continued, "It is a personal task involving my finances, and I need someone I can trust. Do you think I could trust you?"

"Yes. If you want your business to remain private, I can, I will keep it private."

"I thought so. I don't want anyone else in the firm to know my business. You came with excellent references. You are obviously intelligent. I don't even want Ava to know the details of this business."

"Thank you, sir. I appreciate your trust in me. I will keep your business confidential. Where am I to work and will you tell me about the task?"

"Ava is organizing an office for you on this floor." If I had not been listening so intently to Mr. McTavish, I could have counted my heart rate just by placing my hand over my breast. "You will work with the door closed, and when you leave the office, you will lock the door. I have a key, but no one else but you and I can access the space."

He buzzed for Ava who promptly came for me. He instructed her to settle me into the new office, then turned to me. "I will join you in your office in one hour and we'll go over the details." Your office, my office!

I was filled with excitement, over the moon, and had to work hard to control myself. This was a real professional expectation requiring confidentiality and competence. I had trained for this in school. Since my earlier experience in Mr. McTavish's office had clearly produced this extravagant result, I followed my former behavior and removed myself as silently and elegantly as I had been trained.

Mother: I thought those hours you spent in charm school were silly, but maybe something positive rubbed off on you. Just remember, only wear tennis shoes if you are playing tennis, or perhaps if you are a visitor on a yacht.
Lucinda Lee (Me): Yes, Mother. That is exactly what the teacher said.

The office itself actually had wooden furniture, a mauve decor, a visitor's chair, a bookcase and a window. Missing was a telephone, but Ava explained that Mr. McTavish had requested a private line for me, that it would be installed before day's end. This was both good and bad. It meant my calls would not be answered at the switchboard. I would be responsible for answering my own phone with no one taking messages for me.

"Does he want you to do any work that I could help you with?" This was a cagey way for Ava to pry. What she really meant was, "What are you doing for Mr. McTavish? Tell me all."

I viewed this volley as my first test and responded, "Mr. McTavish has not yet given me details. Do you find him difficult to work for?"

"Yes, he is demanding, but they all are."

"I have to tell you I am not big on sharing information. Do not expect me to be a tell-all. I follow the Bar's confidentiality requirements and am not big on in-house gossip."

This was not a particularly kind thing to say as I was implying that perhaps Ava was a gossip, but I wanted to set the stage correctly. I didn't yet know what the task would be. As one would expect, Ava did not tarry. She had probably worked with more difficult attorneys than me.

When left alone in my new space, I opened and closed drawers, found the usual yellow-lined legal pads, black ballpoint pens, and other office paraphernalia. I found two standard real estate directories and one Bar Association directory on the shelves but nothing else to give me a clue about my future with McTavish and Willis.

I hoped there was a bathroom nearby as I began to feel a little squeamish in the nether regions. What if this business were illegal? Could I work in this environment as a loner? Could I do the required job? Mr. McTavish was known to be the paper-pusher. I hoped I would not be ordering coffee filters and creamer.

Luckily for me, Ava returned with coffee and directions to the ladies' room (it was on the fifteenth floor). I sent her out again as I prefer decaf coffee, pretty nervy of me, but here I was, sitting in an office on the sixteenth floor.

When I received my brief from the boss, I was greatly relieved, confident and exceedingly eager to begin. The task at hand was to interface with the Florida bank, representing Mr. and Mrs. McTavish, in the acquisition of a multi-million-dollar coastal property. I would review and familiarize myself with McTavish financial affairs, and I would complete the process from start to finish.

In truth I was no expert in these matters, hardly knowledgeable, but on the asset side, I was a quick learner, could take instruction from Mr. McTavish and could operate independently when needed. I had passed the Bar exam on my first try. I was a good novice candidate for this job.

The sad part, however, was the realization that Mr. McTavish could not, did not, trust any member of his own firm. I think he picked me precisely because I was arrogant and ignorant.

Thus begins my career.

Work, Then Pleasure

We represent the Illinois Hospital Association as well as a large publicly-traded healthcare company that owns a network of hospitals and outpatient clinics. Healing people of their ills often involves legal problems. Customers of these facilities claim they were treated negligently, employees claim they were injured on the job or in some way discriminated against, doctors misdiagnose, do the wrong surgery. Patients are given incorrect medications or fall on floors just cleaned by a conscientious janitor. Survivors claim wrongful death. The list is long. I always thought hospitals were places people went to get well, but apparently that is not always the case. Our firm is all over malpractice. We play golf with hospital administrators, deep sea fish with orthopedic surgeons, shoot skeet with urologists, enjoy symphony with psychiatrists, and occasionally host luncheons for the Nurses' Association. When I say "we," I exclude myself.

None of the male attorneys wants to work on hospital guardianship cases. They prefer the bigger stakes of malpractice. The senior partners have decided guardianship issues are the realm of a female. No man here wants to appear in the Probate Court or get his hands dirty in the murky world of family conflict, abuse, isolation, old age, and illness. My colleagues think I have pulled the short straw. I don´t tell anyone, but I find these cases fascinating and enjoy the feeling of actually making a difference in the lives of real people as opposed to the difference I make in handling real estate transactions for members and clients of our firm. Money, money, money. Guardianship can involve money but if the needy person has money, more often than not relatives have already picked dry the bones and gotten out of Dodge.

I am the attorney considered unlucky enough to have coffee with the hospital social workers. They bring in no income to the facilities we represent, at least not directly. They don't have personal income sufficient to afford days out on Lake Michigan or weekends in Las Vegas. They strike me as hard-working, conscientious people who often find themselves walking high wires connecting the solid brick and mortar buildings of their employers and the gelatinous substances of humanity.

Grandmother Reenie McKay: I don't truck with no social workers. Back when I had babies one of 'em came round and asked a lot of questions. "How many babies you got? Do you know who the fathers are? Do you have running water? How much money you got? Is your husband working?" I told her to get herself on down the road. She thought she was bettern me. I saw her leave some groceries on my front porch, beans and rice and cheese. She didn't even call out my name, just left the bag and high-tailed it. She probably knew I would've got my broom after her.

I have learned that they do bring money into the coffers indirectly, often by developing ethical, workable, discharge plans for patients who otherwise would be taking up hospital beds ad infinitum. Discharges are important because the more times the bed turns over, the more revenue for the hospital. Sort of like a restaurant where the quicker the customer orders, eats, and vacates the table, the quicker the next customer can be seated and the more times the table is filled, the more income for the restaurant. What restaurant encourages dawdlers? The hospital administration wants the patient out, and the social worker wants a plan that provides care for the patient in the community. The social worker also wants to keep his/her job. They have a bad reputation. I think it stems from the 1930s, during the Depression, when people had no money and state social workers enforced the law by taking children away from impoverished parents and placing them in orphanages.

Files for the most distressing guardianship case yet sit on my desk. I cannot get the details out of my head. Last week one of our hospital administrators asked me to join her in a meeting with a physician and social worker concerning a patient they were unable to discharge. The patient, she explained, was elderly and unable to understand and follow simple directions. He was admitted with multiple decubitus ulcers (bedsores), in a badly contracted state, with high fever and delirium. He was unclean, emaciated and had no accompanying caregiver or family member. The patient's immediate basic needs – nutrition, personal hygiene, dressing changes, diagnostics, and medications – had been addressed in the acute care hospital unit, but he could not stay there for custodial care now that the course of IV antibiotics was completed and his condition was stabilized. The hospital required a decision-maker who could understand the options available, to develop and implement a plan for the safe care of this patient. The word "abused" was not mentioned in the initial conversation. However, it was used frequently during the conference I attended last Thursday at the hospital.

I was impressed by the hospital's staff: social worker Lila Banks and by Dr. Parsons, both humane and caring professionals. Ms. Banks said she had practiced medical social work for twelve years, that this case took effort for her to remain non-judgmental. She worked on this case in coordination with Margaret Ames, the community Adult Protective Services caseworker assigned to the hospital's catchment area. Ms. Banks introduced me to Ms. Ames, also in attendance at the meeting. The two social workers presented me with their findings concerning the patient's social and economic status. Dr. Parsons participated by cuing Ms. Banks when she reached a full-stop in the medical part of the story.

After the meeting, Ms. Banks gave me the following summary.

"The patient, John David Strong is an 84-year-old Caucasian male widowed for thirteen years, his wife having died in a nursing home. They had several children whom they brought up on a small farm they squatted in southern Illinois. Mr. Strong was well-known to the county sheriff and to Child Protective Services. He served two years on an eight-year sentence for armed robbery and is believed to have used several aliases, eventually moving his wife and children to Chicago. After several addresses and various aliases our subject, Mr. Strong, managed to keep his children out of school and himself just under the radar of police and protective agencies. Now the only two people traceable are Mr. Strong and his eldest son, Robert. The two live together. Robert clearly had not been an adequate caregiver."

Ms. Ames asked me to accompany her on a visit to the Strong's home. She assured me we would take along a police officer, and she suggested I "dress down."

"Don't wear good shoes or light-colored clothing," she advised. "Wear something washable." She placed particular emphasis on jewelry. "No jewelry is best."

I had no difficulty selecting dark clothing although none of my dark suits were washable but I had to hunt for appropriate shoes. I found a pair of rain-ruined flats in the back of the closet; shoes I should have thrown away but was grateful I had not. The no-jewelry rule was easily manageable as I never wore flashy jewelry. I removed all but a couple of bills from my billfold, keeping enough for a taxi, and placed the rest of the money with the stash I always keep in the apartment for emergencies. For the record, diary, I don't keep the stash in a cookie jar or in my lingerie drawer.

Unsure what to expect, perhaps the worst, I met Ms. Ames and the officer and rode with them to a part of Chicago I had never seen before. En route the thought occurred to me, maybe those masses, especially Blacks, who migrated to this city, hopeful for an improved life, would have found this environment more degrading. No welcoming neighborhood here, no ground to stand on, to own or to till, just broken glass and weeds and brick and deteriorating concrete. Wouldn't a shotgun wooden shack with a door leading to a front stoop, steps to soil be more appealing, more homely than this?

Great-Grandfather Robert Tilson: I reckon you could rightly say we didn't have much in the way of cash money but we always had land. I could step outside where I lived and walk on land. I don't feel sorry for these city people. They problems ain't mine. They made some real bad choices.

The car pulled over to the curb, what was left of delineation between roadway and sidewalk. The house we were visiting had a make-shift well-worn wooden ramp in front. The policeman stood back, wary perhaps of his ability to protect two white, very white women, me with a briefcase and purse.

I readily let Ms. Ames take the lead. She whispered to me, "The police who accompany me on abuse calls never go in first."

Her rap on the door was answered by a pitiful-looking man of indeterminate age who could barely maintain his standing balance. His hair fell over his face; he had not shaved well and he was missing several teeth. He had a look of confusion, maybe born of an inability to understand why anyone would want to enter his home. His television was on, his seat obviously the towel-covered, worn corner of the tattered sofa.

Ms. Ames talked slowly to him reminding him that she had visited him before, that she was bringing me with her, and that I was going to help the judge take care of his father. I wondered if the judge would have found this amusing or poignant. I found it an indicator of this frail man's feeble grasp on reality.

When we sat to talk with Robert, I understood Ms. Ames's instructions about clothing. I tried not to see the roaches but to focus instead on the interview. Ms. Ames asked the questions, and Robert gave his brief responses. He clearly did not have the art of conversation.

After a few minutes, I got the gist. When Robert was a child, the family lived on a farm. Mr. Strong, frequently bedeviled by his own home brew, took out his fury on the children, Robert getting the worst treatment. His tortures were many and horrendous as he was kept chained for weeks on end with the dogs.

Clearly the damage to Robert was both physical and mental. I wondered if he could testify in court. I could not imagine him out of this milieu.

Ms. Ames informed me that the Strongs received two cheques each month, Robert's state Disability payment and an Old Age pension for his father. The local confectionary knew Robert and cashed the cheques. Robert then used that money to buy food, and he paid the rent man who stopped at his home door the first day of every month. He did not have money for medicine and did not go to any doctor. He told a woman at the grocery store that his father was sick and that woman had telephoned an ambulance.

At Ms. Ames's request, Robert showed me where his father slept. It was a baby crib. The odor in the room was strong, repugnant, and I felt weak, determined to remove myself as quickly as possible.

Ms. Ames thanked Robert for talking to us and told him we would meet soon with the judge, that, no, his father would not be returning home.

"What about the money?" Robert asked her.

"We'll figure that out after the judge makes his decision."

I noticed that Robert had never asked about his father's condition, but my thoughts initially were only on getting out of the house, although the air outside was not particularly fresh, it was at least not air in that sad, nihilistic set of rooms.

In the car, after I had gathered myself, I told Ms. Ames I would call the court scheduler, that I felt sure we could get an early date. The court would already have appointed an attorney for Mr. Strong, and I would meet with him or her to see how we could expedite matters. I explained that McTavish and Willis represented the hospital, not Mr. Strong or Robert, and that once the court appointed a guardian – probably a Public Administrator since there was no money involved – Ms. Banks could make a nursing home placement of her patient.

"Will the state pursue guardianship of the son?" I asked.

"No, we do not have enough money or time in our coffers. My supervisor says to look on the bright side. He has a roof over his head and a government cheque. That's more than some."

From Ms. Ames's office building, I took a taxi to my apartment where I stripped to bare skin immediately inside my entry hall. I was tempted to throw the clothing in the rubbish bin but instead put every item in the washing machine, even the dry-clean-only suit, turned the knob to Very Hot Water, Full Cycle. Happy that in my apartment I always have plenty of water, I ran into the shower and turned it on full-blast, soaking my entire body and my hair.

****

Dressed in my usual attire, I joined my Descendants Club sisters in our favorite downtown hotel bar for pre-dinner cocktails. We enjoyed our own private dining room with full attention to service.

Someone asked me, "How was your day, Lucinda Lee?"

I sipped my Scotch-on-the-rocks and replied, "I have had worse." Was that truth or not? I tried to focus on the evening's speaker on the role of American Indians in the War Between the States, our war, but my thoughts were of abuse and the karma in the lives of Robert Strong and his father. I could not prevent myself from thinking about my own past. Was the abuse I endured in my childhood less bad because now I was an educated woman with a somewhat civilized life? Robert Strong, despite his limitations, tried to care for his abuser. Was that a sign of his humanity or was he slowly torturing his father to death? In my case, I saw my father die a quick death, no long-term suffering imposed on him. What is it about witnessing the tragedy of others that makes us relive our own tragedies?

Oh, Scarlett, let us think about this tomorrow. Or not.

Wedding

Mother's name is now Dorothea McKay McKay. I find this extraordinarily funny but she is not amused.

"That's what happens when you marry your second cousin on your father's side." I am such an irritant.

She's been living on the mountain since the accident two years ago. G.W. promised devotion, and he is a man of his word. He is thin and angular; Mother is soft and curvy. They complement each other in appearance. Where Mother can be haughty and self-absorbed, G.W. is approachable, generous in spirit, and a good listener. I like them together. I shouldn't have to worry now about Mother, a big relief for me, although in truth worries about Mother fell on Sam's plate.

G.W.'s business has grown. He is a major player in the water business. Bottling is now done in the valley. I haven't seen the plant yet but feel sure he will want me to see the works. Sam is here for the celebration. He has already seen the plant but wants to go again. Manufacturing, water, chemistry all interest him. I am just interested in G.W.'s taking care of Mother. No, that isn't true. I am interested in the administration of G.W.'s business, how it is organized. That's how my brain works.

Mother and G.W. were married this morning in the chapel once presided over by a Wardlaw. A Presbyterian Church now, the travelling minister performed the service. Everyone atop the mountain was invited as well as people who work for G.W.

Great-Grandmother Mattie Bain: My man were a good man. We married on the mountain near the springs. Married by old Preacher Wardlaw who got drunk as a skunk after saying we was man and wife. All the men got drunk but my man. He picked me up in his arms and ran through a field of purple coneflowers and black-eyed Susans and yellow buttercups so pretty I would have cried except was so happy to be married.

Grandmother Reenie: I couldn't wait to get off the mountain. Henry Lee and I ran off. We got married somewhere in Texas. I wore a new dress bought from a store. It was my first store-bought dress. Later I bought me a hat.

Granny Alexander: We women always remember our own weddings, every detail. You'll learn all about weddings when you have your own. You are planning to get married, aren't you?

Of course, I was the Maid-of-Honor. I teased Sam about how perfect he would be as ring bearer, and he insisted on calling me the flower girl. Sam walked Mother down the aisle, a walk that took about a minute. I finally learned that G.W. stands for George Washington. We have a George Washington on the mountain. I promise not to tease him, or Mother, but saying G.W. is better than having to say his full name. Besides, it makes me giggle, and a wedding is a serious event.

Actually, Sam and I are both happy to see Mother out of the Alexander prison and into G.W.'s warm, protective love. Looking back, I think he fell in love with her at the Zona gas pumps when Sam and I were children first discovering the mountain. Mother doesn't want to talk about it. She is embarrassed to be in love. She may not realize it, but she is too old to play the blushing bride. But today is not for criticism. We are all celebrating. Who doesn't love love?

Mother and I are linked by blood and secrets. I deny our similarities because I see her as dependent and focused on herself more than on Sam and me. I see myself as fiercely independent. I wonder how she will respond to so much love. Will she absorb it all? Will she return it? My guess is that G.W. will indulge her, give her whatever she wants and accept her no matter how she behaves. From battery to indulgence, what a road my mother is travelling. This wedding business makes me introspective. I try to shake it off because I definitely do not want to revisit the past.

After the ceremony, at G.W. and Mother's home, we have "all day singing and dinner on the ground" or maybe it is "all day dinner and singing on the ground, I do not know everyone who is here enjoying the hospitality, but the noise, the food, the presents stacked on a folding table outside in the sunshine, the flies, and the dogs, all contribute to the success of the day. The music was the best. I could have listened to the fiddling all night long."

G.W. has done Mother proud. He has built her a home with a spectacular view of the valley. It has all the modern conveniences. Mother has obviously had an unlimited budget in decorating. G.W. graciously tells Sam and me the house has plenty of bedrooms, and we are welcome to stay any time, but not tonight.

G.W. and Mother are staying in the house tonight, starting their honeymoon on the mountain before setting out for New Orleans. Mother wants to tour plantations along the lower Mississippi and G.W. wants to do whatever Mother wants to do. This marriage may work!

Sam and I are bunking at Aunt Lillian's where even though I am a practicing attorney with a job in Chicago, on the mountain, I have a curfew. Can't argue because I am a guest.

Sam and I have decided he will take me down to Clayville tomorrow to tour the plant. Tonight we drive over to the Wardlaw Garage to catch up on old friends.

Stoke has not changed. His red hair is still too long, and he still has bad posture. He is running the garage now. I ask him if he finished his undergraduate studies at University of Arkansas. He tells me he quit after two years, when his father died. I do not ask him if he remembers our kissing in Aunt Lillian's kitchen because he is married. He introduces me to June who looks sturdy, strong. She has a beautiful smile, dark eyes and shiny hair. She tells us she doesn't like the garage, prefers being in her home. Stoke clears off a seat for her by placing a towel over an old metal folding chair. I like her. She will give Stoke babies, and he will adore her. I see their future and it is good. What is it about this mountain that creates and nurtures deep love?

Chance looks more than ever like Paul McCartney. I wonder if he can sing. He finished two years at a junior college in the valley and is working for G.W. It seems these boys have stamina for two years of college and no more.

"I do whatever needs doing. Sometimes G.W. needs help with the truckers who take the water down the back of the mountain. Sometimes I check production activities at the plant. No day of mine is like the day before."

When all of us are inside, Chance closed the garage door indicating no more business today. He turns on a couple of small desk lamps. We are a cozy group: Stoke, June, Chance, Cyril, Sam and I. Cyril, beside me, says he is working at the Sheriff's Office. He is interested in my work. I tell him a little about the firm that employed me straight out of law school.

"Are you happy up there in Chicago? Do you think you'll ever come back here?"

"I am happy in Chicago, but I am not a Yankee. They treat me differently knowing I am a Southerner. I probably treat them differently because they are different. Sometimes I think no one was taught manners. The work is good, and I have some friends. We do fancy things, like go to hear the symphony."

That is a conversation stopper. No one has anything to say about Chicago or symphony. I could have said, "I enjoy visits to Japan, or to Mars" and I would have received the same reaction.

Chance and Sam stand, tell us they are going "out back" and will return shortly. To get the conversation going again, we talk about the wedding and the people at the party. Chance and Sam return with Mason jars filled with home brew.

"McKay Mash," Sam says, "is well-known in these parts. You fellows have been brewing for generations, right?"

"Yeah, Wardlaws and McKays go way back. The McKays made the mash and the Wardlaws ran it."

Why didn't I know this? I am not in the mood to ruminate over male and female differences but how did Sam learn about McKay Mash? No one ever mentioned it to me.

Admittedly, I don't like the taste. It cuts my mouth like razors. June doesn't drink any but the boys profess a taste for it.

"I don't think I can drink anything that comes out of a Mason jar," I say but no one cares. It doesn't take many sips of the mash for the effect to take hold. I'm thinking I will be driving back to Aunt Lillian's tonight as Sam looks like he is slaking his thirst. Any minute now, the men may start saying things they will regret in the morning.

"Would you like to see an old car?" asks Chance.

Sam eagerly responds, "Sure." Already he is slurring his speech. I think he is not a drinker. I am along for the ride, following Chance and Sam, leaving our cozy dimly-lit nest behind. We walk a path out back and to the east of the garage.

"Over there are some cabins we rent out in the summer." He points and in the moonlight I can almost discern an outline. "Behind the first one, follow me."

I cannot see Sam but tag along close to Chance who shines his flashlight toward an old wooden shack. I´m afraid of snakes. Chance assures me they aren't out at night and I believe him. He unlocks the padlocked door. It seems silly to lock a door of a building that I could push over even with my girlie strength.

"We keep it locked so the tourists don't wander in."

I'm hoping the raccoons and squirrels haven't wandered in and dare not think of any other possible intrusive things that could go bump in the night or that hiss and rattle.

Chance switches on an overhead light and with Sam's help, unveils an old vehicle, maybe from the twenties or thirties.

"It could outrun everyone," Chance says with pride in his voice.

"Where was the booze stored?" asks Sam, walking around the car.

The fellows open the doors and poke around inside. The seats lift out as do the door panels revealing cavernous spaces for hiding contraband.

"Wouldn't the investigators know where to look?" I ask.

"You've been hanging around symphony people too long. 'Revenuers', not investigators." Chance corrects me. "They couldn't catch this car."

Sam and Chance lift the hood and look at the engine. Sam is impressed. "You would get some speed out of this baby."

"Do you want to see my car?" Chance asks.

In for a penny, in for a pound. I am vaguely interested in cars, but it is a pleasure to be with Sam and the adorable Chance. I am enjoying their excitement. This is not like my daily Chicago life.

Chance leads us deeper into the garage to show us his car. It is a souped-up sedan.

"I race this car. You would be surprised at how many tracks there are at the foot of the mountain. I do pretty well." He shines his flashlight on a bulletin board pinned with several colorful ribbons.

Our Chance is a dare-devil!

When we rejoin our crew, Stoke asks Chance if he showed us both cars. "I'm proud of my brother. He's one fast driver."

I turn to Cyril. "The sheriff's not after him, I hope."

Cyril grins. "Not tonight."

Love Hurts

I'm in love. I'm not saying I want to get married, but I am in love. He is special, extremely well-educated, sophisticated, ultra-intelligent and very New York. He comes from a family similar to mine in that religion and family are top priority. He was devout earlier in his life but became more worldly when he was an undergrad at Harvard, or maybe when he did his doctorate at Yale. He speaks fluent French and is an Assistant Professor in Microbiology at Northwestern University. We live in the same building. I call him 9D. I'm 7A.

A mutual friend, actually the doorman, introduced us when we were both coming inside at the same time, umbrellas, rain dripping. It was very romantic. We had seen each other in the elevator but had not been introduced. His name, I'm excited writing about him, is David Weiss, Dr. David Weiss.

We have the same birthday, not the same year. He is thirteen years older than me. I like knowing his bar mitzvah occurred the year of my birth. He is knowledgeable about everything and very interested in my work. He says he cannot imagine the human suffering I encounter in my guardianship cases. He is less interested in my real estate transactions and asks silly questions that make me laugh at his naiveté. He may know a great deal about DNA but he isn't very keen on investments. And, on popular culture, he is hopeless. I teach him about Delta blues and The Eagles.

We are an item at symphony, have season tickets. He pays for his and I for mine. We do not mingle our money. During intermission I introduce him to colleagues from McTavish and Willis. He is charming and they are impressed with his position at the university.

I am the subject of office gossip. Mr. McTavish's private secretary bribes me with tea. She brings a cup to my office, green tea with lemon, and tarries too long at my desk. She wants "just a little information." My firm is a total gossip mill. Granny Alexander always said, "No one is good for more than two weeks." I find comfort in that. I can tolerate two weeks.

I buy all new lingerie, matching bras and panties, lots of lace. I shop at Saks Fifth Avenue. Everything I buy is sexy but not raunchy. I indulge in a gorgeous turquoise peignoir – otherwise known as a matching robe and gown – but in the Lingerie Department it is a peignoir. It cost a fortune but it makes a statement.

I am down to size six. Unless we go out to dinner, I have no appetite. On Sunday nights I go to David's apartment and we have Chinese or deli food and watch Masterpiece Theatre.

Did I write about his intelligence? We read the *New Yorker Magazine;* late Saturday nights we pick up the Chicago edition of the *New York Times.* We read the newspaper in bed on Sunday mornings. We talk about politics. I have insights about local politics because I keep my ears open at the firm, but David knows about international politics and enthralls me with his assessments of the news.

I buy a Jewish cookbook and make the effort. David says my chicken soup is delicious. I read stories by Isaac Bashevis Singer and we discuss Jewish culture. I love every aspect of Judaism, Reform, and Orthodox.

For our birthdays we celebrate with David's family who fly in from New York, Boston, and Philadelphia. One of the aunts asks me if I want babies. I am reminded of my own family's comments. I think all families are alike. I flippantly tell her that I prefer marriage first.

I do not reveal my judgment that David could not tolerate the changes in life required by children. He is a devoted scientist, dedicates his energy to the laboratory. In many respects he is obsessive-compulsive, more so than I. Children upset order. I think my contribution to this relationship is my openness to thinking outside the box. He may be brilliant but I do detect restriction in him. Freud would say, anal retentive.

David's family approves of me. I do not admit it, but I would have no difficulty becoming Jewish. My family wouldn't care. They have always admired the value Jews place on education, and David is a Ph.D. and a university professor.

David travels in August to France, meeting cousins and touring about for two weeks and five days. I cannot leave Chicago in August although I would love to escape the heat. I am working on two guardianship cases that need preparation for court hearings as soon as possible. And more to the point, David did not ask me to accompany him.

We renew our season's tickets for symphony, and prepare for a second winter together with theatre and dance society tickets as well. I am in cultural heaven.

****

We accept dinner invitations from law office colleagues and from David's university peers. We entertain at restaurants. I learn to appreciate exotic drinks like Lillet with lemon peel. We chat about authors and plays and guest violinists. We are urbane and I feel beautiful and sublimely happy.

****

Second birthday together. Hanukkah. Christmas. No proposal. No ring. I open a large box: ice skates.

****

David begins having headaches that interfere with our social life. My headaches are gone. His are making him miserable. He consults his physician, has multiple tests. The physician says his headaches are stress-related. David denies stress at work. He finds happiness in his laboratory. He consults his rabbi. It seems I am the problem. I am the cause of David's stress.

I ask David if he would feel better if I converted to Judaism. He replies that it is not his place to express an opinion on that topic. I feel quite lost.

We no longer have sex. I watch Masterpiece Theatre alone in my apartment. I leave the turquoise peignoir in David's closet. I never want to see it again.

I don't know if I will ever love again. David was the love of my life. No one in my family expresses an opinion.

My Personal Stalker

Living in the same apartment building as David is difficult because I occasionally run into him in the elevator. Once he asked me when I planned to pick up the blue robe that I left in his closet.

"Turquoise, not blue," I say just as the elevator door opens and I quickly step across the threshold to the seventh floor. I feel good that I have left that little correction in the air behind me. I never want to see that robe again, but David doesn't seem to understand. He probably thinks a robe is merely a robe, but to me, it was purchased purposely for its effect. He doesn't get it. It must bother his sense of order to see it hanging among the shirts in his bedroom closet. I get no joy out of his discomfort. Our relationship was not supposed to end. I have let him go but the sadness lingers.

The answer to the problem is a basketball team. I need to date several men at once, get involved deeply with no one – meaning: don't have sex yet. I need, not just want, to be wined and dined, to have several possible dates for art museum lectures and theatre. I want to play tennis in the afternoon with one adoring man, come home to change clothes for an evening with another adoring man. Is it wrong to want many adoring men?

Everywhere I turn are men, married men. I am not ready to date a married man. I have principles. The Illinois Bar Association has asked me to serve on the Ethics Committee. For once I am not a token female. There are two other women on the committee. This committee has more women than most which speaks to the known ethics of men in the Bar. That was naughty. I should not have written it.

My life is McTavish and Willis. I made junior partner and continue to enjoy my special relationship with senior partners about whom I know a great deal. My singular role handling everyone's real estate transactions has given me access to the secrets of several of these fellows. I know where the money is hidden. Because of this unique position, I have no doubt I will become a full partner.

Money has become a non-issue for me. I think about where to invest. As the firm's in-house real estate specialist, it is amusing and ironic that I am a renter. A major client of the firm is building a high rise in Midtown, not far from my current apartment. I like the location and put "look at the drawings" on my list of tasks.

I do enjoy a swimming pool. On weekends, when I am not at the office, I spend summer Saturday and Sunday afternoons sunbathing beside our building's pool. It is placed adjacent to the high-rise I call home, on the west side. Sun is best in the afternoon.

Like every other single woman, I arm myself with water, a book, beach towel and plenty of sunscreen. I call it sunbathing but actually I don't want to tan. I turn red in the sun and break out in a heat rash.

Granny Alexander: My mother never let me expose my skin to the sun. We had croppers who picked the cotton. I never even went out of the house without covering my arms and wearing a hat. That's why I have no wrinkles. Porcelain skin is what you want and you'll have it, if you stay covered in the sun.

Sitting by the pool is an act of wish fulfilment for me. It allows me to shed the inhibitions of my Austin-Reed black suits and Ferragamo low heels with the tidy toe bow. Instead I wear fabulous two-piece swimsuit ensembles with stylish cover-ups and colorful sandals.

Sometimes I lounge next to a rather butch Ph.D. Speech Pathologist. I enjoy her stories about her clinic's efforts to help inner city children. She has asked me to join her for drinks several times, but I have begged off. I would probably enjoy myself so I tell her today that I accept.

It was at the pool that I met a large, boisterous French-Canadian man named Frank Lucas. Not another scientist, I told myself, but yes, another scientist. Dr. Lucas burst into my life as he succeeded in jumping from his second-floor balcony into the ground-level pool, terrifying those of us who were more-or-less soaking in the ray's poolside. He was only inches from injury, barely missing the concrete pool surround.

One of my fellow residents, Mr. Johnson, immediately arose from his lounger, slipped on his sandals, wrapped a towel around his shoulders and walking rapidly through the side door into the building, ran to the Manager's Office to report Dr. Lucas's dangerous, out-of-order behavior. Dr. Lucas, having splashed all of us with displaced water, appeared to be enjoying paddling about in the water. He yelled up to his balcony where other people were gathered, drinks and cigarettes in hand, applauding his dare-devilry.

"Jump. Dare you to jump," he excitedly called out to his friends.

Emerging through the blue door connecting the pool to the interior of our building was our highly coifed and girdled Mrs. Rosen, our beloved manager. She is always efficient in collecting rent and is a willing receiver of packages. Her desk faces the doorman and she seems to miss very little of the comings and goings in the building.

We have no lifeguard. It is a "swim-at-your-own-risk" pool but standard rules are posted: no running, no glass, children only if supervised.

Mrs. Rosen grabs the long metal pole used by the pool maintenance man, and she runs toward the pool holding it as though she were jousting. Frankly I think her maneuver was difficult as on the run she balanced the pole carefully, aimed it at Dr. Lucas, jabbing him on the left shoulder blade. He was involved with his friends, shouting, daring them to jump and at first swatted the pole as though it was a mosquito landing on his back.

"Turn around, Dr. Lucas. Over here," she screamed in an authoritative manner.

Dr. Lucas obeyed. He seemed stunned by the manager's poking a pole at him. He grabbed the pole and if Mrs. Rosen had not at that very moment dropped it to ground, she would have joined Dr. Lucas in the deep end.

The scene struck me as a cross between frat boy on spring break and slapstick, but it wasn't funny as Dr. Lucas's dive was dangerous, not to mention immature. Who at his age, and with his bulk, jumps off a balcony into a swimming pool two stories below? A crazy person, that is my answer.

Dr. Lucas pays little heed to Mrs. Rosen because he has spotted me. It is a moment of supreme embarrassment as he yells out, "I give myself a ten. What do you say?"

I am mortified at being singled out by this wild man. Before I can give him a sharp reply, the Speech Pathologist responds, "We give you a zero. You could have killed yourself."

She gathers me up like a beach towel, and hurriedly guides us from the pool. Mrs. Rosen and Dr. Lucas remain to sort out violation and consequences. I am relieved to escape.

The poolside episode was only the first in the Lucas saga.

About two hours after the incident, he knocks on my door and asks me to join his party on the second floor. I decline. I am certain he is drunk.

The next day the doorman tells me Dr. Lucas has asked for information about me. Am I dating anyone? Do I date men? What is my profession? Where is my office? Do I go out at night? The doorman asks if I want him to answer Dr. Lucas's questions. I say absolutely not. Do not give out my personal information.

That evening Dr. Lucas again knocks on my door. He asks me out to dinner. I decline. I tell him I have plans. I do have plans. I am meeting one of my Descendants' friends at a local bistro. It is a relief to say no honestly but if I hadn't had plans, I would have lied.

I think I am saved from the daring, crazy Dr. Lucas and dismiss him from my thoughts until he impinges once again on my life. During the main course of my escapist dinner, I see Dr. Lucas walk in. He walks straight over to our table, pulls out a chair for himself and sits down.

I hate to be rude but he is unsettling. He talks about the restaurant, asks if the food is good. Before we can respond, he begins talking about our apartment building, how happy he is to have such a great apartment to live in for the next nine months, how he has driven his van down from Quebec, has no family, will work on a specified project (the details of which I do not catch) for a contracted period, how he is single and he never seems to stop. I rise from my chair while he is in mid-sentence. Even an attorney can identify mental illness or drugs or just craziness.

"Dr. Lucas, you are wearing me out. My friend and I just wanted a quiet dinner." He has no manners. Correction: he has bad manners. No one invited him to sit. He is talking incessantly to me when there is another person at the table, a person whom he has never met. I am a Southerner. I cannot say, "Dr. Lucas, please leave. I do not like you. You are rude and intolerable." It seems I cannot directly say what I mean in a social situation if my words would hurt someone's feelings.

"Excuse me. I didn't mean to impose. I don't know anyone here in Chicago."

I am both vilified and ashamed. What he has just said is a lie. Who were all those people on his balcony?

"Perhaps another night," he says and leaves.

I explain to my Descendants' friend Diana[1] that Dr. Lucas is a boisterous mad scientist. She is sympathetic and wants to know the entire story. I am happy to have someone to talk to about this drama in which I seem to have a key role.

The next day eighteen red roses are delivered to my desk with a note: "I'm sorry. Dinner tonight?"

This man just doesn't quit.

At least six or seven people walk past my office trying to get a glimpse of the bouquet. I say to no one in particular and everyone who is nosy, "Do you think I'm the only one who receives flowers?" This does not address the questions nor stop the interest in my personal life. I close the door.

In the afternoon, Dr. Lucas telephones McTavish and Willis and is connected to me. I am on the verge of calling the police but mentally replay his behavior and decide the police would not think Dr. Lucas warranted their involvement.

I tell Dr. Lucas I will meet him that night at a neighborhood restaurant. In my office I write a script, much like I used to write court statements. I want to be fully prepared to tell this Romeo-on-steroids that I will file harassment charges against him if he persists in chasing me. I do not see us on a date. My plan is more along the lines of a session in which I logically express my case.

We meet for dinner. He is surprisingly sane. Is it due to medication or have I misjudged him? He is a perfect gentleman and carries on a normal conversation showing appropriate interest in me and my life. I am almost convinced that I was too hasty in my judgment of him. I leave the script in my purse.

---

[1] The "Diana" mentioned here is your author. I have purposely deleted mention of myself in Lucinda Lee's diaries but the exception in this case is necessitated by my witnessing the event. While in other areas of Lucinda Lee's experience, I have tried to be non-judgmental, in this instance I can truthfully testify to Dr. Lucas's intrusive and obnoxious chatter. L.L. did not encourage him and seemed displeased and embarrassed by his behavior.

We return to the apartment building. He rides the elevator with me to the seventh floor. I unlock my door and thank him for the pleasant evening. He maneuvers his bulk so that I am blocked from entering my apartment. He places his hands on my waist or maybe one hand on my waist and one on my shoulder, and I am suddenly without options. I can't move forward, backward, or sideways. There is probably some wrestling or boxing term for the position he has me in. He leans over and kisses me on the mouth, a ghastly kiss, his mouth open, his tongue at my tonsils. As I try to pull away, he pulls me harder toward his body and rubs against my breasts. I step on his foot and try to position myself to knee his crotch when he pulls away, thanks me for the lovely evening and walks to the elevator.

I quickly step inside my apartment, close the door, double-checking that it is locked. I am stunned. I have a problem.

****

Granny Alexander: Maybe all men from Canada are like him. You should only go out with Southern men. Their mothers taught them good manners.

****

For the next ten days, Dr. Lucas seems to be everywhere I go. When I leave for work in the mornings, he greets me on the sidewalk in front of our building. When I return home at night he is in the lobby and asks me to join him for drinks and dinner. I do everything I can think of to avoid him. I am thinking of telling him that I am married but I would have to talk to him and he would undoubtedly ask me the whereabouts of my husband or he would egotistically believe my being married would have no impact on my having a relationship (an affair, sex, whatever he has in mind) with him.

****

Two weeks after the big pool splash, the doorman opens the door for me just as David is emerging from the Manager's Office. He greets me with a friendly smile, the kind that makes me wish we were still together. Even though I have an intellectual acceptance of our split, emotionally I am still healing. Where once was a broken heart is now a hairline fracture.

I do not want to engage in conversation with David. We have nothing more to say to one another but we find ourselves waiting together for the elevator. Because the moment is difficult, I say, "Have you seen the latest exhibit at the Art Museum?"

He replies, "I am dating the curator."

As my irritation begins to bubble in my tummy – never ask a question unless you know the answer – the elevator doors open and out bursts Dr. Lucas. He seems bigger than life.

"Perfect," says Dr. Lucas. "I hoped you would have supper with me tonight."

Something about his eyes and that slurred "s" tells me he is high on alcohol or God-knows-what illegal substance.

****

There is no place to run.

David rushes into the elevator. I am left alone with the lunatic. If I didn't know before now, David is not my knight in shining armor. No rescuer, he.

****

"No, Dr. Lucas. I cannot join you for dinner. I have business with the manager."

I edge toward Mrs. Rosen's door, open it without knocking, enter and close the door behind me. Mrs. Rosen is fortunately alone, sitting at her managerial desk, the credenza behind her stacked high with loose papers, file folders, color charts for paint, and three-ring notebooks. I don't like this kind of disorder, but at this moment it is not my primary concern.

Mrs. Rosen is very pleasant to me. It occurs to me that she probably knows about my broken romance with David Weiss.

"I need to talk to you about a personal matter," I say.

"Yes, we need to talk. Dr. Lucas is a nuisance."

I think this lady is more savvy about people's characters than I have given her credit for.

"I am considering a restraining order. In truth, I am also considering the purchase of a condo. I think it is time for me to move. I have loved my apartment and most of the residents, but I need to move on."

"Dear," she begins. I do not like to be addressed in this way, but today I do not mind a little mothering. "Dear, you need to leave town. Just for a month or so. We are going to evict Dr. Lucas. I cannot tell you how many complaints this office has received about his loud parties. The people that go in and out of that apartment have been threatening and scaring the doormen. We cannot have Dr. Lucas here."

"He is causing problems for me as well."

She continues, "He has not paid his rent. The last cheque he wrote bounced. He told me you would cover his overdue debt."

I am stunned. "The man is crazy. I most certainly will not shell out any money on his behalf. I want him out of my life. He follows me everywhere."

"Leave town. I think it will be easier for all concerned if you are not here during the eviction. I anticipate a security problem but we are prepared. I am so sorry that you have had to deal with a tenant of his caliber."

I like her idea. She instructs the doorman to walk with me to my apartment. He is a little elderly man who could not protect me even if he wanted to but I think it is a sweet gesture. I will remember him with an envelope.

I telephone Mr. McTavish, something I rarely do outside the office. I explain the problem to him and he agrees for the sake of my safety, I should leave town. He means, but does not say, that he does not want a crazy person disrupting the firm. All our staff and clients are, of course, sane.

Mr. McTavish becomes avuncular and jokes that I need to "go on the lam." He suggests the Highlands. I tell him I have a close alternative. I assure him I will be safe, that I have people who will look after me.

Our agreement is that I will come in to the office tomorrow morning and neaten my cases, arranging for any necessary coverage. Fortunately, none of our hospitals is pressing me right now about a guardianship case. This is particularly to my current benefit because these cases demand prompt attention. I have two real estate transactions that someone else will have to handle. Neither involves restricted deeds and I have completed most of the ground work.

I telephone Zona, visit with Mother and have serious discussion with G.W. who, if I asked, would fly to Chicago tonight to stand guard at my door. I tell

120

him I can make it through the night, that tomorrow I will drive down, down, of course, being the direction of the South. Driving is relaxing for me. Tomorrow after stopping at the office, I will be on the road. The problem of Dr. Lucas will be in the able hands of Mrs. Rosen.

Road Trip

Driving in Chicago is both madness and unnecessary. My little Corolla is parked happily year-round in a garage attached to a neighboring apartment building. The fee is slightly high but does not approach the cost of insurance which is stratospheric. The question arises, why bother to keep a car? The question is fair. The answer is not logical. The mere existence of the car, my car, gives me a sense of freedom. No, not logical. It is just there "in case."

Before today, I have never identified an "in case" situation but now is the time to call in the freedom card, to play it in triumph. My ego is boosted in the knowledge that I am prepared for this urgent need to "get out of Dodge," to leave Chicago in the capable hands of Mr. McTavish and Mrs. Rosen.

The work on my desk is an enticement to stay, but my better judgment prevails as evil thoughts about Dr. Lucas course through my brain. What nerve, telling Mrs. Rosen that I would pay his rent. I review my conversations and encounters with him and cannot blame myself except I have regret about going to dinner with him. My naiveté astounds me, but I cannot dwell on the past, and I am not one to focus on my limitations or errors.

Even using the interstate, it takes an hour to get out of Chicago. The Chicago skyline is striking. I study it in my rear-view mirror until it is impossible to see the tallest skyscrapers. I experience both the achy feeling of regret about leaving my adopted home and the excitement of the road. Granted, my little Toyota is no sports car, but then I'm no hotshot driver.

My plan is to drive to Springfield, have lunch and maybe explore the city, see the capitol building and the Lincoln home museum. Lincoln did, after all, play a significant role in the life of my forebears, and I owe him respect as President of the United States. None of the guest lecturers at our Descendants' meetings has educated us about Lincoln's life in Springfield. The least I can do for the chapter is to pick up some brochures. I believe the house is decorated in Renaissance Revival furniture and that will interest those who have no interest in the politics.

After an hour in the museum that was once the home of Abraham and Mary Lincoln, I have had enough of the exhortations about Lincoln's greatness, his depression, his fraught relationship with his wife, his exceptional skill often using humor at leading the split nation. Having listened in my high school American History course, I have already been taught most of what I was told this afternoon by the eager docent. I never said "I'm a member of the Descendants. My people were on the opposite side of the war." That would be rude, and possibly irrelevant. I guess these scripts written for docents are meant for tourists who never learned history in high school or university.

I am impatient. I leave Springfield headed for St. Louis. I'll spend the night in or around St. Louis. I have not seen the Arch and it would be fun to see that Gateway to the West.

Like Memphis and Argenta, my home ground, St. Louis is on the Mississippi River. I have many associations with the river and want to see the bluffs at St. Louis, and I have read about the Eads Bridge, the iron structure that I will drive over from Illinois into Missouri.

Missouri was a border state, declaring neither for the North or the South. Some of my father's family who lived in southern Missouri responded to the call of the Union. Others had differing views and loaded their rifles, gave out loud Rebel yells and shot at their own kin. But that is the past.

****

Approaching St. Louis from the Illinois side of the river did not disappoint. The Arch is truly an arch. I imagine Conestoga wagons driving through it, heading west.

Granny Alexander: The Alexanders came west on the Southern route, from South Carolina down through Georgia and eventually up the Mississippi. They stopped at Natchez. They didn't make it as far north as St. Louis. I knew someone who went to St. Louis in 1904 for the World's Fair.

Great-Grandmother Mattie Bain: Our people come west from Virginia, first to what is now Tennessee, and when it got too crowded, they went west again. The Bains and the Tilsons just wanted to be left alone. No, we never were in Missouri.

I am staying at a roadside Holiday Inn just beyond St. Louis on Highway I-55 South. The day on the road has been wonderful. As a tourist, I would deem it a success even though I didn't have time to see Lincoln's tomb. As a driver, it was okay although the two big cities, Chicago and St. Louis, were painful to drive through.

The scary truth is that I have seen a Chevy van that may be following me. I first saw it on the other side of Springfield, and then spied it again when I was having lunch. When I crossed the bridge into St. Louis, it was a few cars behind me. Am I paranoid? Chevy vans must be everywhere. It is just that Dr. Lucas has a van. He said he loaded it with his possessions and drove it from Quebec to Chicago. I must be paranoid.

The song plays repeatedly in my head: "She's gonna love me in my Chevy van." That is definitely not all right with me. Now that it is dark I am having frightening thoughts about an old Twilight Zone (or maybe The Outer Limits) television program about a truck relentlessly following and terrorizing an innocent couple.

****

Today's task is to focus on the road, to aim the car toward the Arkansas Ozarks and to arrive safely in Zona.

Driving today is less fun because I am feeling vulnerable. I should have telephoned G.W. last night but I didn't want to make a fool of myself. He would have told me to stay in the motel until he arrived. I know he is busy, and I hate to be dependent. I thought I saw the Chevy van when I stopped for lunch at Blytheville but not after that.

Climbing the mountain in my little Corolla is a breeze. At the "heaven or hell" sign I cling to the mountainside and drive slowly. No need to take risks. At the other side of the hairpin curve, on the road opposite, I see the van. Dr. Lucas is driving. I can see him clearly. He has no passengers.

I could have stopped but I did not. At this point I am exhausted and infuriated and don't think I could control myself. Instead I press the accelerator and speed forward. These roads are familiar to me. I have the advantage.

I am far ahead of him when I turn left past the post office and make my way over the rutted road to my safe house, not really mine but it feels a comfort.

Mother was in the yard waiting for me. She was pretending to care for the rhododendron bushes along the front of the house. She waved as I pulled my car off the county road onto our private road. I parked at the side of the house, slumped over my steering wheel in relief and breathlessly got out of the car. "You won't believe what is happening to me."

"Never mind," she says, "we have other matters to discuss. Let's go inside and have tea." She means iced tea which is fine with me in the heat. With those words, she successfully minimizes my problem. We have the tea and cool off. I offer suggestions to Mother about her shopping trip to Memphis which is what she has on her mind.

If I am a Flower of the South (and I am), Mother is a Flower of the Mountain. She is surrounded by men all of whom seem willing to serve her and overlook her personal foibles. Don't they see how self-involved she is? What amazes me is how G.W. adores her, no matter her selfishness.

I cannot but wonder how she will get along with Sam's wife. Sam and Cynthia have a place in Clayville so that Sam can be near the plant which he oversees. G.W. lucked out having a Georgia Tech Chemical Engineer in his family. The arrangement works for both Sam and G.W. I hope it works for Cynthia. Before long this business could be on Wall Street.

"Is Cynthia going with you to Memphis?"

"No. She's working. She's updating the books for the quarterly audit."

"I thought you weren't interested in the business. Surely G.W. can hire a firm to do the accounting." I am goading her, and I know it, and I should stop.

"He could. We don't talk about it, but Sam says Cynthia likes working."

"More than shopping." Stop it, Lucinda Lee. Let these two women be themselves.

"She is flying to Dallas with your brother next month."

"I get it. She's going to Neiman Marcus and you're shopping at Memphis department stores."

"Nothing wrong with Memphis department stores. I purchased my full-length mink from Goldsmiths." I am grateful I am not expected to compete.

"Yes, Mother and you look lovely in it," I give up and become a toady.

"Don't you think it is time you stopped working and got married?"

"I love my work."

Mother rises, patting my hair then running her fingers through it, gently but firmly pulling it off my face.

"You would look better if you combed your hair differently."

The conversation is over as far as I am concerned. It is always a tug of war, and Mother always wins. I should learn from her. She has less wisdom than Granny Alexander but is sharper and quicker in her remarks.

Tonight G.W. and I will sit on the porch and I will pour out my heart to him. I will look at that magnificent vast valley and with luck will drink something other than McKay Mash or iced tea.

****

The best adjective to describe G.W.'s reaction to my story is controlled. Sitting on the porch enjoying our whiskeys, we are calm and able to discuss Dr. Lucas and his threats to me as though I have related a fictional account concerning a character other than myself. Both of us are motivated to keep the mood light. G.W. doesn't want to upset me or see me in an upset state. I don't want to break down because I don't want to cause stress to G.W.

Ashamedly, for all my feminist faith, I feel a bubble of safety under G.W.'s protection. By the second whiskey, I am not concerned about anything. Life's problems are all resolvable.

Mother retired early. G.W. doesn't want to spend his relaxation time with me although he is too well-mannered to leave me alone on the porch. We say our good-nights and I go downstairs to the suite of rooms assigned to me. I promise G.W. I will not worry. I wonder where Dr. Lucas is. My rooms are on the ground floor of the house but around the back. I can't imagine Dr. Lucas would be fool enough to come onto G.W.'s property. There are no locks on the door from my sitting room to the back porch and patio. I close it and do what I have seen in the movies. I place a chair in front of the door. For extra protection, I put a handful of coins on the chair. If Dr. Lucas tries to open that door, the coins will fall to the floor and surely I would wake up. Too bad, G.W.'s guns are locked in a cabinet upstairs.

****

To my delight Chance Wardlaw joins us for breakfast. He is just as adorable as always. We linger over coffee to catch up on a few aspects of our lives. He is still working for G.W. and is continuing to have success at racing.

"I'm keeping you from working," I say as I spy G.W. in the kitchen doorway, giving Chance a gesture that I think means "stop talking and let's get to work."

As Chance rises from the table, he says "We'll have time to talk later. Want to join me in Clayville tomorrow for the last day of the Peach Festival?"

"My big chance for time with you? I wouldn't want to miss the Peach Festival. Seriously, I love peaches."

Chance glances at G.W. "Maybe G.W. will make peach ice cream tomorrow. He's got the best recipe."

"Why did I ever leave this heavenly place?" I never lived in Zona but no need to nitpick. We all know my life is in Chicago but why admit reality?

About the time the men leave, Mother joins me for coffee. She asks if I got to talk with Chance.

"He spent the night here last night, walked the grounds. I hope he is going home to sleep now."

"I had no idea. Does he do that often?"

"No, silly. G.W. seemed to think it was a good idea in case we had intruders last night. Did you bring some problem with you from Chicago?"

I didn't know whether to tell Mother or not but didn't have to make a decision.

"I really don't want to know if you did," Mother said.

****

The Peach Festival draws five or six thousand visitors over a weeklong celebration. Carousels, a Ferris wheel, twirling teacups, and other fairground rides, scheduled pie eating contests, a 5K run and plenty of food for sale, judged produce, and picnics attract locals and folks from all over the state including Chance and myself. Saturday's highlight is the crowning of Miss Peach, always a coveted title for eighteen to twenty-one regional beauties.

Chance and I walk around the exhibits. I buy peach preserves to take back to Chicago, and we shop for the freshest peaches we can find and buy a bushel for G.W.'s use in making ice cream. I am happy.

By late afternoon I need a break and excuse myself in search of a Porta-Potty. Disgusting as they are, I am grateful to find a free one behind the cotton-candy stand.

The fairgrounds are not that big. I agreed to rejoin Chance near the pageant stage. Walking slowly, enjoying the general atmosphere, I see the back of a man who looks like Dr. Lucas. I feel nauseated. The man, not a hundred feet from me, turns around. It is Dr. Lucas. The maniac. I quicken my pace although I am not sure I can go much faster without throwing up.

"What's wrong? Sit down. I'll get some water." I find this funny. We make water. No, that's not what I mean. We bottle water. We sell water.

"No. Don't leave me."

Chance fans me with a paper program for tonight's event. "Does this have anything to do with your stalker?"

"You know about him?" Of course G.W. has told Chance. That's why Chance was patrolling our grounds at night.

"G.W. is concerned about you. We are all concerned."

"He's here," I say. I place my hand on Chance's arm both to steady myself and to assure myself that he is at my side.

"Can you show me? Where did you see him?"

"I don't want to talk to him."

"We don't have to talk to him, but I would like to see him. Are you up for it?"

We walk toward the cotton candy stand. Beyond, exiting the public parking lot is the Chevy van, Dr. Lucas at the wheel.

"There," I point excitedly. "Do you see him?"

"Yes. Canadian license plates."

"That's him."

Problem Solved

Zona is in a dry county. Chance and I buy Grape Nehi and junk food, as though we were teen-agers. We cross the road from the general store-cum-cafe-cum-filling-station and walk a few yards to the side entrance of the garage.

The single grease-laden bay is occupied by an old Ford. We walk past Stoke who is sitting on his heels deep in conversation with the person underneath the truck. Stoke nods in recognition but does not allow our presence to interrupt the technical nature of their discussion.

The garage's substitute for an office is a counter laden with maps, calendars, automotive magazines, and stack upon stack of brochures and advertisements. Chance reaches into a drawer, sifts through loose jingly-sounding odds and ends and produces a key which he triumphantly waves in the air.

"Such talent," I gush. "You actually found a key among all this splendor." I make a broad gesture encompassing enough of the garage to support my sarcasm.

"Make fun of me at your own peril," he replies. "Follow me to paradise."

"You braggart." I love teasing him.

We walk to Wardlaw Tourist Cabin #8, strange because only three cabins are visible. Are five more hidden away?

Chance unlocks the cabin door. "I could answer that question you are dying to ask, but I think I'll keep you guessing."

"So now you are a mind-reader." I think maybe he is.

The cabin is a small motel-like room that honors the sign's promise of "kitchenette included." The rest of the set-up is the pretty standard woodsy outdated furniture you would expect. At least it is clean.

We stash our food and Nehi for later, sit on the side of the bed enjoying the moment. We are here for a reason. Rather quickly we are touching each other. I cannot keep my hands still. Chance puts one hand over mine and saying nothing, touches my face. It is a sweet gesture, full of warmth and caring. That's the kind of sex we are going to have, I think, and we begin undressing ourselves and each other. Chance kisses my neck, and we fall together onto the bed, bodies touching. I feel all of him. He doesn't notice my matching lingerie recently bought in Memphis. He doesn't notice my un-plucked eyebrows or the tummy I constantly try to suck in. He looks at my face. He feels with his hands and his body. None of me is untouched. I shudder when he places his hand just under my breasts, on my rib cage. I shudder again and again until that spectacular feeling of fullness and inevitability comes to me. He recognizes the physical need and moves both slowly and forcibly. I am gone and aware of him as a part of myself. I have moved beyond thought and hold onto him until we are both breathless.

"You've done this before," I say when finally I have the will to talk.

"There's a saying on the mountain: women are scarce and goats are scared." He laughs.

I am muddled and do not see the humor in this.

"Just laugh," he says. "Don't think too much."

I become docile and take instruction. In minutes we are both asleep under thin motel sheets and a pink chenille bedspread.

****

It is still daylight outside. I am on curfew again and have to be back at G.W. and Mother's house by 9 p.m. This is our agreed-upon arrangement. G.W. says he will assume the Canadian wild man has attacked me if I am not home at the strike of nine o'clock. I actually appreciate his concern.

"You don't have to worry about that curfew business," Chance informs me from the other side of the bed.

"Seriously? You're releasing me from my promise to G.W.?"

"Things have happened that you don't know about," he says.

"Is this something I want to hear?" I am an officer of the court, in Illinois.

"Are you going to turn me in? Or G.W.? Or Cyril? Or Stoke? What about your brother? Besides, we haven't done anything illegal."

"What have you done?" I am calm, curious. I desperately want to know what happened.

"On television, they talk about hypotheticals so what I'm going to tell you is what could happen or what might have happened. I'm making it up right?"

"Cut to the Chase, Chance!" I giggle but possibly because I know what is coming, and I am going to let Chance tell me even though I know it is going to be unethical at best, illegal at worst.

"The idiot was hanging out at the Dog House in Clayville, drinking and talking. He kept asking people in the bar if they knew you. He said you were hot stuff in Chicago. I'm not going to repeat what he said about you. I know it wasn't true."

"This is really making me angry. I had no personal relationship with him."

"Keep in mind, this was in the afternoon. At one point he went out to his van and Cyril watched him shoot up. We think he was doing meth. Hell, we know he was doing meth. That's when we decided to get him up here on the mountain."

"Does this have anything to do with Mother's insisting I drive with her to Memphis?" I'm starting to think there was method and planning kept secret from me.

"We didn't have an exact plan. Your brother wanted you in a safe place, and he didn't like the idea of your mother driving alone to Memphis. It just worked out that way."

The entire five days we were in Memphis, I had no clue. I forced myself to go, although I love Memphis, and I did get to see the Alexander cousins. Who doesn't love the Peabody Hotel? The ducks are especially cute; the service is what service should be. My thoughts stray.

Chance continues, "I made small talk with him, let him tell tales about you and convinced him that he would love McKay Mash and some time with the locals. I told him to follow me up to the garage and we would tune up his van and give him all the liquor he wanted. I didn't promise meth but I let him think it was part of the deal."

"And he drove up? Followed you, I guess."

"The long and short of it is that he got pretty drunk. We gave him the brew made with hog feed. That stuff is strong. It's like sliding down a razor blade into a bottle of rubbing alcohol. About midnight – it could have been later – we dared him to keep up with me driving down the mountain. He couldn't see straight but got behind the wheel of his ratty van and tried to follow my tail lights. No sober person would have taken me up on that dare."

"No lights on the mountain roads, right? And you drove fast, I'm guessing."

"At the heaven or hell sign, he made a choice."

"Has he been found?"

"Oh, yeah. Cyril's bunch is handling the investigation."

"I guess I know what that means."

Chance stood up and stretched.

"I'm going to take a shower. I'll get you back to G.W.'s before nine. He'll show you the newspaper write-up. The headline is something like 'Drugged and Drunk Canadian Man Drives Off Mountain'. Somewhere in the article it says that our county sheriff led the search for the body and is conducting a full investigation, yadda, yadda, yadda. You'll see in the story. No one suspects foul play. It was an act of pure stupidity by a crazy person. There's no one to blame except the man himself."

"It's over." I hardly believe it.

Preacher Wardlaw and Great-Grandfather Robert Tilson: We take care of our own.

Preacher Wardlaw: Dust to dust.

I decide I need a shower, too.

Business

G.W. passed a spiral notebook to me and identical notepads to Sam and Cynthia. Mother poured coffee. We are seated at a round, wooden table, cypress, I think, a wood that matches the kitchen cabinets. There is an abundance of cypress in these mountains, especially in the nearby national forest. While we have plenty of trees, there is also an abundance of quiet, stillness that belies the activity of wild turkey, deer, and boar. Even bears find a home in our mountains.

Around us are windows that frame the property at the back of the house. There is a long sweep of cleared ground and outbuildings for cows, goats and chickens. I suppose you could keep a horse or a mule out back in the barn which now houses G.W.'s tractor.

Beyond is a scene that draws my eye, mountain peaks and valleys and the grand blue clear sky. It is an effort to focus on the work at hand. I change seats with Cynthia so that I am not distracted.

We are doing a task unnatural to our setting. We are talking business. Not fishing, not hunting, not plowing, or roadwork but business of the commercial kind, a set of tasks, a new way of life especially for G.W. While Sam and I are educated professionals (I should include Cynthia in the list. Although she does not have advanced academic degrees, she is a legitimate certified accountant.), G.W. has a high school diploma, one for which he barely qualified. It embarrasses him. He overestimates the knowledge Sam and I possess.

"I called this meeting because as a family we need to address the growth of our business. It's time we organize and recognize we have potential to be a major player in the bottled water market. I'm no expert in these matters. You kids are better educated than I, but I have the drive and the persistence, and I own the water and the land it sits on. If we pool our efforts." he paused, grinning at the pun as if pleased with himself. "If we pool our efforts, we can become wealthy enough to ensure our independence for the rest of our lives."

He reached for his coffee cup as if surprised he had spoken so many words. "I think we should start where we are today. Cynthia has the financial reports."

Cynthia is always organized. She reached into her designer purse-cum-briefcase and produced packets of reports for each of us.

"If you want, I can bring everyone up to date on our current status. I've also prepared some projections." For the next hour, we review the figures, our production and distribution costs, our marketing fees and our incoming revenue. We have been in business for two years and are not yet in profit due to the cost of building the small bottling plant and the high cost of trucking the water from Low Glen down the mountain to Clayville. We've been funding all our costs with our own money but it is clear we cannot continue at a loss. Sam and Cynthia need salary, and G.W. and I would like a return on our investment. Yes, I have put a bit of money into the project.

Cynthia says she has projections but first we should hear from Sam concerning efficiencies in water delivery and bottling.

Sam explains to us that the cheapest way to produce our consumer product is to accomplish all tasks at source. We have some specific problems due to the location of the source, namely we sit atop a mountain with limited infrastructure. Sam is an engineer. He loves design and detail. He too has a briefcase with folders for each of us. We decide to review them during our break for lunch. I am grateful as I am hungry. Something about the mountain air affects me that way. In Chicago I usually eat at my desk, a take-out salad, a microwaved Lean Cuisine. Time is money in law firms. Only when I am entertaining a client over a meal do I really get to eat and then I am concerned about the business more than the food.

On the mountain I am ravenous at mealtimes. So far my clothes are still fitting me but I don't want to return to Chicago requiring alterations of my suits and looking fat.

Mother has set out cold ham, cole slaw, and tomatoes in the kitchen. In a galvanized tub on the front porch she has Zona water bottles on ice, and we help ourselves as we automatically remove ourselves from the interior of the house. We are drawn to the back porch where we can clear our minds of thought and enjoy the fresh air and the views.

Rocking back and forth in a big locally-made over-sized rocking chair on G.W. and Mother's back porch is one of the comforts of life. Add a sandwich, Zona water, family, and I am in hog heaven.

"Pretty good stuff, this spring water," I say to the others enjoying the view and the break from the same vantage as I.

"Someone ought to bottle it," Sam says, and we all laugh. "Who would have thought ten years ago that there would be a market for bottled water?"

"We've got the best in the world, right here," G.W. says and none of us disagree.

****

As we begin our afternoon session, I remind the family that I return to Chicago in a week. No one wants me to leave. I feel guilty but offer to do all that I can do locally during my remaining so-called holiday. No one mentions Dr. Lucas.

Sam has drawn up plans to pipe the water down the back of the mountain, directly into the bottling facility. Cynthia has worked out the cost savings as G.W. owns that property.

Property ownership fascinates me. The Tilson family bought up 160 acre lots in 1860, when the purchase was part of an Act of Congress that made provision for the sale of public lands. A couple of years later the Civil War swept down on the mountain and the Tilsons, who has not been interested in war, were more or less recruited by the Union Army. They left their wives and children to tend the land. Not all of the Tilsons returned to the mountain, Mother's great-great grandfather having fallen in battle. The ones who returned took up their plows and rebuilt their lives on their own land, as remote from the rest of the world as possible.

G.W.'s family, the McKays, and the Wardlaws fought for the Confederacy, having enlisted before the Union recruiters made it up to the heights of the Ozarks looking for cannon fodder. They came home to poverty, reunited with their families and plowed their land alongside the Tilsons. No one had any money until Prohibition when they had a desirable product. Armed with money, G.W.'s family bought up several plots of land, including one that had belonged to my great-grandparents. People on the mountain sell to other people on the mountain. Outsiders have never been welcome.

The land Sam talks about is one of those sections acquired by the McKays who saw the possibility of building a road up the back of the mountain. Either that was their dream, or they just wanted to be surrounded by impassable land.

Sam tells us that the projected path of the pipe he is recommending is currently strewn with rocks but its steep incline would allow gravity to do the job currently being done by trucks negotiating the trail never meant for heavy traffic or heavy loads. He envisions the pipe as a direct connector between the spring and the bottling plant.

In addition to drawing up the plans for the pipe, Sam has initiated chemical tests on our water and is assuring compliance with state and federal standards for clean water. Sam loves these details and explains everything to us using flowcharts and spreadsheets. If we fulfil our growth projections, we will need to hire a person to do our quality assurance and control. In the interim we will rely on Sam's knowledge of hydrology and his meticulous attention to standards and regulations.

Sam and Cynthia are a perfect match. Each, in his/her field is a perfectionist.

As interested as I am in the engineering and compliance side of business, I am equally interested in our financial health. We have personal relationships with two banks: the bank where we have the company account in Clayville and the Alexander Bank in Argenta. I agree to accompany G.W. to meetings at both banks to explore our credit opportunities. I also want to explore land deeds and water rights to ascertain our definitive ownership of all properties. I am keenly aware of the family lore about ownership, but nothing trumps the actual deeds and official records. In my way, I am as meticulous and Sam and Cynthia.

After a brief afternoon break (I think G.W. took a nap), we reconvene in the great room. I announce that I can contribute a six-figure sum to our venture but it is time for us to decide how we will divvy up ownership. Clearly we are a family enterprise, but we want to minimize the possibility of feuding in the future over profit and shares. We agree to revisit the incorporation documents which list G.W. and Mother as sole owners. I boldly ask for 25% of the business. G.W. wants 51%, controlling interest, asks if Sam and I will split the remaining 49%. In this family Cynthia's share is considered embedded in Sam's 24.5%. Cynthia does not voice a difference of opinion although we wait to allow her time to absorb what has been suggested. She does not speak up. We are therefore in agreement and toast with fresh spring water.

I now own 24.5% of Zona Water Company.

G.W. has an additional surprise. He announces that he is legitimizing a business that McKays and Wardlaws have been in for decades, at least for two generations. We can guess.

He and the Wardlaw boys have decided to turn their special recipe into a legal product. They have placed an order for barrels and have already expanded one of G.W.'s outbuildings into a warehouse. They consider themselves master producers, are tidying their distillery in order to pass requirements for state licensure. They've consulted an attorney in Clayville who helped them with the business papers and applications.

I am afraid G.W. will break out the mash which I cannot tolerate, but he seems to understand the difference between aged whiskey and McKay Mash and he serves us from his small supply of Maker's Mark.

I visited Maker's Mark distillery in Kentucky during one of my wilder college days when I had no money and could only take a break from studies and work when someone else was footing most of the bill. There was a boy (isn't there always a boy) with a VW van, and I took off with him for a week or ten days. We had a fabulous time. We also toured the Jim Beam distillery and tasted it as though it was a new experience.

Granny Alexander: Everything happens for a reason.

I can understand G.W.'s vision. He wants a boutique distillery. He wants to make the best whisky, not just a whisky.

"To G.W., the mega entrepreneur, to the Wardlaws and Alexanders, may our businesses thrive," says my brother.

"May America's thirst be quenched by Zona Water and McKay Whiskey," replies G.W.

G.W. and Mother's ancestor John Henry McKay: Put a lightning bolt on the label.

Where are the Wardlaws? We need them here to join the celebration.

Last Day in Zona

The sun hasn't risen yet when I awaken to the sound of a light rain tapping against the window. The room is cool and I wrap myself first in a long cotton robe, one I have borrowed from Mother, and when that is not enough to ward off the chill, I lift a colorful well-padded quilt from the bed. I slept under two quilts, both made by Aunt Lillian.

Mother and I plan to visit her later this morning and I will tell her how much I admire her work. I will call the quilt "art" and she will deny it. We have had this conversation before. She will say she makes quilts out of necessity, because it is cold on the mountain. Anyway, I fortify myself against the cold with the long robe and the quilt, and a pair of boot socks (another borrowed item), and climb the stairs to the main floor of the house. Mother is not yet up but by the look of the kitchen, G.W. has already had coffee and juice. He is probably feeding the animals.

I want something hot, make a quick cup of drip coffee and situate myself on the back porch. No morning chorus in the rain and no visible glorious sunrise, just crisp mountain air and the outline of the distant mountains welcome me to the day.

I have this lovely peace to myself for a time before I hear the opening of a door, and see Sam emerging from the house. He and Cynthia spent the night since we retired to bed late after catching up on the details of our lives.

Sam and Cynthia have "wants." They want a new house; they want a baby; they want the business to prosper; Cynthia wants to garden; Sam wants help with the administration of the company to free him to invent and innovate. I could listen to them all day. They are filled with hope and vitality. Beside them, I feel jaded, happy yet not as exuberant. Maybe I have just seen a sadder side of life.

"What is it like to live in Chicago?" Cynthia asks.

"Not much different than Memphis," I reply, "only bigger and faster. Chicago has incredible skyscrapers and fabulous shopping. You would love Marshall-Fields. You could spend days wandering around the store from department to department. Chicago has industrial history, ethnic neighborhoods. In the summer you can spend every weekend in a different neighborhood, eating different food, seeing people in ethnic outfits. They always have music and dancing. It is like travelling around the world and the entire time you are in Chicago."

"Sounds exciting. I'm glad you get out on the weekends. What about work, Sis? Are you still satisfied with McTavish?"

"I like my work. If we can ever make any money with Zona Water, I would like to strike out on my own. My dream is a practice focused on elder law. I have had enough of the real estate world. The people I have to deal with, the drive for a buck, the cut-throat competition. I can handle it but I would rather not. You might not believe it, but not everyone I work with likes me."

"Not possible, sis. What's not to like about you?"

"One attorney I encountered," I start but hesitate, "his client owned acreage in a prime spot, a piece of land one of our clients was desperate to own, overlooking the lake. That attorney became frustrated with something or other about my position. Maybe it was the offer we were making. He turned to me, in front of my client, and said, 'You think as slowly as you talk'." I pause for effect.

"Oh my God. What a jerk," this from Cynthia for whom the word 'jerk' is the worst epithet in her vocabulary. She is probably hearing her mother tell her to wash her mouth out.

"What did you say?" asks Sam of me.

"I burst out laughing. I believe my laughing surprised everyone. I can still see their faces."

Sam and Cynthia start smiling because I am smiling, broadly smiling with my mouth and my eyes and my entire face.

I say, "Don't you think that is the cleverest put-down ever? I thought it was brilliant. I could have replied, 'Does it matter when I am getting the better of you?' I'm such an ego-maniac, I know my thinking skills are well-developed. I'm confident. He was the one who was frustrated. I don't know. Humor is impossible to explain. I just found it hysterically funny."

"Did you complete the deal?" asked Sam.

"Yes. I'm a professional, right? Sometimes these negotiations remind me of child's play. 'Sticks and stones', remember?"

Changing the subject, Sam says, "I dream of teaching. I want to succeed in this phase of my career, and in the next phase become a professor, teach at Georgia Tech or U of A. That's my goal."

"I hope you can reach it," I respond. "These are good times, sitting on the porch sipping hot coffee, listening to the rain, and talking about our experiences and hopes. Let's remember this instead of the bad times, Brother."

"I don't know how you can be sentimental and hard-nosed all at once, Sis, but I guess you have been that way all your life, you slow-thinker, you."

"I'm going to regret telling you that story, aren't I?"

Cynthia goes inside and we follow. Rain or no, we have the day to live, tasks ahead of us. Cynthia and Sam are driving back down to Clayville. Sam will check on the springs on the way. Mother and I have our plans for the morning and I hope to have a little time with Chance. Tomorrow I travel to Little Rock where I will do research at the Land Office, then onto Argenta for two days with Granny Alexander. Chicago is at the end of this rainbow. By next Monday, I will be back in the office at McTavish and Willis.

The rain has stopped. The sky is the color of a poorly bleached old bed sheet.

G.W. asks me if I would like to accompany him to the distillery. I never saw the old still set up by G.W.'s grandfather back in the day when no one in these parts wanted to pay liquor taxes. The new operation is on the same site, larger now and legitimate.

The truck gets us part of the way. G.W. parks in a lean-to and we walk on a muddy trail, crossing over a rapidly moving stream to the newly-constructed corrugated aluminum building. It is an assault on the landscape.

Inside, the concrete slab is hard and unforgiving underfoot and the sound of water dropping onto the tin roof reminds me that this is a solid enterprise, one based on water. The thought occurs that both our businesses are grounded (funny word) on water, and I should be ecstatic that it rains. I will forever be grateful for rain. I will and should rejoice in rain. I do rejoice in rain. I should write a book entitled, *The Happiness of Rain* or maybe *The Joy of Rain,* like *The Joy of Cooking.*

I see Chance at the far end of the warehouse. He is inspecting barrels, not just standing beside a barrel giving it a momentary glance. No. He is on the floor, half inside the barrel.

"I give up, G.W. What is he doing?"

"He's smelling it. The aroma of the barrel will affect the taste of the whiskey. Does it pass the smell test, Chance?"

"I think we did okay with this lot. I'll test the others but this one has a rich nutty smell. I like it. Hello, gorgeous Lucinda Lee. Did you have a good night?" Chance gives me a classic aw-shucks grin. I have to remind myself that I am in this warehouse with my step-father and I have to "dance with the fellow who brought me" or something like that.

"You're a cutie, all right. I slept like I always sleep on the mountain, the sleep of the innocent. G.W. tells me you are now a bona fide business."

"There you go, using those Chicago legal words. We're making whiskey. That's the beginning and the end."

"The alpha and omega," I say as a knee-jerk reply.

"Whatever you say. What I know about is making whiskey."

"And smelling. You know about smelling."

"Big, darn deal. I can smell!"

G.W., quiet during this adolescent exchange meant to cover our secret past, says he will show me around, but there is not much more to see in this tin box of a warehouse. He leads me through a door at the far end, and we are in the actual distillery. G.W. explains the process to me, more the kind of information welcomed by Sam, the chemical engineer than by me, the Chicago lawyer.

"Wave good-bye to Chance," G.W. directs as though I am four years old, and we trudge through the undergrowth and soggy soil back to the truck and to home.

The entire outing has taken no more than forty-five minutes, important as I have promised to accompany Mother on a visit to Aunt Lillian.

****

"What were you thinking?" Mother says when she sees me looking bedraggled and damp. "Put on dry clothes, something pretty to cheer up Aunt Lillian." As an afterthought, Mother says "A little make-up would help you look less washed out."

"Yes, Mother." What am I, a child or an adult?

Granny Alexander: Blessed are the meek. Honor your parents.
Helen Reddy: I am woman, hear me roar.

****

Aunt Lillian is old. Can a person be both frail and strong at the same time? We sit in her small parlor, the same upright piano on the far wall, the same crochet doily on top draped just so. Framed photos adorn every surface of the room. The walls are bare except for a framed picture of Jesus, and two large oval-framed pictures of Aunt Lillian's mother and father. She invites us into the kitchen, the real center of her house. She has placed for my benefit her collection of family photos on the familiar wooden table. Some of the photos are in albums, others (Kodak 4 inch square black and white photos, very old sepia studio photos, some Polaroids) are in no order in empty Whitman's Chocolate boxes.

I love Aunt Lillian and her kitchen smelling of homemade bread, her weathered skin now cold to the touch, her white hair pulled back into a bun at the nape of her neck. She has removed her apron because our visit is a social call. She offers us fresh coffee, boiled on her wood-fueled kitchen stove. Refusal would be rude but drinking one cup of that coffee would give me jitters for the rest of the day. I accept but ask for her to make mine half milk, half coffee.

"I made this fresh-baked bread this morning just for you, Lucinda Lee. You always liked my bread. I guess you don't get any home-baked bread up there in Chicago." She pronounces it SHY, ka, go. "Help yourself to the plum preserves."

"Did you make these preserves?" I ask, meaning, did you can these yourself or "put them up" which is the correct local jargon. I already know that she did, but I want to tease her lovingly and emphasize her skill.

"Oh, yes. Do you think I would buy preserves?"

Spreading preserves on the thick slice of bread, biting into it and savoring the sweetness and the texture is one of life's pleasures. Like sitting on the back porch at G.W.'s and listening to the rain. I think my expression shows Aunt Lillian how happy I am when I am in her kitchen.

"You're still just as busy as ever then, haven't slowed down?" I ask, trying not to focus on her frailty or any necessity to slow down.

"I can't quilt anymore. I can't see the needle eye well enough to thread it and these old fingers are too stiff, but I guess I have made enough quilts in my time. I miss it mighty. My quilts have been good company to me."

We talk about quilts. Mother knows most of the patterns and recalls several that her mother and grandmother had made. Aunt Lillian has two quilts that she is giving me for my home in Chicago. She has already folded them, tied them with strips of fabric torn from an old sheet or similar worn-out piece of cloth.

"I'm proud to have these, Aunt Lillian," I say knowing it is a completely inadequate expression of my feelings. Her kindness almost overwhelms me and I have to hold back tears. "I will always look at these quilts and think of you." Aunt Lillian has no time for this kind of sentiment over quilts, and she reaches for a Whitman's Sampler box.

We spend an hour or so looking at photos and reminiscing about past years and identifying children, now adults and adults, some departed.

Uncle Jack is still outdoors, working when we leave. I regret not seeing him, but he is doing his life's work each day of his life. I understand he would not want to be a part of a "woman's circle."

Leaving Aunt Lillian saddens me, and I cannot hold back the tears. I am afraid I will never see her again. I cling to the quilts, pulling them to my heart.

****

Mother and I drive to the cafe for lunch, my treat. Even though we shared time together during our trip to Memphis, and I am staying in her house, we never seem to say anything of value to each other. Our relationship is built on appearance.

I ask, "What do you think about our business plans?"

"What do you mean?" she asks.

I realize Mother is not interested in our businesses. She has not asked me any questions about my life in Chicago nor has she spoken of Dr. Lucas. I struggle to find a topic.

"Are you happy, Mother?"

"Yes. Sometimes I think of your father. Not all of our life was bad."

This is not the topic I want to discuss.

"I am sure G.W. wants you to be happy. How do you pass the time of day?"

"I keep busy. You know I don't have easy access to shopping, but thank goodness we have a post office. I order whatever I want from catalogues. If I don't like what I buy, I send it back. All of G.W.'s clothes come from L.L. Bean and Sears."

"Sounds convenient."

"After you leave, I'm redecorating the downstairs bedrooms. I've seen several spread sets that I like. I was going to set up a canning kitchen in one of the out buildings, but G.W. is too occupied with his whiskey to help me. Maybe he will do it next year. This year I'm planning on helping Aunt Lillian with her canning."

"I loved seeing her. She never changes."

"She is older. You probably didn't notice. She wants me to take a few of her quilts down to Clayville to sell, but I'm going to buy them from her. She could use the money, and there is no market for quilts in Clayville. Oh, and I have decided to learn to play the piano."

"At Aunt Lillian's? On that old upright?"

"No, I'm buying a piano. First I have to find someone to teach me. I've always wanted to play piano." My mother always surprises me.

The waitress brings our cheque. I reach for it.

"Are you sure you have enough money?" Mother asks me as though I am a poor student. I do not bother to inform her that I am a successful attorney currently funding the Zona Water Works. She wouldn't care. She has her world. I find peace in the belief that she is happy, has interests, is loved, and seems to have good health.

****

Chance and I carve out two hours to escape to Cabin #8.

"Still no tourist renting #8? Must be off season." Teasing Chance is easy.

He is in a mood. "You're leaving tomorrow." It is a statement of fact. Our love-making is uncoordinated as though we are trying too hard to please each other, to give and to get every pleasure possible, as though our lives are compressed into this clock-controlled segment of time.

We do not linger in bed. We don't know whether we want more privacy or to escape the walls of #8.

"I have things to say to you, Chance." I realize he is running away, quickly dressing, handing clothes to me, urging me along.

"I don't want to have this conversation," he admits.

"You are not staying on the mountain, and I am not about to live in Chicago. That's a laugh. Me in Chicago. I don't even want to be a tourist in Chicago. I do not want to talk about it further."

"Okay, okay. Will you let me tell you how grateful I am for everything you have done for me?"

"No. Go home."

"Chicago? G.W.'s house?"

"Take your pick."

Letter from Sam

Dear Sis,

Picture the Zona Water bottle, now 80% plastic, on the bottom of the ocean floor. Beautiful fish float around the bottles that are there forever emitting toxins into the water. Eventually the once beautiful fish become sick, die. Some develop strange tumors or adaptations. In time the ocean floor is covered with plastic, once to a depth of a few inches, now increasing daily to mountainous stacks of unusable plastic.

This is what happens when plastic flourishes. We as human beings eventually annihilate our water supply.

During the period of our business development and growth, Zona Water has relied on bottles made utilizing state-of-the-art production techniques. In my judgment we have been diligent in consideration of material and manufacturing.

In America and other western and European countries, a concern about ecology and protecting the environment has led me to conclude our next focus needs to be research and development of a 100% recyclable, reusable and compostable bottle, one using and emitting no toxins. The exploration will begin with plant-based materials. Of particular interest is tree bark. Anticipation in the laboratory leads to an interdisciplinary approach with botany and the new specialty area of bio- or ecol-botany.

Let me know your thoughts about research in this area. I have a personal interest in that I care deeply about the future of this planet, for Janet and Sam, Jr. They will be around long after we are gone. Plus, I find it fun to learn in a new area, just as you do.

We have made a lot of money, Sis. Now maybe it is time we can make a real difference.

Love,
Bro[1]

[1] Letter was found folded inside one of Lucinda Lee's diaries. It is the author's opinion that this marked the beginning of the mega status of the company. The letter was dated 1979, no month or day.

Brotherly Wisdom

Thanks to Sam, and his laboratory, our big breakthrough came in 1982. Zona Spring Water in totally eco-friendly biodegradable bottles hit the market and made a splash for our company and thrilled environmentalists.

Shortly afterward we had the joy of ringing the opening bell on Wall Street. G.W. did not like New York but was on his best behavior on behalf of Zona Water. I can't say whether New York liked G.W. but I witnessed a great many handshakes and even one or two mentions of McKay Mash. I guess G.W. will be the talk of the town if we make enough money for these folks.

Sam brought his wife, Cynthia, and I showed up on my own, as usual. They left Sam, Jr. and little Janet at home but had lots of stories for me about their cute behavior. Cynthia is pregnant again but barely showing. I can't help comparing myself to her. I am thirty-seven years old, still single, and likely to stay that way. Chicago is filled with attractive men, mostly married or gay. The fact that I am a successful attorney, decent-looking (I work-out every morning, watch what I eat, get my hair done regularly), and by most standards am well-off, doesn't seem to matter. Could it be my personality?

We begged off social events in New York. Considering G.W.'s attitude to "market types" (as he called them), and considering my experience with the sneering man in the back row of the photo taken to memorialize our achievement, we thought it best to keep to ourselves for the afternoon and one night we were in the Big Apple. Moments before the photo was taken, the sneering man had told me he thought I was exotic (exotic!). Then he told me what he could do for me. If the camera had now been on me, I would have taken swift action against this forward, inappropriate, disgusting Lothario.

Granny Alexander: I think now is the time to tell you what happened during the Depression. My family and the Alexanders owned quite a bit of property from Argenta up toward Memphis. Taxes had to be paid or property was repossessed by the banks. But the banks had closed. All the debt was bought up by a Company, I'll just call it that, in New York City. We were able to pay our taxes. It just about killed your Great-Grandfather Alexander and my poor father couldn't afford to pay the hands, and had to do most of the work himself. We kept our land. The taxes were paid first, before food. Of course, we grew most of our own food so we were luckier than people in the cities. We paid our taxes and we kept our land, but we watched over and over again as our neighbors and friends couldn't pay their taxes. Their homes were sold on the courthouse steps, sold for taxes. Guess who bought those homes. That Company, those dirty, uncaring, thieves from New York City. Listen to me carefully. NEVER do business with that Company. NEVER.

I think G.W. would have been happy to leave New York as soon as the bell was rung and the photo taken but I did manage to persuade him to take a helicopter tour of the city that he enjoyed, and we had a great dinner at the hotel. I predict G.W. will consider this his one and only taste of New York.

Even though we are publicly traded now, the family still has control. For the sake of investment and the chance to grow, we share the board room with two major institutional investors. It doesn't really matter as Sam's patent has brought huge upside potential to our growth (the business people like this kind of talk). It is no longer solely about money for us. We are concerned more about maintaining quality and some semblance of freedom to make decisions in areas that affect our family's destiny. It is not always easy to explain our objectives to the people G.W. calls "market types." Actually, that's not correct. It is easy to explain. They just don't always choose to understand.

****

Returning to Chicago, Mr. McTavish summoned me into his inner sanctum.

"While you were in New York, we voted you in as a partner. Congratulations!"

I looked around his office. Little has changed in thirteen years. He sits behind the same grand desk. His Highland scenes still adorn the wall to my left. He still enjoys the magnificent view to my right: the lake, the skyscrapers, the movement of the traffic, commerce that built Chicago.

149

Mr. McTavish has not changed either, except for a few extra pounds around the middle that he tries to hide with exquisitely tailored suit jackets. Most important about him is the fact that he has survived. His persistence, his intelligence, his wary lack of trust in his own people, his courage, his very believability have contributed to his success and longevity in practice. Summing him up in one word would be simple: solid.

I hitched my wagon to his horse. Years ago he gave me a chance to forge a career. Under his protection, I have flourished and now he is offering me a partnership. The moment is sweet.

"We appreciate your work for our hospital clients and your expertise in all private real estate matters. No one knows better than I that you are capable and discrete. No doubt you hold secrets about several of us. The partners now have one thing to ask of you."

The speech was interrupted by his secretary who pushed a coffee cart into the room. She was smiling at me, the smile of one who knows today will be a celebration.

Upon hearing the click of the closed office door, Mr. McTavish continued, "The partners and I do not understand your withholding access to Zona Water, your very own family business. You sit on the board. You obviously own a sizeable portion of stock although you have kept details from us. I didn't even get notice of the IPO. This is disdain, undeserved disdain as we have treated you with respect. This firm has resources, international expertise that could benefit Zona Water yet our people have had no opportunity to present our case. Here's my offer. You join us. We join you."

"I don't speak for the Zona board."

Now I understood it, and it was as if that fabulously luminous brilliant blue sky turned nimbus black. Mr. McTavish had always said: Be clear and direct about your position. And he was following his own advice. In the process he was turning what should have been my joyous moment into his opportunity. He made clear what he wanted. Would he allow me to pursue my interests if Zona Water were not on the table? The idea was absurd. His condition was crystal clear.

I lost my naiveté years ago. I understand quid pro quo but this feels like a threat. I thought of the board: G.W., my mother (who dressed up for every board meeting and saw them as social events), Sam, Cynthia, and the two investment partners (one from the state's teachers' retirement fund, the other representing the state's largest independent bank). Chance Wardlaw sat in, even owned a small number of shares, but not enough to impact any voting. From the beginning G.W. had declared the company's allegiance to Arkansas. Where possible we have done all our business using local resources, even national distribution by truck and rail.

I wondered whether the board could continue with this provincial way of thinking especially in light of our desire to market globally and to strengthen our development of ecologically-sound bottle technology. In honesty, could Zona Water grow further without a major overhaul of structure? Did we need McTavish and Willis?

"Perhaps we do need a more sophisticated approach," I said. "You realize I can't accept your offer today because of the contingency. How much time is it on the table?"

"We would like some indication of openness immediately."

"I understand. I'll fly to Clayville in the morning."

****

Since the establishment of the company, I had flown back and forth many times from Chicago to Little Rock. Clayville's little airport, in existence only because farms in the area use crop dusters, cannot handle large airplanes or little jets. I fly to Little Rock, shuttle from Adams Field to Clayville in a private-hire helicopter. Usually Sam or Chance or Cynthia meets me in Clayville and we travel the few miles north and west to the bottling plant where we hold our meetings. This saves me the trip up the mountain and allows me to make the round-trip in a day, a long workday.

Many thoughts were going through my mind as I left Mr. McTavish's office. Superimposed was burgeoning anger. How dare they make my partnership conditional? I was prepared to buy-in, but this deal was more than a buy-in. I'm expected to deliver Zona Water to them as though it were prime rib, rolled out on a platter for the slicing. In this scenario was I the waiter or could I possibly be the prime rib? My anger was confusing me.

We do need to expand dramatically. Have we hit a plateau? Do we need different management to help us move to the next level? We have a viable business plan for the next five years, but are we too provincially-minded to fulfill our plan?

I thought of the differences between Chicago and Clayville: the major metropolis of over two million people with its fabulous John Hancock Center, the incredible Art Institute, the world-renowned symphony orchestra compared to the county seat of less than ten-thousand souls. The vast cultural and ethnic diversity of the powerhouse contrasted with the home of the annual Peach Festival. Yet, I came from Argenta, not much bigger than Clayville, and my mother's family have roots in the even more isolated mountain town of Zona. Maybe I have overreached myself. For the first time I wondered about the effect of an expanding Zona Water on the town nestled in the arms of the Ozark Mountains.

What of myself in this vast cosmos of law and business, family and friends? Can I continue to separate, to compartmentalize my lives in Chicago and Zona?

The questions were flooding my mind when I boarded the helicopter in Little Rock. I knew the pilot. He had flown me many times, this short hop from Little Rock to Clayville. He had a nice smile, a buzz cut, and a wedding ring. They all do, I thought, have wedding rings, that is. I closed my eyes and tried unsuccessfully to empty my mind.

I saw Sam's SUV on the side of the prefab building that served as control tower for Clayville and within minutes was sitting beside him as we traveled the short distance to the bottling plant.

I always reacted to the noise of the plant. "It's the sound of health," Sam yelled to me. "We reduced the noise significantly since we introduced the biodegradable bottle."

"I can tell," I yelled back, "Significant change."

****

Doors closed, sitting comfortably in the conference room, I placed my yellow lined notepad and pen on the table in front of me. I have made extensive notes in preparation for this meeting.

The first words out of my mouth are a realization: "I don't need these notes." I put the yellow lined notepad back in my briefcase.

"I want to present the offer made by my firm." I proceeded with an almost verbatim account of yesterday's meeting with Mr. McTavish and concluded with, "There it is, the reason I wanted this meeting. Am I to get my partnership? Are we interested in hiring McTavish and Willis?"

Silence followed. Sam finally spoke.

"Sis, with all respect, you know I admire you and love you and want the best for you, but you need time-out. You've lost perspective. We can't make a decision to hire a Chicago firm because your career depends on it. There are two issues here: first, your career goals, and second, Zona Water's business needs, two separate issues."

"I'm going back to work," G.W. said. "Sam, talk some sense into your sister."

For the next hour Sam and I worked our way through the sticky spider's web of my future. Afterward I saw more clearly my relationship with McTavish and Willis and knew what my answer would be regarding partnership.

Consolation

True to my word, I bought a condo following the business with Dr. Lucas. I explained to Mrs. Rosen my desire to extricate myself from bad and sad memories. David was not one for change (except where women were concerned), and I judged he would never be able to cope with the stress of moving all his books and belongings from one apartment to another. He would be a fixture in the building until the high rise crumbled. No threat that he would follow me to my new location. Even with Dr. Lucas out of the picture, I would encounter David and sometimes David plus his current love object, in the lobby. Finding another home was my only choice if I expected freedom from my past.

I thought initially that I would buy into an ultra-modern glass skyscraper being constructed by one of McTavish's clients. I had worked on the deal and knew the value, but when I began looking at older properties, I fell in love with a high-rise conversion near the University. The location suited me but it was the period detail that ultimately won me over. The developer had remodeled the kitchen and bathrooms but had had the good sense to leave the moldings and parquet floors. The first time I viewed the unit, I fell in love with the two bedrooms and two baths off the front hallway and the maid's room, bath and storage room off the kitchen. The large living room and dining room were ample, too fine for my post-university make-do furniture.

For six glorious months, on weekends, I frequented country auctions and antique shops. I began to feel better about my unsuccessful encounters with men as I lost myself in furnishing a new life.

I flew to London for a two-week holiday in May of that year and came home with Royal Worcester, service for twelve. Silly, but the shopping was fun, and I told myself I might entertain in the future. My married acquaintances had all registered for china and silver, actually filling their china cabinets with the help of their friends. Sam and Cynthia had enough Waterford and

154

Wedgwood to serve twelve. I reasoned: I should too. I overlooked the fact that I had to pay for my indulgences out of my own pocket.

With this new-found (newly-purchased) household, I decided I needed a maid to keep it in order. I began to ask around the building and received a reference for a woman who had done day-work for a family who were moving out. Maggie Deadman.

I interviewed Maggie, checked her references and hired her for three days a week to clean, iron, shop, and cook. I told her I didn't want someone who swept dust under the bed. I wanted a true cleaner and a self-starter because micromanaging was not my style. We agreed on wages, and I arranged to pay her Social Security as I explained to her the need to assure a future income. High-flyers often failed to pay Social Security for the help, unethical, uncaring and even illegal. I vow to behave properly and respectfully.

"You may not always be able to work. Who would support you?" I asked Maggie a few months into her employment.

"I have a son," she said. "He would look after his Mama."

****

Ellis, the garage man, told me that Maggie had a visitor while working in my apartment. Clearly Ellis disapproved. A retired Chicago policeman, Ellis kept a close eye on the comings and goings of residents and guests. I thought he was particularly watchful of me, and I felt safer because of it. When he called to my attention Maggie's having a guest in my apartment during her work hours, I took notice.

"Who? Who was her visitor?"

"He said he was her son. I think he is an ex-con. You should talk to Maggie."

"I will. Should I be afraid of him? Is he still upstairs?"

"No. He's left. I told him not to return unless you approved."

"Quite right, Ellis. I will talk to Maggie."

****

"He was in jail," Maggie said, "but he has done his time." Maggie and I sat at the kitchen table, and she defended her son. "He stopped by to pick up house keys. He didn't mean any harm."

"Why was he in jail? What is he doing now?" I have never gotten over the habit of asking more than one question at a time.

"He was in prison for possession of a little bit of drugs. He got in with the wrong people."

"Maggie, no one goes to prison for possession of a little bit of drugs."

"When they stopped him, he had drugs and an unlicensed gun in the glove compartment. I didn't raise him to have a gun and drugs."

"I'm sure you didn't. He's on parole now? What is he doing for work?"

"He's looking for work. He found Jesus inside, and he is preaching on the street. He would like to help young people stay off drugs."

"I would like to meet him. I might have something for him. Tell him to bring me the name of his parole officer. What's your son's name?"

"Darnell Deadman."

I wrote down, "Darn Deadman."

"No," Maggie reached for my writing hand correcting me, "Darnell Deadman."

****

Ellis wasn't easy to convince to hire Darnell Deadman to work for him, but when I offered to pay Darnell's salary for six months, it was an offer Ellis couldn't refuse. Our agreement was that Ellis would supervise and provide work in the garage (parking, washing and detailing cars, helping residents load and unload), but I would have use of Darnell's time for my personal and professional odd jobs. After six months we would reassess. If Darnell screwed up before the six months were up, he would be fired immediately.

On Darnell's first day in the garage, Maggie spent as much time in the office as Ellis. She said she wanted to be certain Darnell got off to a good start. Ellis complained about the infringement on his space and sent Maggie upstairs because she got in his way. He assured her he would keep a close eye on Darnell.

By Christmas, Ellis and Darnell had bonded. Maggie said the men occasionally had drinks together after work hours, and Darnell was trying to upgrade Ellis' clothing choices to a more "hip" style.

At my little Christmas gathering at home, catered by Maggie, I handed out gift cards to my three employee/friends. They gave me a glass bluebird that I placed on the kitchen windowsill where the light could shine through. We called it my bluebird of happiness.

Technically Ellis was not my employee but he clearly was part of my household. After a few cups of holiday spiked wassail, I told Ellis about my stalker experience.

"If anyone threatens you again, I'll know how to take care of him."

I believed him.

Lowlife

The man with the thin winter jacket sitting at the lunch counter stared at the newspaper open before him. He squinted as if to narrow his vision to a single line of print.

Chicago attorney Lucinda Lee Alexander will address the Illinois Bar at their monthly meeting. She will speak on changes in eldercare law.

"Lucinda Lee Alexander! How many Lucinda Lee Alexanders could there be?" His narrow lips slowly expanded into a broad smile revealing a silver capped eye tooth slightly longer than its partner.

"She'll be wealthy now with all that Zona Spring Water money, and she's a Chicago lawyer to boot. I think she'll be very happy to see me, maybe happy enough to share some of that fortune with me. Elder care, my foot, I'd say Roger care."

Roger Phillips did not finish reading the newspaper.

****

That was how it began, or how I imagined it began: with a seemingly simple man sitting at an ordinary lunch counter reading a notice in the newspaper.

****

I think twelve years is enough time to establish my legal credentials and to learn what I need to learn from McTavish and Willis. I hold no feelings of ill will toward them but they were greedy, wanting a piece of Zona Water as a prerequisite to my becoming a partner in their firm. Forget it, I said to them. I think it is unreasonable to form a relationship of fondness for your employer. At least that is what I have learned. I think the word to use is appreciation. I appreciated what I learned at McTavish and Willis. Now I am equipped to begin a new chapter of life.

The idea had been in my head for some time. When I presented it to my friend, Diana Reed, she was interested. She was my choice because first of all, we are friends and I think she would be easy to work with and secondly, she is a licensed, experienced social worker. We have had many discussions about our practices over the years.

We formed a partnership and opened for business under "Elder Law and Care Planning" in an architecturally-important turn-of-the-century high rise near the University Medical Center. We had exemplary experience between us and many community contacts. Additionally, we joined the Speaker's Bureau sponsored by the Chicago Geriatric Alliance and began a series of educational lectures to familiarize the community with each of us and our firm.

I would be lying if I said I didn't love the process of setting up and organizing our firm and protocols, not to mention the joy of working with the architect and decorators. We were successful from the start, and my days were filled with the satisfaction of meeting a need and doing it well. I had the professional collegiality with Diana whose ideas were usually right on target and confidence in my maid Maggie who competently took care of personal life, assuring that my home was in good order and that the refrigerator and cupboards were full.

The receptionist announced the arrival of a new client via telephone to my friend and now business partner, Diana Reed, LCSW. Diana emerged from her office, traversed the labyrinthine hallway toward the lobby. Introductions were cordial and brief, with the reassuring formality that communicates professionalism and capability to the client. In her office Diana asked the client's purpose for coming, then listened intently, her body language expressing total absorption in the client and his or her concerns. With an awareness of the client's needs, Diana provided information about the services offered by the firm covering a broad range including estate planning and asset management (overseen by the well-known – if I do say so myself – attorney in the field: Lucinda Lee Alexander), other legal services including medical directives and guardianship. Diana herself, in collaboration with the elderly person involved, and possible medical services, could provide counselling regarding retirement planning and care options and information about community benefits and services.

"We are a full-service firm. Currently our clients include an aging population and the adult baby-boomers who are interested in addressing their parent's needs." At this point, Diana introduced a packet of material for the client to take home, to peruse, and help in determining the next phase. "I will retain your intake form. If we haven't heard from you within two weeks, we will contact you regarding your desire to continue with our firm."

If no further issues were identified, Diana then rose, opened her office door and escorted the client back to the lobby where the client scheduled another appointment and was thanked for his patronage.

Diana and I developed this protocol after review of professional literature and consultations with a number of specialists in the field. Our firm was one of the first to utilize this interdisciplinary approach.

We benefitted greatly from demographics and the growth of the aging population. As Diana's husband told me, "You gals have hit on the right idea at the right time. Plenty of people in your Descendants' group have aging parents to think about. Word will spread quickly. Hell, we're aging, we're all aging."

I would be lying if I said I didn't love the process of setting up and organizing our firm and protocols, not to mention the joy of working with the architect and decorators. We were successful from the start, and my days were filled with the satisfaction of meeting a need and doing it well. I had the professional collegiality with Diana whose ideas were usually right on target and confidence in my maid Maggie who competently took care of personal life, assuring that my home was in good order and that the refrigerator and cupboards were full. It was Nirvana for me. Unlike my work hours at McTavish and Willis, now my schedule was reasonably under my own control.

I found myself free on weekends. I could enjoy an art exhibit on a Sunday afternoon without guilt. Occasionally when the Development Office of the Art Institute called me, I consented to sponsorship of an exhibit. It pleased me to support the museum while simultaneously enjoying elegant advertisement of the firm.

I suffered only when it snowed! A child of the Deep South, I never accustomed myself to snow and ice.

Except for occasional minor drama at the office – someone out sick and someone else complaining about extra work or dealing with a temperamental copy machine, my life was neat and tidy and peaceful. And then it wasn't. It was all at risk all to unravel.

****

"Where did this letter come from? Who delivered it? When?" I think of myself as composed and graceful under stress, but that aside, I became anxious, raised my voice and illogically fired more questions at the receptionist than she could be expected to remember much less actually answer. I muttered to myself, "I don't believe this is happening to me." Why not happen to me? I felt myself losing control. "Forgive me." I groveled to the receptionist. "If you would, give me about five minutes, then come into my office."

On my desk was the letter.

Dear Lucinda Lee Alexander,

Maybe you remember me from the time your daddy was in the Burn Unit. I remember you. I was his day nurse and saw his horrible suffering. He had moments of lucidity and could talk. You may be interested in the letter I've been holding all these years, sort of a keepsake, like an Ace I am playing now. Your name is in the letter. I feel sure you would like to see it. Meet me at 6:00 tonight at the Lunchroom Bar. You can buy me a bottle of Zona Spring Water! Yours truly, Roger Phillips.

The nerve of that man. After all these years, he is threatening me with a letter. What letter? Precisely, that is why he knows I will meet him. Should I go alone? Who would I take with me? Until I know what is in this letter – if he even has a letter that is authentic – I best see it for myself, alone. Deep breathing.

From the receptionist I learn it was delivered by a service, a youngish man in a uniform, the usual bicycle delivery. She received it within the last hour. I assure her I am past my "tizzy" and there is nothing for her to worry about.

I am worried, no, concerned. My schedule this afternoon shows two appointments. I refocus, as I am able to do, and push my personal agenda to a remote compartment in my brain. I am good at dealing with the issues at hand.

I decide to arrive late at the Lunchroom Bar. No need to appear anxious. Appearances belie emotion. Who said that? Probably that came from Granny Alexander. I believe in Granny Alexander, from whence cometh my strength.

Granny Alexander: I also said to be bold, stand up for yourself. Don't let anyone act like he has the better of you. I'm right behind you, or out in front, if you want.

I would love it if Granny Alexander were in front of me right now, if I could follow her into the room knowing she would cut this Roger Phillips down to size.

So-Called Letter from Home

I walk into the Lunchroom Bar located under the El. What a perfect place to meet, I say sarcastically to myself. At least, no one I know will be here. Two lone men are sitting at the bar. The room is dark but I detect a thin blond man rising from a table near the back. Light from the small lamp on the table catches something shiny on his face and for a brief moment I am blinded. The light fades, and I hear my name. Immediately I know this person summoning me is low class. No man of dignity or stature would greet me by calling out my name in a public place. This thought is foolish. Of course he is low class. The floor is sticky. I wish I wasn't wearing Ferragamo shoes.

I do not wait for an invitation to sit. This is not a genteel, social situation. Facing him, I see a reasonably attractive man with an incongruously honest, open face, blue eyes, hair short in back and long in front, sweeping over his face. My first association is cowboy, probably because he is wearing a plaid Western-cut shirt. I do not recognize him.

"You've aged," he says, his silver capped tooth identifying itself as the source of the earlier blinding flash of light.

"Maybe you have never seen me before," I replied.

"I've seen you all right. Your daddy was in a bad way. He screamed out in pain because of you. Oh, and he died."

"Say what you have to say and be done with it."

"Oh, yeah, I'm going to have my say but you're not going to be done with it."

"Who are you?"

"I was working as a nurse in the Burn Unit when your old pappy was admitted. Man, he was in bad shape." At this Roger Phillips shook his head as if in disbelief that a person could have terrible burns. He took a sip of his beer.

"Want one?" he asked Lucinda Lee in an odd gesture of conviviality.

"Get on with it, Mr. Phillips, if that is your name."

"Yeah, that's my name."

"Prove it."

"You're trying to catch me out, aren't you? Do you think I'm an ignorant hillbilly? Speaking of the Ozarks, how is your new family? That Zona Spring Water must be making a fortune."

"I don't know what I am doing here. Unless you have something to say to me, I am leaving."

"I wouldn't advise that. Before he met his maker, your daddy told me what happened that day, in Argenta, in his own back yard."

"Everyone knows what happened, Mr. Phillips. It is a matter of public record."

"Yeah, but some of us know more than others. Here's what I've got." He reached for his windbreaker draped over the back of his chair. I glimpsed the TRANSCO logo, familiar to me because Zona Water had contracts with TRANSCO. It was a large trucking company, headquartered in Chicago, a reliable outfit. At least, Zona Water never had any problems with them.

From an inside pocket Roger Phillips produced an envelope which he placed on the table. "Of course, this isn't the original. This copy is just for you so you know I mean business." He removed a paper from the envelope, unfolded it, and turned it to enable me to read the words typed on the sheet.

"Another beer for me" he called to the bartender. "Nothing for my friend."

It wasn't a letter. Before me was a declaration of sorts, brief and to the point.

My daughter, Lucinda Lee Alexander, threw a lit match on me, causing me to burn up. If I die, it is her fault.

The typed statement was dated; it was signed with a shaky *X*. Under the *X* were the words: *witnessed by* and the signature of Darlene Simmons, L.P.N.

"You can see why I knew you would be interested in this piece of paper. You're a murderer, aren't you, counselor?"

"You are a lowlife. There's no proof that this *X* was made by my father."

"It's got a witness."

"That is not proof. My father was under physical and emotional stress. Who knew what was going through his mind? He might have been hallucinating. He committed suicide. It's in the record."

"Maybe you could convince your friends, and your family, that you weren't the one who killed him, but would you like them to see this letter? Wouldn't it make them wonder, just a little bit, about what you might have done?"

"Slime. You're beneath my attention." I got up to leave, grabbing the so-called letter, stuffing it into my purse.

"Next time, I'll see you in your office, say in a week. Maybe you'll have a little, no, a big, gift for me. Green is my favorite color."

My Friend, Benke

Benke Dawson. I awoke after a pill-induced sleep, feeling sluggish but sure I had the beginnings of a plan. As I lay in bed under one of Aunt Lillian's quilts, I pictured Benke Dawson in my mind. Norwegian, but that didn't factor. A tough lawyer. She rarely represented the innocent, or so it appeared. Speaking of appearances, I wondered if she dyed her own hair – solidly red – or if somewhere in Chicago existed a hairdresser who could mix a color so unnatural. Nevertheless year after year when Benke Dawson appeared before the Law Board Ethics Committee, her hair color never changed. I suppose she will have that horrid color when she is eighty-years old.

I can count at least half-a-dozen times Benke has come before us following misconduct complaints. Although we've censured her, slapped her with fines, and reminded her repeatedly of standards, she has always prevailed and returned to her slimy practice.

She made a very fine speech before us on the committee a year or two ago. I remember her reminding us that the law is a set of guidelines not a rigid book of instructions, "guidelines," an interesting view of law, especially for those who do not want to be bound by definitive, rigid "thou-shalts" and "thou-shalt-not" rules.

There are clichés for my current circumstance. Get the right person for the job. You don't take a silk purse to a fight or maybe it is you don't take a cat to a dogfight, or something like that. I'll look it up later. I feel quite certain Benke is the right person for the job that needs doing. She'll be my dog in a dogfight.

****

"I am sure we are not here for a fashion show. Is this the way the Ethics Committee is now doing business – taking your subjects to lunch? I like this better than the last time we met. What's on your mind?" For two women who

166

came from such different backgrounds, different influences, different career specializations, we looked just like the suburban women in the tearoom, women who had dressed for lunch and who were bright and engaged in chatter, "ladies who lunch." We were all enjoying the tearoom atmosphere, the salad and fruit plates, the fizzy water and cucumber drinks.

"I need a lawyer, and you immediately came to mind." I tried to underplay the significance of my words, to sound casual, as though I frequently talked to my luncheon partner and as often asked for her help.

"I'm flattered." I think she was.

I showed her the statement supposedly signed by my father on his hospital deathbed.

"You want someone to handle this for you? Are you too genteel to solve this problem yourself?"

"My grandmother would say a genteel person does not have to proclaim gentility. I am what I am, Benke. I don't want Roger Phillips to squeeze me for money now or ever. I don't want this note made public. In short, I want this problem to go away, and I am of the opinion that you know more about handling this kind of business than I do."

"Tell me the entire story, or at least give me the highlights."

I did.

"He is not very good at blackmail. He is giving you time to develop a plan. He has given you the name of the witness, and you know where he works. Do you intend to pay him? Once you start, it will never end."

"No, I don't intend to pay. I don't want him to go public, but why would he? I want to discredit him."

"Discredit, one of your genteel words."

"I have means to locate the witness. I don't know exactly yet what I want you to do. You have a reliable investigator, right?"

"Absolutely."

"Do you have means to get information about Roger Phillips? Perhaps find out about his relationship to TRANSCO. As you can guess, in my practice, I don't have need of the kinds of services you use. I don't have the contacts."

"Cash, Lucinda Lee. Whatever this is, whatever it becomes, it will cost you. About my fee, you've got two options: pay me a large amount of money or pay me back with your support next time I come before the Ethics Committee. That's clear enough."

"You are lots of laughs. I choose option one. I'll pay you. I shouldn't say this to an attorney, especially not to an attorney like you, but cash money is not my problem." Did I just say "cash money?" What am I, a hillbilly? "When this business is over, we are over. Next time you come before the Committee, you cannot count on my support. Otherwise I trade one yoke for another."

"Deal. She wrote a figure on a napkin. This is for basic costs. Due today. Messenger it over. If Phillips shows up at your office, buy time, not with money. Give him a carton of Zona Spring Water." I think Benke thought she was funny. She added, "I don't know about you but I'm having dessert. We're on your dime."

Rescue Plans

Having clients' problems to focus on is a god-send. It is difficult to obsess on your own problems when you are immersed in the interests and concerns of others. I learned this lesson in childhood.

Spring weather in Chicago is unpredictable. It was cool and clear when I met Benke at the Women's Tearoom, but in my office after two appointments, I look out my eyebrow window and see that it is raining heavily. No more clients are scheduled for me today. I ask our receptionist to hold my calls, and I return to thoughts of my personal issue.

I have a plan. I am clearly a planning person. I reach for the telephone.

"Cyril, it's Lucinda Lee. How is the sheriff business? Are you keeping busy?"

After Cyril's post-election public victory party two Novembers ago, I joined the private celebration at the Zona garage. Everyone was there including the star of the show, Cyril. All the boys are married, even my favorite Chance and of course their wives were present as were Sam and Cynthia, Mother and G.W. (I seem to be the only single person in the world). We enjoyed McKay Mash as we told silly stories about Cyril's childhood. The bolder and braver among us drank the powerful white lightening as familiar to all present as co-cola and Nehi grape. After all it was the Wardlaws who sped that brew down the mountain and into the bellies of anyone with cash and a dry mouth. If the family had a motto it would be something like: Fastest men in the Ozarks. No, make that fastest men on wheels in the Ozarks. Not very catchy.

Cyril joked: "We Wardlaws are never on the right side of the law; we're usually out front."

"Yeah, out front of the revenuers," someone shouted.

"Is that why your campaign slogan was: Vote for Cyril Wardlaw, a true leader?" asked Stoke, bring down the house, or in our case, the garage, with laughter.

Good memories, I tell myself.

But today's telephone call to Cyril isn't about memories. It isn't even a social call.

"Are you keeping busy?" I asked trying to focus on Cyril and not myself. "Are you still a 'true leader'?" Answering my own question, "Of course you are."

"What's up, Lucinda Lee?" I guess Cyril can tell I am not myself. I am a foreign anxious, uneasy person, speaking from another world. In this partnership, Cyril is the steady one. "As far as I know your folks are doing okay. Your Mother's flying up to Chicago next weekend, right?"

"Yes, for a fund-raiser, but that's not what I'm calling about, not Mother, me."

"Spit it out. You can tell me anything."

"I'm being blackmailed. Me, the straight and narrow one."

"Anything can happen to anyone, Lucinda Lee. How can I help?"

I told him the entire story. Before I had asked him for specific help, he said, "You want me to check out Phillips and the witness." It was a statement, not a question. "I'm on it now. Why don't you come on down here? We'll take care of this problem."

"I can't keep running to Zona every time someone threatens me. Just do what you can. Unfortunately I don't have a lot of time."

"This Phillips was a nurse. Do you have any contacts in Little Rock to check out his licensure status? If he is on a registry, you might be able to find out where he is working, if he is working as a nurse."

"Great thinking. I might have a connection to that information."

"I'll try to find the witness. If she is in Arkansas, I'll find her. Give me 48 hours."

"Okay. Thanks, Cyril. Not a word to family, please. I'm sure Mother is looking forward to the gala. She's been to Dallas for a new dress. I don't want to spoil it for her."

"Agreed. Talk to you soon. Lucinda Lee, call me if you need me."

****

170

My weekend was miserable. Neither Benke nor Cyril reported progress. I initiated contact with my acquaintance at the Chicago Hospital Association. She gave me a name of her counterpart in Arkansas.

Tick tock, and I am anxious.

One finding: Roger Phillips has no criminal record.

****

The weekend was rainy. The wind swept through the city in waves. No one was on the streets. My mood was low mirroring the misery of the weather. I tried eating comfort foods but had little appetite. Sunday night, I was tucked into bed, alone as usual, quilts wrapped around me, watching *Mystery Theater* when the phone rang.

"I located our witness, Darlene Simmons. She still lives in Little Rock. I met with her this afternoon. Our county isn't that far from Pulaski County. I called Sheriff Smith, and he tagged along with me. Ms. Simmons lives on the north side of town with her daughter and grandchildren. She is retired from nursing; said she loved her work as a nurse but only worked about three years in the Burn Unit. She said it was a very stressful place to work."

"Did she remember my father or Roger Phillips?" It was all I could do to allow Cyril to tell the story in his own time. I bit my lower lip to remind myself not to interrupt.

"Yes, she remembers both. She said she never saw your father draw the X on the paper. She questions whether he could have held a pen. She said Phillips brought the paper into the nursing station and folded it so that she could not read the statement. Just the X was visible. He asked her to sign where he had written the word *Witness.* She said she signed without thinking about it until later when she got home and reviewed her day over a beer with her husband. Her husband is the one who questioned her signing a document when she had not seen the patient sign."

"But the reason she remembers is that some weeks later there was an incident involving Roger Phillips who was a staff nurse at the time. Ms. Simmons said Phillips clocked in as usual, as did she. While they were taking report, two security guards entered the nursing conference room and escorted Roger Phillips off the premises. Of course, this created a stir and a great deal of gossip about why this had happened."

"What did Ms. Simmons think happened?"

"The rumor was that he had made sexual advances to not one but several young women, relatives of patients. He would get information from the medical chart and show up at the homes of patients while they were in hospital. One woman filed a complaint with the hospital, and I guess the hospital didn't want the publicity of legal action. They simply had him removed from hospital premises."

"So, he is a sexual predator, scum. I couldn't find any conviction record though."

"I think his name was struck from the nursing registry. I didn't travel down that road but I can if you want."

"No. You've done enough. I think I have what I need to solve my problem."

"I don't doubt you have the ability to handle this creep. I'm sorry you have to deal with this kind of lowlife. Why don't you abandon Chicago and come live with us? You know we love you. No one here is going to blackmail you."

"Oh, Cyril. For a sheriff, you're a softie. I'll keep your suggestion in mind. Got to get clear of this mess first."

I missed the ending to the story on *Mystery Theater*, but armed with mud to sling at Roger Phillips, I slept more easily Sunday night.

****

Still raining on Monday. Everyone at the office had Monday morning blues. Diana came into work and told us all we should embrace our unhappiness. That's the kind of thing you would expect a social worker to say. I retreated to my office, not wanting to learn methods of embracing my mood.

I telephoned my Arkansas Hospital Association contact and received confidential data I should not ethically or legally have been given. Sometimes back channels work in my favor although I am boasting as underhanded tactics are not my norm, but needs must. Complaints against Roger Phillips were filed; he pleaded guilty to charges of gross violations of several regulations governing nursing practice. Consequently he lost his license to practice.

We ordered out for pizza. By the time the last of the pepperoni was downed, I was in a much-improved mood. I think the pizza helped all of us. It was probably Diana's idea.

In the afternoon I closed shop early and taxied over to Benke Dawson's office. Over a cup of too-strong coffee, I updated her with my newly-collected information.

"I have a few bits to add," she said. Her man had infiltrated (her word, not mine) the TRANSCO truck yard where he learned that Roger Phillips was not very popular, not "one of the guys." He was described as a "prima donna," a fellow who thought he was better than the other guys. No one liked him but he showed up, did his job. He usually ran short hauls in and around the city. No one knew where he lived or anything about his personal life.

"I think I have enough to work with." I was beginning to feel more confident about my advantage against Roger Phillips. "What are your thoughts about how I should handle matters when he shows up at my office."

This discussion concluded in about thirty minutes. The only place I wanted to be was home wrapped in a chenille robe with a glass of chilled Chardonnay and something dramatic on PBS.

Better Not to Ask

On Wednesday, I worked at home, giving Diana full run of our offices. Maggie quietly commenced with her tasks in the front of the apartment while I concentrated on files and documents in the room advertised as the maid's room but now converted into my study-cum-office. The room was located behind the kitchen and felt remote and removed from the rest of the condominium. Books lined one wall and a large recliner filled one corner. A two-drawer wooden file cabinet doubled as a lamp table beside the comfortable chair. I sat at the desk, positioned in front of the two large sash windows.

The risk of working at the desk was the distraction of the great beyond on the other side of the windows. It was tempting while working to put pen down, stand up to stretch, lean across the desk and look to life below on the busy street. Today I let myself be distracted. Although I legitimately have paperwork beckoning me, my real purpose today is a negative: to be somewhere other than my downtown office.

Maggie senses something is up. She can always read my moods. Ellis and Darnell are in the garage, but Darnell has checked on me every hour. That is not usual but is the mode of operation for today.

Mid-afternoon I receive the call from our receptionist. "He arrived, the man you told me about, the blond cowboy. He asked for you, said you would see him without an appointment."

"How did he react when you told him I wasn't in?"

"At first he seemed puzzled. I don't believe he is a quick thinker. He talked really slowly. Anyway I told him what you said, that he was expected at the office of Benke Dawson, and I gave him directions. I thought he was going to make a scene in the waiting area, but he didn't. He was actually kind of calm, like maybe he wasn't surprised. He's gone now."

"Did you telephone Ms. Dawson?"

"Yes, I let her know he had left our office."

"Super. You did great. You won't see him again."

"What is this about, Ms. Alexander, or shouldn't I ask?"

"The latter," I said.

I wanted a sip of victory Scotch but decided it was too early in the game to celebrate. I used the word "game." It was a game in the Sherlock Holmes's sense. It was not a game in the sense of play. I was in it for real. Would it turn out well for me? Would Benke be able to close the deal? I hoped so.

Maggie usually left around 4:30 p.m. I found her cleaning the guest bathroom, a room unused since the last time she had cleaned it.

"Take a break, Maggie," I said as she was scrubbing the counter top, her hands covered with rubber gloves, the smell of ammonia overwhelming the room. "You shouldn't be in there. You'll get sick or pass out from all that ammonia. Gloves off, please. Come join me for tea."

Maggie obeyed, followed me into the kitchen where I reached for the tea kettle. As deft as any football blocker, Maggie placed herself in front of the sink, grabbed the kettle from me and using hip motions redirected me to be seated at the kitchen table. I knew better than to argue with Maggie. I accept that she runs my household.

"Sit with me, Maggie," I cajoled, almost begged. I wanted her company. "Talk with me. How are your grandchildren?" Darnell, married or no, had two children he claimed were his, and Maggie loved them and loved talking about their adorable attempts at communication and their mischievousness.

Maggie refused to sit at table with me but she did prepare a cup of tea for herself which she drank standing up by the sink. She told me animated stories about the children. She managed to say a few kind words about Darnell who enjoyed his work in the garage, showed up on time, did what Ellis told him to do and stayed out of trouble. Thank you, Ms. Alexander.

I stopped her at the point of adoration of me. It made me uncomfortable and kept wide the barrier between us. But, of course, there was a barrier between us. I am aware that my ancestors are eager to intervene in this relationship by giving me advice and opinions from their experience, but I suppress it. I don't want to hear about slaves being called servants, or the importance of boundaries with the help. I love Maggie, and she is a wonderful human being who loves her family and has well-deserved pride in herself. So there, ancestors.

Just as Maggie was leaving, the telephone rang. I was expecting the call.

"Good news?" I asked hopefully.

"Maybe not. Phillips was here. I asked him to show me the original letter, as he calls it. Interestingly enough, he had it in his wallet. He was angry, wanted money, the usual blackmail routine, except I don't think he is very smart. He kept insisting he could ruin you and by the time he left, he was saying he could ruin me too."

"What did he say when you told him he didn't have a chance, that no one would ever take that statement seriously?"

"He was incredulous. He said if he waved the letter around your friends, it would embarrass you and maybe worse."

"He's right about that. You weren't afraid of him, were you?"

"Are you kidding? I've had worse ones in my office. Besides, I am never without protection. My man stood outside the door. One yelp from me, and he would have taken care of Phillips."

"It may come to that," I said under my breath. "Thanks, Benke. I know you will let me know if he returns to your office."

"I don't think he wants to see me again."

****

Door keys in hand, I pressed the elevator button for the garage. I rode down alone and was grateful for the moments of solitude.

"I may need your help, Ellis."

He was a boxy man, tall and wide, chocolate in color with gray hair cut in a fashion twenty-years out of style. He had the weathered look of a man who has seen too much tragedy. It might have been my imagination, but he seemed to twinkle when he saw me. An ex-cop who twinkles, I doubt it. Anyway, that was my perception.

He said we could talk in his office, a tiny hut near the garage entrance. He stepped aside to let me enter first. A desk, two chairs, two telephones, several security monitors and scores of keys filled the space.

Before I could say anything about how he needed a larger space, he offered, "I know what you're thinking. Darnell is skinnier than I am. He usually sits at the desk and watches the monitors, but sometimes I do the job. We make it work. How can I help you?"

I told Ellis the story of Roger Phillips. I told him everything: his losing his hospital job, his probable forging of the document that he claimed bore my father's *X*, where he worked in Chicago, the steps I was taking to try to get him out of my life.

"I'm not asking you to do anything, Ellis. I am just alerting you that I don't want access given to this person. If he rings my condo from the front door, obviously I won't let him in. Maybe he would try to come in through the garage."

"What's he look like?"

I gave a description to Ellis.

"Mother is arriving tomorrow, and I don't want any sign of this man to interfere with her having a good time."

"Yeah. Darnell is picking her up at the airport. I'll be here, keeping an eye out. Don't worry. It's easy to say, but try not to worry. I know a few men over at TRANSCO. They wouldn't like having a pedophile among them."

"I don't know that he is a pedophile."

"Sex maniac, predator, pedophile. Take your pick."

I decided the finer points of definition were not appropriate in our situation. For Ellis's kindness and support, I wanted to hug him, but that was out-of-bounds in our relationship. I endeavored to behave appropriately with Ellis to preserve the trust between us. We had an unspoken code incorporating respect, fondness and distance. I knew my place.

I had no appetite for dinner but heated a Lean Cuisine and tried to eat. About two forkfuls into the decadent lasagna, the in-house buzzer rang announcing a visitor at the front door. I pressed the video button and saw the face of my blackmailer. A rush of adrenaline enabled me to contact Ellis on the in-house telephone.

"He's at the front door." The response came not from Ellis but from Darnell. "I need to speak to Ellis," I said.

"Is the man who is bothering you at the front door?" this from Darnell.

"Yes."

"We'll take care of it. Don't worry, Ms. Alexander."

I never heard again from Roger Phillips. I haven't a clue what happened to him, but I know not to ask. Sometimes, problems take care of themselves. Tra la.

****

Mother arrived on Friday. She brought three suitcases for the long weekend and was excited about being able to dress up. Apparently in Zona, she doesn't have opportunity to wear her jewelry and furs very often. I do not have the heart to tell her that wearing fur coats is no longer the done thing.

We enjoyed a lovely charity gala and auction at the Art Institute. Zona Water was the corporate sponsor, the company represented by my mother who looked ten years younger than her years. As it turned out, many women wore fur coats. I guess the word hasn't yet reached its target.

Mother flirted with all the men who sat at our table, and two who were straight, responded. Who said: in order for a vacation to be memorable, there needs to be a little sex? I think for my mother the flirtation was enough, at least I hope that is the case.

Diana and her husband sat nearby; Diana elegant in Oscar de la Renta. I had a chance to tell her I would return to the office on Monday. We shared shop talk for a few minutes until we were pulled apart by my table partner, an erudite art critic who could read the history of the cosmos into any painting. I must admit art critics always sound intelligent and sophisticated even if I never follow their in-depth analyses. Maybe I should have studied more Greek mythology, more Bible, and more astronomy. I bid on and took home a cityscape of Chicago painted by a local artist. I had a sentimental connection because I could identify most of the historical buildings in the foreground. When my partner began interpreting the scene based on an obscure Bible passage from the Old Testament, I ordered champagne.

Reunion

Thirty years separate these unknown people from the young, troubled high school graduate whom I barely recognize as myself. Copies of our high school yearbook, bound in gold, are displayed on tables in the lobby of the Doubletree Hotel.

We cannot meet at our school because decay has set in, an environmental and social upheaval has changed the all-white proud bastion of football, white aligned teeth and Confederate flags into an all-black wasteland of poverty, broken window panes and overgrown lawns.

No one speaks of the efforts of today's students, of their challenges and triumphs. Over cocktails and canapés served poolside, still bouffant, back-combed women with blue eye shadow flutter eyelashes at well-groomed, girdled men who are laterally glancing at waitresses young enough to be their youngest daughters.

I feel quite alone.

I flip through pages of the yearbook looking for pictures of myself, hopeful that I can find an identity, can determine my place within this horde of people who seem so at ease with each other, so accepting of who they were and who they are now. They seem to know one another, to have intimate conversation even after all these years. Maybe I am wrong. Maybe it isn't conversation.

Where do I fit in this world?

I laugh at myself. Isn't this a cliché? Don't most people have difficulty "going home again?" Aren't there movies and books about people returning for reunions only to feel out of place in time and in space?

Ronnie is recognizable. He was a swimmer, a life guard with a Vee-shaped torso, his wide shoulders and narrow hips attractive as he confidently strolled around the pool at age eighteen. Not the brightest of students, he satisfied himself with academic performance at the low end of the high bar. Who is he now? He greets me, remembering my name. I was after all, at the high end of the high bar, memorable I think to those few who surrounded me in our academic achievement. Or maybe he remembers me because we danced well together. I like that memory and remembering the dress, seafoam green, strapless, although Mother insisted that ribbon straps be added.

"You were always one of the smart girls," he says. The tailored woman beside him has the same confident air that Ronnie had when he monitored pool behavior. She looks directly at me, pulling my eyes from Ronnie to her. I don't recognize her. She does not identify herself. They are warm and cool, a partnership, a joint presentation to the world.

"What are you doing now? You don't live here in Argenta." As an afterthought, he adds, "This is Karen, my wife." The barest of introductory information gives me little clue about where to take this conversation. I follow the least heady path, the path of every day, ordinary tittle tattle among people with superficial interests in each other.

"I went into law, live in Chicago. And you?"

"Ph.D. Education. Run the school board."

"Wow. Nice."

"Yeah. Who would have thought it?"

Karen continues to glare at me, daring me to withhold any meaningful memory of a past that did not include her.

"I hope you have found happiness," I say in benediction and turn toward a noise coming from the diving board end of the pool.

Charlie has entered the party, Charlie the football hero, the quarterback who led our team to State Championship. He has a healthy, fit look, clean shaven, hair cropped short, very short. His eyes are bright and alert as though he is scanning the field for a receiver. He is walking fast and a group forms around him, the mass moving as one. He is the magnet attracting the loose filings. I step back to allow the unit to pass. They do not and stop instead, a few feet from me. I watch a woman touch his arm. He pushes her away, a flash of anger lasers from his eyes. His movement is a definite aggressive physicality. Perhaps he learned that as a football player. Perhaps that was a defensive move or perhaps he is accustomed to ridding himself of adoring fans. I do not like the gesture and generalize to disappointment in our hero.

Great-Grandfather Tilson: Charlie got too big for his britches. Put him out on the mountain some night and see if he could find his way home. Striking a woman is against the way of the Lord. My wife was a quiet, God-fearing woman. I never would have shoved her and if anyone else had, I would have found my shotgun, that's for sure.

This night is not going well for me. I have no fans, no supporters, no one to push away or draw near. Who among us has not been in my position? Success in adult life counts for nothing. At a reunion we are all returned to our seventeen- or eighteen-year-old personas. We are once again a member of this or that clique, the smart girl, the football hero, the summer lifeguard. It is as if no time, no event has occurred between that time and this. We are who we were not who we have become. Rumor flies that the cheerleaders are meeting to practice. They will reprise their glory years for our entertainment before dinner. Does anyone find this sad?

I am not depressed but I could be. No one mentions the tragic death of my father. Too polite perhaps or maybe uninterested. Old news is old.

At breakfast I learn that one of my former classmates is now a sheriff in a nearby Mississippi county. Over coffee we have a decent chat about legalities in Chicago versus rural Mississippi, and I manage a few mutually-interesting comments about criminal life in Clayville. This is the more equalizing topic for us and we finish breakfast feeling we have made a reasonable connection after all these years, although we never were acquainted thirty years ago.

I am avoiding the bus tour of Argenta, do not want to remind myself of highlights and lowlights of the past. I relax in the quiet hotel, walk to the adjacent mall for lunch, book a manicure, take a nap and prepare for the evening banquet.

Music from the 1960s and 1970s screams from the ballroom as we who are almost at mid-life boogie into the balloon and crepe paper strewn room. I should have volunteered supplies of Zona Water to this event but came late to the party, truly was not involved in any planning. Even though Zona Water is one of the largest industries in the state, no one from my high school seems to notice that it is my family business. If they don't notice, I won't make a show of it.

I am transported to the turmoil, sex, political upheaval, hope and uncertainty of my adolescence and young adulthood. It is the music that engulfs me and brings it all back.

181

I fill my plate at the buffet and carry it to a table where one empty seat remains.

"May I join you?" I ask, noticing the sweet Nancy, Nancy Calkins, seated next to an older man, unknown to me.

"Please do. I've wanted to talk with you." She introduces me to her husband who is in "the cotton business (except she pronounces it bidness). She looks the same, short and round, round face, expressive round brown eyes, a round mouth smiling broadly. I think she is still wearing Estee Lauder Youth Dew. I used to think she bathed in it. Maybe she still does."

Always the perfect girl, sweet was the adjective, sweet and good, kind, the girl who always obeyed, always did the right thing, my high school friend Nancy.

"I'm sorry we haven't had more time to talk," I said to her, trying not to roar above the growing din in the room.

"Goodness but that is a large purse," she said unexpectedly, "Didn't you bring an evening bag?" Her ornate petite purse is placed on the table beside the selection of dinner forks.

"No. It doesn't matter," I said trying to hide my embarrassment at this fashion faux pas. I hang the purse by its straps on the back of my chair. All the angst of adolescence returns. In the background I hear "She's sixteen. She's beautiful and she's mine." Reality hits. This is ridiculous. Nancy with her perfect evening bag and round, well-fed face probably has a daughter who is sixteen. I am sitting here with the "wrong" purse, and I am feeling embarrassed.

Nancy doesn't seem to notice my discomfort. She chatters on, filling me in on thirty years, telling me about her first failed marriage, then her perfect second marriage, her perfect husband who loved her dearly, her beautiful home, lovely children, the country club, the charity work. She occasionally touches her left hand to her face in a gesture I recall from our ingénue days. Her rings sparkle.

I told her I was happy for her, that I always expected she would have a happy family life. I shared details of my life gloating a bit about the good life I led in Chicago. Reunions are not about focusing on failure. Nancy has never been to Chicago. They might go some day but for now they are very involved with their family, golf, football games, church and the like. When they travel, they usually go to Hilton Head or to the Gulf Coast, but I raise an interesting possibility.

"What possibly?" I ask.

"Travelling north," she says, and I catch the full meaning. I am some sort of reverse carpetbagger, a turncoat, guilty of something.

The eight of us at the table shared several bottles of wine, one of the men taking charge of the bottle openings and the pouring. I didn't count glassfuls but before coffee was served, Nancy returned her attention to me.

Grandfather McKay: Whisky is better. Wine is nothing more than grape juice. When I first started drinking, my choice was whisky. Times were hard during the Depression, and I drank whatever I could get my hands on. In the end I drank Everclear. Be careful or you'll end up like me.

"Do you remember that summer you stayed in Atlanta? I think it was after junior year. You were dating Jimmy Stafford. You said you were in love with him but you let him come back here alone for the summer and you stayed in Atlanta."

"Yes, I had forgotten about Jimmy, the only other person from our class who went to Emory. Where is he? Why isn't he here? I haven't seen him since University days."

"I slept with him that summer."

"My boyfriend?"

"You stayed in Atlanta. You let him return to Argenta."

"You slept with my boyfriend. When was that? Twenty-five years ago?"

"Yes."

"Why are you telling me now?"

"I just thought you would like to know."

Granny Alexander, what do you say to that? Why would the once-angelic (or so I thought) Nancy have sex with my boyfriend and tell me about it twenty-five years later? Enough of this. I don't want to continue this evening or this weekend. Over. My return to Argenta is over. The door is closed on the past. I am going to take my big purse and return to Chicago.

Granny Alexander: Nancy Calkins is jealous of you. She has been holding that anger against you, just waiting for an opportunity to fling it in your face.

Dear, I'm afraid your sweet Nancy isn't sweet, angelic, and kind. Take comfort in the fact of her feeling guilt these past twenty-five years. Close the door on these people. They add nothing to your life.

You should always pack an evening bag.

Grandmother Reenie McKay: You should have spilled wine on Nancy's evening bag.

Great-Grandmother Tilson: Turn the other cheek. Be thee forgiving.

Big Life Changes

On reflection, I think my decision is right. This morning I spoke with Diana and shared with her my determination to sell the legal side of the partnership. She has been my dearest friend, she and her husband my Chicago family. The business we developed together has thrived and without boasting I can say that we have made a profound difference in the lives of our clients through education, guidance and intervention. I am satisfied with this accomplishment and yearn for change, discovery, and adventure.

I am not bored; I am not burned out. What am I feeling? A sense of readiness for something new.

Enduring love has not found me. Putting life on hold is an option for the afraid and timid amongst us. Flower that I am, no one can call me timid.

Surely there is no cruelty in my decision. Diana is capable and while we have enjoyed collegiality, she has the ability to utilize her skills with other attorneys. I daresay she will teach them about elder law.

She asks if I have anyone in mind, anyone who is interested in buying out my part of the business. I do. I almost doubt if I should reveal the name for fear Diana will light up in joy. I do not want to believe she could be happier with another business partner but this is an immature thought. In sober moments I realize my future happiness will be lessened in knowledge that I have left problems behind. I want her to be happy.

"You do know what you are doing, where you are going, what is next for you?" asks Diana hurriedly and excitedly breaking all the rules about asking clear direct questions. We are sitting in our small conference room, just the two of us, sipping coffee. I recognize her concern for me, her lack of focus on the impact of my decision on her own future.

"Diana, think about yourself. I understand you are not ready to retire."

"Retire? Oh, my goodness, no. I love this work. I want to continue but with the right partner. You are turning my life upside-down, you know."

"I´m sorry for that but can promise you that we will have no end of candidates to buy me out."

"Brings me back to my questions. What are you going to do with yourself? Are you sure this isn't some mid-life, post-menopausal crisis?"

"Brace yourself. I'm going to sell everything and travel. I want to see the world, have new experiences. I'm single. I have plenty of money. I'm ready to write the last page of this chapter and move on to the next."

"You plan to travel alone?"

"I would rather have someone to travel with me, but I don't, so yes, I'll do it on my own."

"You will sell your apartment?"

"Yes, I have already had inquiries, but first I want to settle our business, find a good business partner who will carry on with our philosophy and goals."

"And suit me."

"Yes, and suit you."

"We won't have a problem. I have met several attorneys over the years who would love to buy you out, and of those individuals, there are a few that I would like to work with." Diana named two attorneys we both knew and respected. I began to feel jealous. I did not know there were other attorneys Diana would like to work with. The feeling passed when good sense overcame me and I pulled myself together to reply, "I´ll make some contacts, begin to spread the word. I'll telephone the two attorneys you mentioned. A plan?"

"Yes."

We discussed timing and after detailing current business matters needing attention and completion, we agreed on a target for my vacating premises (sounds harsh), pending satisfactory sale of my partnership.

"You know my husband and I will miss you terribly. I cannot accept that you will be out of our lives."

"I will be in Europe. It isn't the moon. You can visit me."

"Where?"

"To be announced."

****

Preparations for my leaving Chicago, leaving the United States for Europe have begun. Maggie and Ellis have boxed my china, silver and other keepsakes. I've sent these to Clayville. Sam and Cynthia have storage space in their basement. Eventually my precious Royal Worcester, Waterford and sterling will get passed along to their daughters.

Most difficult to part with is my prized collection of American pattern glass. After deliberation I ask Sam to set aside these boxes for my return from Europe. The glass will form the basis of a life, a new life after the upcoming European new life. It is my only thought of life after Europe, a thought not fully formed, a "just in case" or "in the event of" a return to the country of my birth.

Granny Alexander: I understand completely. Pattern glass goblets will form the basis of a new household should you return to the country of your birth. You can always decorate around pattern glass.

Grandmother Reenie McKay: One of my boys, your uncle, is buried in Europe. You could visit his grave. He married a crazy French woman. She might be dead too.

Great-Grandmother Mattie Bain: I always wanted to go to Little Rock, but my man and children kept me on the mountain. I guess I was happy enough. I didn't know no better.

I pack clothing for all seasons. Everything else is sold or given away or carried off to the rubbish bin.

I stand in the empty condo and feel the rush of emotional attachment. Happy memories reel through my mind. I refuse to remember sad times. Triumph is the proper emotion.

I came, I saw, I succeeded.

Ellis, Maggie and I have said our farewells. Ellis gave me a mass card. He explains that he has paid to have his priest include me in his prayers. I cried to think of his kindness, and his service. Maggie is not as sentimental. She shushes any attempts I make at expressing my feelings and insists "what is meant to be, will be."

The geriatric partnership is no longer in my name. Diana is undoubtedly coping well, as she does, enjoying the challenge of a new colleague. She has blessed my leaving, has wished me well knowing our friendship will survive separation. I recognize now that she was always the heart of our business. I was an adjunct, an important adjunct, a necessary adjunct, a legitimizer of the service provided by Diana.

I am emotional about leaving these people who have meant so much to me.

Good-byes have been said to the Descendants but my lifetime membership is paid. No chance of separation from my ancestry. The Art Institute staff has expressed their sorrow at my leaving. Some of those bright folk – I almost said, "young people" because they get younger every year – will actually miss my personal interest in the collection and new acquisitions. Others will miss my availability for exhibit sponsorship. They gifted me with a To Whom it may Concern letter of introduction that I can utilize to make my presence known to any museums around the world. It is a fine gift but of doubtful actual use to me. I cannot envision myself arriving at the Louvre entrance waving this letter and demanding special treatment.

I drive today to Clayville, a few more boxes in the car. My intention is to spend time with Sam, to check in on Mother and G.W., to leave my car with whoever wants it and to schedule flights to somewhere in Europe. First I have to develop an itinerary. A journey of a million miles begins with one step, and having an itinerary helps.

Diaries Five and Six
1995–2015
Retirement – Death

Good-Bye to All

Mother and G.W. seem to have no opinion about my trip to Italy. They are indifferent to me and my plans. Last night they threw a big party in honor of my visit, but the shindig was really an opportunity for everyone on the mountain to celebrate the twentieth birthday of our businesses: Zona Water and McKay Mash.

I am shocked at how old everyone appears. The Wardlaw boys are married and have children ranging from toddlers to adolescents. Sam and Cynthia's daughters are strikingly beautiful, and while they care little for formal education, they do seem interested in Zona Water. Odd, their interest in Zona Water. You would think they would want to spread their wings and explore the world. Here I am at fifty (egads), ready to explore. Maybe they will feel more adventurous when they are older.

The older daughter is working in the administrative office of Zona; I cannot understand what the younger daughter is doing. It has something to do with the Peach Festival, organizing entertainment and the like. My nephew is not able to join us. He is still in University. Sam tells me he hopes his son will eventually join Zona Water. Truth is, I am not that interested. If the children were in need of me, I would want to help them, but they are securely on their own paths as am I. My mind is wandering constantly to my own future.

If I stay here on the mountain or in Clayville, I fear I will begin to age, literally find myself getting older. I will become satisfied with life in a cocoon. I can see that Sam and Cynthia will never leave. They have everything they want within a few miles of their house. I tell myself: do what you need to do and get out. Don't be mesmerized and paralyzed by the love and beauty of this place. I am still in the game. I am still in the game.

****

I allay my anxieties by over-planning. I provide Sam with access to all my business affairs. I arrange my visa, sign up for Italian language classes in Florence, hire a Florentine lawyer to help secure the permesso di soggiorno necessary for long-term residence in Italy. I book flights, hotels and make lists of must-pack items. I kiss everyone good-bye, fearing silently I will never see G.W. again. He has aged more than anyone, proof that imbibing McKay Mash does not extend life. Oops, my logic is incorrect. Maybe McKay Mash has extended G.W.'s life. We will never know.

Great-Grandfather Alexander: You are wrong if you think whisky doesn't extend life. I drank a toddy every morning of my living days and survived until eighty-five years. I would have lived longer if Tiny Grant had not been speeding and had been more vigilant. Dang cars. Pardon my French.

****

If I ask myself why I left Chicago, why I am relocating to Italy, I would say I feel my legal work is complete. Unlike many people who retire to cast aside a life of drudge, boredom, and unhappiness, I was satisfied with my work, with the years of my career. I liked my business associates; my clients appreciated the service offered to them; I had the respect of my colleagues. My personal life in Chicago wasn't bad either. I had a lovely condo, the Descendants, the Art Institute, the occasional ballet, opera or symphony matinee. I had (and have) family in Zona and money is no problem. What wasn't to like about my life?

My answer is not an answer, it is more a call and response. The life I built for myself was good, well-organized for a full well-rounded existence. So why give it up? I asked myself this question many times during the past year, and I remind myself as many times of my reasoning.

Grandmother Reenie Tilson: If it ain't broke, don't fix it. You should leave well-enough alone. Life could be worse over there in Italy.

Motives are always complicated. I think my decision is an indication of readiness for new challenges. Maybe I want to start over for the fun of it. In Chicago, been there-done that. I want to surprise myself, to travel the Via

Appia, to become more worldly, more sophisticated, to be something other than the woman born in Argenta, Arkansas. If I start in Italy, who knows where I could end up?

Grandfather Tilson: We are alike. I retired at fifty, gave up work and took up alcohol.

Great-Grandfather McKay: I died in harness, plowing those familiar mountain fields. When I was a boy I worked alongside my grandfather clearing those same fields. It was back-breaking work, but I provided for my family. Dying in that field was like dying in my own bed. I don't understand retirement. I understand the "tired" part.

If I were honest with myself (and why not be honest in a diary?) I would admit I am going to Italy for sex and art, the light, the beautiful language, the food, the many layers of history and for sex. Proof that I am like everyone else, like the second sons and aristocratic wives seeking escape and "culture" through the Grand Tour, like E.M. Forster's repressed English women travelling to Italy only to be faced with moral questions about sexual choices, like the movie stars of the 1960s who drunkenly threw themselves off yachts into the bay of Portofino caring nothing for the ruined mink coat or the sunken Ferragamos.

I reach for my travel guide and vow to discover Italy first, myself second. If that adventure includes romance under the magnificent ceiling of the Sistine Chapel or on the vaporettos of Venice, all to the good.

Granny Alexander: Isn't Italy full of Catholics?

Memphis cousins: The Descendants will miss you. There is no club in Italy. Ladies do not travel alone.

****

I looked over my diary entry above and am embarrassed at my comments about sex. I wouldn't want anyone to think badly of me.

Granny Alexander: Never put anything in writing that you do not want the world to see.

Grandmother Reenie Tilson: If you always did what everyone wanted you to do, you would never have a life. There is nothing wrong with sex. I had twelve children. I can't count the number of men on two hands. Go on. Enjoy yourself. All this frettin' ain't good for a person.

This obsession about why I am leaving is self-absorbed, and I decide to focus on other matters. I walk the grounds with G.W. He tells me not to worry about Mother, that she is well looked after by family. He tells me not to worry about money, which I never do anyway. He tells me I always have a home to return to.

"I was in Italy during the war (World War II), around the Po Valley. Fighting was fierce. The Italy I saw and the Italy you see will be different. After the war I came home to Zona and I have never wanted for any other place to live. You can see for yourself how your mother and I have built a fine life here. You go on and do what you have to do to have peace in your life. Come see the plans for the new labels for the mash."

These may have been the most personal and revealing words G.W. ever spoke to me. I was very moved by his feeling free to speak like that to me. I would have liked hearing more about his experience in the war, but know it is better not to ask. He is such a kind man. Mother is a very fortunate woman.

With G.W. and Sam nearby, I will not worry about Mother. Sam, I will miss.

Habits Considered

I refused an offer of marriage in Italy out of habit. The fallback position of brushing teeth after meals, wearing matching panties and bras, reading before lights out provide no inspiration but comfort the soul in their regularity. Marriage of the minds, the ties that bind, the vow to love, honor, and obey interfere with singular inhabited life acted out daily, hourly, minutely in concert with no other mortal. I accuse myself of lacking a heart, of lacking courage, of swimming in shallow water. I taunt myself. Dive in. Risk it. Make a list.

Pros about Mario DeBenedetti
1. He is handsome and attentive.
2. Wants sex all the time.

194

3. Presents me with skimpy lingerie that he allows me to wear for about a minute.
4. He says my body is hot. (This ranks high since I am fifty years of age although I have not told him my true age.)
5. He owns and runs a business.
6. He is ten years younger than I am (if he is telling the truth about his age).
7. Mario worships me.
8. He speaks beautiful, mellifluous Italian.
9. He loves Italian pop music.

Cons about Mario DeBenedetti
1. When we are together, life is totally about him.
2. Sex all the time.
3. He insists I accompany and admire him at motorcycle rallies, car races, downhill skiing tournaments.
4. He has no interest in art, opera or cultural activities.
5. He lives with his parents.
6. Mario voted for Berlusconi (and bragged about it).
7. Yes, there are more. Items 1–6 just scratch the surface.

The bare-faced truth of it confronts me. How could I possibly marry a man who voted for Berlusconi? I am weary of sex on the kitchen table, in the bath tub, surprise sex while I am hanging damp laundry on the rooftop clothesline, sex on the motorcycle, sex in restaurant toilet rooms, roaming fingers on aisle four of the grocery store. No more. I have had enough.

At one time I longed to be an "S O," but not now. Significant other: yes. Sex object: no.

Grandfather Tilson: Where does he stand on the issue of whisky? My understanding is that those "Eyeties" like their wine, the kind with corks and fancy labels. Even in the old days my people (your people) were not Catholic. We wore Orange in Ireland and were proud of it, but you do what you want. Ask him if he ever drank Ripple.

Granny Alexander: We never talked about sex in our day. I will say this about your grandfather: he was considerate.

****

Alone I have reviewed my pro and con lists while sipping a cup of *caffe molto caldo*. It occurs to me that Italy is not a soft, voluptuous, curvy country. It is a boot, a vertical rectangular shape with a heel! Everywhere I see sexuality, men in red trousers announcing their attractiveness, women on *passeggiata* teasing all passersby with swaying hips and low-cut t-tops. Even the nuns in their long habits advertising their celibacy are reminding us of their views on sex.

Great-Grandfather Alexander: I don't think much of a man who wears red trousers. He sounds like a peacock to me. You can do better.

Mario sexts me. I respond using an Italian-English pocket dictionary to help me form reasonably-grammatical sentences. Some of the words we use are not in the dictionary.

****

It is time to leave this blissful, exhausting playpen, to tick this experience off the bucket list. I have gotten lost in the back streets of Venice, and I have been sexually sated in Florence. What more does life offer? At some point we all have to give up our toys.

Tempus Fugit

The brilliant sun is to my left, slightly behind my shoulder. Ahead, clear and seemingly close is the distinctive Gibraltar outline almost touching the Atlas Mountains across the Mediterranean in northern Africa.

The three women walking toward me look just like me, dressed in spandex pants, hoodies and trainers. We pass each other. They must be half my age, thirty, thirty-five. But then, I don´t look my age thanks to cosmetic surgery, semiannual botox, filler and inherited good skin.

Why am I thinking about Mr. Haley, my eighth-grade algebra teacher? The days, two days actually, are clear in my head. Twenty-eight of us, twelve- or thirteen-year-old adolescents, our minds on basketball, the opposite sex, best friends and the weekend, the one coming and the one just past. The bell rings and we are seated, quiet, watching Mr. Haley, an ancient white-haired man in grey baggy pants, strict, the father of one of our classmates. She is my chum and sits near me. I know her well and she tells me secrets about her father.

Mr. Haley walks to the chalkboard and writes in the upper left-hand corner, "Tempus Fugit." He turns to face us and proceeds with calling roll, simultaneously handing out yesterday´s tests, now graded. Mine is marked A+ because I completed the extra-credit question in addition to the ten proofs in the test.

After class I lingered.

"I´m going to show this to my father. He always expects me to get A´s."

"If you do, promise me, you will also show him papers marked lower, even ones you fail."

"I never fail." I was petulant, could not understand why Mr. Haley thought I might fail.

"For you, an A is failure."

Students for the next class were entering the room and Mr. Haley began shuffling his papers, clearly an indication that I should leave.

197

The next day in algebra class, I felt tension as Mr. Haley stood immobile in the center front of the room. All desks were occupied. He did not call roll but for a few minutes scanned the room, gazing sternly into the eyes of this or that student.

"Who knows what this means?" He pointed to the words Tempus Fugit, still on the chalkboard. No hands were raised.

"I understand that you do not know what these words mean, and not knowing something is acceptable, but I am very concerned that no one asked what it meant."

We students understood that we were being reprimanded and we began to slide low into our desks. One of the boys spoke out without being called on.

"What does it mean, Mr. Haley?"

"It is Latin for 'time flies'. You can think about what those words might mean to you but to be very clear, the lesson today is about curiosity. If you don't know something, speak up."

This triggered a discussion mostly among the boys. We "smart girls," the few of us in the class, said very little as was our habit when the boys were animated.

After class, Mr. Haley asked me if I showed the A+ test to my father. I told him I had. Emboldened by his interest, I asked him why anyone would want to raise a hand and say, "what is that?" Who would want anyone to see their ignorance? Wouldn't it be better to pretend to know or to pretend it didn't matter?

"Time flies. How else will you ever learn anything new if you don't first recognize your ignorance? Is your life meant to be spent pretending to be something you are not?"

Years later, I wrote the words "tempus fugit" at the end of an email to one of my nieces. She never asked about it.

Surprise in Firenze

Dear Diary. It seems strange to write those words. I have experienced ten divine years of married European life, a busy, all-encompassing life during which I became absorbed, enmeshed even, in relationship. I wanted to be part of something special, and I was. For ten years, I willingly, enthusiastically became one of a married couple.

I am old to be keeping a diary. In years past I decided to change the name to "journal," a more mature word for a more mature phase of my life. "When I was a child, I spoke as a child. Now I am an adult."

Old is the correct word. The life cycle is predictable. It is trite to say "I never thought I would be this old." Truly, aging was never an issue, until now.

As I sit in this overstuffed much-worn chair facing a window, shutters opened to our glorious garden, I think I have accomplished thus far in life everything I could have dreamed of when I was a child hiding in the closet.

Firenze, Florence, is my city, mine to share with millions of tourists each year, mine to share its fascinating history of despotism, fanaticism, creativity, and corruption. Did I mention beauty?

I haven't a clue about the origins of the garden, the identity of the genius who chose the trees and organized the geometry of the flower beds, but I know this building is fifteenth-century, at one time housing supplicants to the Medici family.

Aaron and I purchased this apartment not long after we married. He loved it. We loved it together, and now I am left to fill all the spaces he inhabited, left to sit at this widow admiring the garden and remembering.

The first time I visited Florence, I stayed in a hotel near the Piazza della Signoria, a perfect location close to the Uffizi Gallery, the Ponte Vecchio, the Duomo, and the other sites beloved by tourists. For three months, I immersed myself in the language, food, and culture, meeting a few people but focused more on the physical environment than the personal.

Other cities, other countries pulled me to their hearts: Athens, Paris, Rome, and twice I joined groups, one exploring the Netherlands and Brussels, another touring archeology sites in Turkey. Always Florence called me home.

Who knew I was a gypsy?

My solo life ended in Florence when the owner of my favorite hotel introduced me to his father. David and I were on first-name basis because of the many times I availed myself of his hospitality. On my installment some years back, David said he had invited his father to join us in a welcome-back celebration. I was apprehensive, tired from my journey, ready to settle into my room with a glass of wine and a good book, but David was persuasive.

"You will like my dad. I'm just suggesting a drink in our lounge. Mom died a year ago, and Dad thinks he needs to find another partner soon, before he gets too old!"

"I'm not in that market. I've never been married. I like men, David, but I am not looking for a husband."

"You don't have to marry him. Just have a glass of wine with him. What have you got to lose?"

"Okay, because the invitation comes from you. Tell me a little more about your dad."

"Mother said he was good-looking."

"Did he work? Where does he live? Does he have a sense of humor? You aren't Italian. Where did you come from? How did you end up in Florence?"

"Americans. You want to know everything. Dad is from London, moved here to expand his business back in the sixties. He lives up in Fiesole. My brother manages the business now. I have my hands full running this hotel."

"Is he my age?"

"You are definitely younger than him."

"You're scaring me."

"Have patience. Wait to pass judgment until you meet him. You will find him full of life."

"What is his name?"

"Aaron Greene."

"'E-r-i-n'? You're Irish?"

"No, 'A-a-r-o-n'. We're Jewish."

That conversation was the beginning of enormous changes in my life.

****

The first thing I noticed about Aaron was his snow-white hair both atop his head (where one would expect it to be, although many men of his age don't have so much) and covering his jawline. The second was his general suave, James Bond bearing evident in his clothing and his grace. Yes, I said "grace."

He talked for hours that first night. I didn't notice when David left us after minutes, I guess. In retrospect, I believe I knew immediately that I would marry Aaron. Strange, after living the single life for over fifty years (granted, some of them as a child), that I would know in that moment, that I acquiesced in my own mind, to a future with a man so unlike the men I had grown up with, studied with, worked with, dated, and rejected. Maybe Aaron reminded me of Dr. Weiss, David Weiss. I detected a similar sense of humor, the slightly goofy, slap-stick humor of jokes. But no, Aaron was his own man, unique.

Later in our relationship, Aaron said he was shocked when he met me, that David had not prepared him properly. He said he had no idea he was meeting a beautiful blonde. Aaron, not a man to express his emotions, admitted to being smitten at first sight of me. I loved hearing Aaron say these words. I am not, was not, a beauty, but maybe I was to Aaron.

The joy of romance with Aaron was interwoven with the joy of life in Firenze. We were never bored, never without options. We could fill our calendar with exploratory strolls, endless hours in museums, churches, and cafes.

Aaron introduced me to his fabric business. He stocked exquisite silks and woolens, the highest quality, so sensual that I wanted to uncoil the fabrics from the bolts and run my fingers over each one. I could envision the beautiful coats, dresses, suits that could be made from this or that gorgeous, desirable material. It was no wonder that Aaron's customers were the best-known designers in Italy.

Originally, Aaron ran his business out of London but as his clients increasingly came from France and Italy, he felt a move to Italy was justified. He explained the conflict involved in his decision. Should he move to Milan or to Florence?

"Boo hoo. What a crisis!" I had little sympathy for his dilemma.

"I decided on Florence because I fell in love with the city's history and art. Not everything about Florence is perfect, but the art makes up for the negatives."

As for me, I never cared about the sewage problems or the difficulties of modernizing buildings six centuries old. I cared for Aaron, a man who loved all things beautiful and sensual, and me.

****

We married six months after we met, a small ceremony in the Fiesole town hall. I wanted to carry magnolias or gardenias, but we got married so quickly that I didn't have time to organize flowers.

The first years of our life together were spent travelling. Once I calculated that we were in hotels or holiday apartments for twenty months of the first two years of our marriage.

It took us two years to find, purchase, renovate and furnish our apartment on the Pitti Palace side of the Arno. I was in decorator heaven, although we did experience the nightmares of dust and neighbors unhappy with our noisy workmen.

For five years Aaron and I lived together in our comfortable open-plan twenty-first century digs in fifteen-century skin.

Among the ironies of our simpatico relationship was Aaron's lack of family history. Always defining myself in the context of past generations, I struggled to accept Aaron as a "one-off." He knew next to nothing about his ancestry. His father died in the Second World War. His mother died in the Blitz. As far as he knew, his family had come from Eastern Europe.

"How can you live without knowing who you are?" I was dumbfounded, gob smacked that he was not bothered by his lack of knowledge. How could he exist without having the details of his ancestry?

"I am who I am. I am the man you married."

"But who are your people?"

"I imagine they left Eastern Europe during a program, and made their way to London."

"That's a start. I wonder where they lived in Eastern Europe. How did they travel across that distance, and when?"

"It isn't important. We'll never know. Shall we go out for dinner?" He always redirected the subject when I asked about his family. I still don't understand how a person can have confidence and strength without the back-up of family. Even now, an ex-pat all these years, I keep up with family. Even now, I hear the voices of those who came before me. Even now, I think that within me lie the vestiges of my ancestors. Literally, my DNA comes from all of those who came before me. That can be said of every living person, including Aaron.

****

Now that Aaron is no longer among us, I hear his voice more than any other. He tells me to relax, to enjoy the moment, to let go of the past and not to worry about the future. I hear him call me "Honeybunch," and my eyes fill with tears. He did so much for me.

January 1, 2015

This is the year I will celebrate my 70th birthday, though not until December. I have been a widow for two years, returned to the single state I existed in, survived in, thrived in for most of my life. Aaron was twenty years older than I. He told people he saw me in a baby carriage and told his companion, "I'm going to marry that baby someday."

Around me are widows trying to build new lives. I do not want to be yet another lonely widow isolated in a foreign country enjoying outings to the grocery store, hoping to encounter someone familiar who will say hello to me. Silly thought because the most common meeting place is the pharmacy.

I miss Aaron. I miss his consistency, his reliability, his total commitment to scheduled activity and organized existence. Mostly I miss his ability to respond to questions with assured exposition, even when he did not actually know the answers. He would have made an apt attorney, no, an even better politician. He was always sure of himself.

I am thinking about intimacy. I reread Erikson's stages of development, and I cannot find myself. Linking psychological growth to ages and to cultural activities strikes me as arrogant, spurious, and inelegant. For me, intimacy did not arrive in my life until I was in my fifties. Does that mean I was slow in my development? It did not seem like it at the time. Here I am at sixty-nine addressing isolation, again, as I had addressed it earlier, not so much in my professional life but when swimming up the waterfall of a single young adulthood.

I am nostalgic today, looking back at this moment thinking about what I have lived through: the trauma of childhood, the turmoil of the 1960s, Kennedy's assassination, segregation, the Voting Rights Act, the Equal Rights Amendment (when will it ever be ratified?), the Pill, the Beatles, Rolling Stones, Jim Morrison, Chuck Berry, Janis Joplin, Bob Dylan, Watergate, Viet Nam, even the Korean War in my time, marijuana and computers.

During my single days I accompanied a co-worker to her niece's home for Thanksgiving. Around the table were perhaps ten people connected only to the hostess, strangers to each other, I being the exception as I did not have a former relationship with the hostess, just an acquaintanceship with her aunt. The dinner was potluck, delicious as I recall. I don't recall what I brought, probably a bottle of Scotch. We ten people were mellowing over cocktails and appetizers, turkey and wine, sharing more information than necessary about ourselves but like travelers seated next to each other on an airplane, we were freed by the knowledge that we would never see one another again. After the main meal, dessert and coffee, we lingered at the table, sipping more alcohol, feeling the tryptophan kick in.

After the usual going around the table sharing what we were most thankful for, our hostess asked, "In your life, what has been the most significant invention?" Among the answers were the automobile, rocketry, I said television and one ancient man said, "the safety match." I wish for a do-over of that day. I still do not understand his response. Perhaps the man was a reincarnated version of himself or perhaps he grew up in a remote location which time forgot because the safety match was invented in the nineteenth century. Is it possible he was that old? I googled on "safety matches" and guess the old man was talking about matchbooks that contained both matches and striking surfaces, to him an invention that allowed him easy portability of fire. Funny how the mind goes back to childhood. I remember my brother Sam as a Boy Scout. Sam once told me, before one of his troop's camping trips, always to be prepared, the Scout's motto. Can't forget the safety matches.

If my grandmother were alive, I would ask her. Fire. Are we as a civilization still talking about access to fire?

Annually on New Year's Day, my favorite day, new beginnings and so forth, I invited friends to my home in Chicago for a southern meal. I had to serve late in the day in consideration of my guests' needs to recover from their New Year's Eve's celebrations. Always there were twelve guests, white linen napery, sterling silver, and Royal Worcester cobalt dinnerware. I could serve sixty for a stand-up party but only had seating for twelve at table. To make the table interesting I used my grandmother Alexander's collection of Waterford mixed in with my collection of everyday pattern glass goblets. Her Waterford was Comeragh (which to Grandmother's annoyance, my mother called Gomorrah), the 19th century goblets were variously Paneled Forget-Me-Knot,

Rose in Snow, Minerva, Moon and Stars and the beguiling Three Face. My rarest pieces were probably the early Flint glass, Bellflower, or the delightfully-named non-flint pictorial Westward Ho. If nothing else, these mementos of the past created a conversation topic at the table.

My loyal Maggie did most of the cooking. Her family had migrated from the South in the 1930s, tired, I suppose of lynchings and falling-down shacks hot in the summer and cold in the winter. It seemed to me they had not won much in this lottery of life as Maggie's son was in prison, and she was consigned to cleaning other people's homes, raising other people's babies, but with me, no babies, just an apartment to keep clean and a grateful employer to please. I paid her Social Security and gave her extra money at holidays, even paid her double on New Year's Day. She never turned me down, and I like to think we had a bond of affection one to the other.

We feasted always on spiked wassail and finger foods (spinach balls, cheese balls, always balls and dips), salads (over the years these changed as Maggie and I consulted *Bon Appetit* and *Southern Living* magazines), greens (usually cabbage for a prosperous year, green because American paper money is green), black-eyed peas (two recipes: one, with salt pork or hog jowl for flavoring, the other Tex-Mex), corn bread (never sweet) and crown pork roast or herbed pork loin. The dessert options always included the Alexander pecan pie, (done when a silver knife stabbed in its middle comes out clean), and a home-made (of course) cake. Each year I made the cake.

How did we keep our shapely figures? I eat very little these days and seem daily to expand around the middle. At times I think I look like Mother's mother, Grandmother Reenie, but she was taller than I. No, I think I have Granny Alexander's body, petite in stature with a bottom sliding down my upper thighs. Granny also had a tummy, but she hid it with pretty blouses, always floral. As I write this, I see her planting pansies in the wooden flower boxes running alongside the patch of land outside her kitchen window. If I believed in an afterlife, Granny would be in the garden or the kitchen eternally baking cakes or tending vegetables or planting dainty little flowers.

Bless Maggie, no longer with me, probably sending her last grandchild to university. May they rise ahead of the tide that lifts all boats. May they know who they are, what their ancestors have overcome. Now I have Maria, a woman with a different history and no appreciation of my culture. I embrace hers to avoid loneliness and to stimulate my brain still eager for education.

Aaron and I did not have food as part of our New Year's ritual. We did nothing on New Year's Eve except awaken to the sounds of fire crackers and what sounded like cannon fire. We did on New Year's Day always listen to the BBC's coverage of the Vienna Philharmonic Orchestra's concert. The overwhelming beauty of it always made me cry, a feast to every sense, and a reminder of days past, of the Chicago Symphony, the fine art museums and dance concerts. If only Aaron had been there with me to enjoy those gifts.

Not today, not any day now, but in the past around New Year's Day, I always reviewed my five-year financial plan, when I was single, that is. An attorney-friend of mine back in the day had shown me his spreadsheet method encouraging me to develop one for myself. It was good advice as I have become increasingly independent financially, never counting on the goodwill of others. Aaron and I never had joint finances and by the time we were married, I had sufficient funds to play a little, to enjoy freedom, to treat Aaron. Who am I kidding? I had a fortune in Zona money, managed, invested, and productive. It is another of my pretenses, that I enjoy financial freedom because I am oh so very careful.

I laid no claim to Aaron's accumulations nor he to mine. This year, I just look quickly over my little hedge fund, the money I manage myself, a hobby really. The rest of my (dare I admit it) wealth is remote, only seen in annual reports, moved around, grown, combined, split, packaged, taxed and touched by unfamiliar hands. I am well-fixed on my own. It is the only way I can cope with life, with pride at what I have done for myself. The entirety of my part of the Zona fortune will go to my nieces and my nephew. Money goes to money.

I dream of a Cartier tank watch and a pair of earrings I saw on the website, but where would I wear them? I remember asking Mother where she would wear her mink coat, and she said, "To take out the garbage."

I made a small list today of my year's goals. Writing them is a habit left over from earlier days when I wrote SMART goals (specific, measurable, attainable, realistic and time-based). I confess to this journal that I did not remember what SMART meant and had to turn to my computer for an answer. I have always been an organized person and find these little gimmicks, like setting goals, helpful. My goals now are not so structured. They are:

1. Eat more vegan meals.
2. Advance from regular exercise to a cardio fitness program.

3. Finish reading Montaigne's *Essays.*

4. Accept all luncheon invitations, even those from or including people I do not enjoy.

5. Drink more red wine. (It is healthy.)

6. Explore Mother's paternal genealogy; learn more about the clearances in Scotland.

7. Be more tolerant of fools. (This needs to be operationalized.)

8. Increase monetary gifts to Sam's children. They will be decision-makers for me in my old, old age.

I should add something about the new medicine I am being placed on to prevent sudden death from coronary disease, but it is too boring to talk about health and visits to specialists. In the waiting room of the Cardiology Clinic two days ago, I met a man who is about my age, an amateur historian especially interested in history of Scotland. He asks the usual question after we exchange pleasantries.

"Are you from the South in the States?"

"Yes," I reply thinking that will end our conversation.

"Where in the South? Perhaps near Virginia?"

"Yes, near Virginia. I am from Rock Hill, South Carolina."

"I knew it," he says triumphantly. "I've been there, in Hilton Head."

Why did I say Rock Hill? My family has not lived there since 1852.

To the Best of My Recollection

I have reinvented the truth so many times over the years that I now have difficulty recalling the truth. The secret to making reinventions believable is to vary as few of the details as possible from actual truth. A person can easily stumble if reconstruction is too large or too far-fetched or too remote from the actuality.

For example, the story I told an airport limousine driver was almost true. The journey took about an hour, and I knew I would never see the driver again. What did it matter, making up a story to pass the time? The opportunity was at hand, just two of us in the limo, no one to intervene, no one to remember the tale and remind me of it later.

"Limo drivers are usually men," I said to start us off, to establish rapport. "Do you find the job difficult, carrying luggage and dealing with strangers all the time?"

"I know how to work with people," she said. "I got this job on recommendation of my ex-husband."

"So you've been through the divorce wars." It was more a statement than a question.

"Yes, thankfully we had no children."

"Same for me. It was the loss of intimacy that I found difficult," I contributed.

"I don't miss working all day, then going home and working, like another job at home while the ex just curled up on the couch and snored."

"A common complaint," I said knowingly. "My divorce was horrible because I really loved my husband. It was very painful because he rejected me. He wanted out."

"He met someone else probably."

"Yes, but I was the detritus, the fall-out, the cast-aside adoring wife." This was perhaps a bit too strong. "I should have seen it coming."

We carried on expressing sympathy and understanding toward each other. I don't think I have had another trip to the airport so entertaining.

I was single at the time, never having been married, or divorced but I had had a loving relationship a few years earlier that had ended sadly for me. The issue was not another woman, at least not to my knowledge. I did miss the intimacy, and I did feel sympathy with the limo driver. I just failed to tell the truth. I blurred the edges to present myself in an understanding, empathetic manner. No one was harmed. What is the saying, no harm, no foul.

The biggest story I ever told concerned my father, my violent, abusive father's death. To begin, I do not think I am an evil person, and I do not believe one evil act defines a person. I was twenty-four years old at the time and had finished two years of law school. Since then my life has been successful. I have made a difference in the lives of others through my guardianship work. My trustworthiness has been recognized repeatedly as I handled multiple real estate transactions for my colleagues, often involving epic amounts of money. I am proud that I maintained a loving, respectful, satisfying marriage. But I do have moments of guilt, a visitation of primordial feelings of responsibility and survival.

Parent-child relationships are always complex and mine were not unique. It was not my fault that I was born into an abusive family, an alcoholic father who violently abused Mother and terrorized my brother and myself. Not my fault.

As I became aware of my circumstance, I could never satisfactorily answer the why question. Why was I born to this abuse? I have learned that abused children often blame themselves, ask what have I done to cause or deserve this abuse? Perhaps thanks to Grandmother Alexander who gave me a history to be proud of, or thanks to my childhood friends who had imperfect families, or thanks to my own brain and determination, I realized my father's abuse behavior was not the result of my existence, or my intervention. I could get myself, and my brother Sam, off the hook. At least intellectually I had a grasp of my lack of culpability. With Sam, it was never a question in my mind. He carried no responsibility for our father's unacceptable, cruel behavior.

With Mother, the explanation, the analysis has always been more complicated. At some point Mother and Dad had experienced an attraction to each other, although maybe I am wrong in this assumption. They married in haste, but it was wartime. If their circumstances had been different, if they had

had more time to consider needs and wants and habits and expectations, would they have come to a different conclusion? Would they have confronted each other with recognition that they were oil and water? I think time would not have helped them as in later life they showed no evidence of insight and motivation to adapt. Would my father have been abusive in any marriage or was his abusive nature ignited by my mother's breath? When I have obsessed about their relationship, I have found myself walking in mire, never able to get solid footing. I might as well have been trying to stroll in the Louisiana wetlands. Not possible as any fool knows.

Ultimately I conclude that it was the interaction between the two that was foul. Not A, not B, but AB, simple, two touching live wires creating a spark dangerous to anyone nearby.

That metaphor is ironic given my father's death by fire, a suicide according to record. There were three people present, two able to tell the story, now just one. I am the only one living, and my truth is memory clouded and revised by the hundreds of re-livings of that day.

The story I write now is that muddled truth. It is probably not the story I told back in 1969. In 1969 I was concerned about what other people would think about me if they knew the truth about my past. I was also concerned about legal liability although even today I hesitate to say that concern if no longer present in my thoughts.

To the core, I am a trained, experienced and accomplished attorney. I know the impact of a written confession. I write now the truth, again, I emphasize, my truth, because in the depth of my personality, of my soul as some would say, is a desire to be understood. Being liked is unimportant to me at this stage in my life. Sam always admired me, and Aaron loved and needed me. Others whose lives intersected with mine knew a portion of me, that portion which furthered our mutual paths.

To be understood, I have to place myself back in those days surrounding my father's death. I nod to my own subjectivity. I was there, in that moment and can relate to the before, during, and after of the event. This may seem an intellectual process, but it is not entirely that. When I place myself into that horror, I feel a sadness that encompasses me. It isn't overwhelming now that so many years have passed. It is more a sadness that Sam and I had to experience fear and trauma. Wasn't it unnecessary? Now I understand the admonitions about life being short, live it to the fullest. What is the need for creating pain in others? Would not it have been just as easy to approach life with the intent of bringing joy to others, particularly to family? I say this to my father.

"Dad, I feel pain and sadness because you did not know about the joy of life. You didn't understand that giving is receiving. Such a basic notion and somehow you missed out on the secret of life. This tiny omission in your understanding created anxiety, anger, and pain in all our lives. Today, I no longer care where this omission originated. I simply feel bereft that you had misery and created more misery."

I sense my father's response. He would not have listened. He would have walked away. It is irrelevant now, however, because I have said to him many times the things I felt, sometimes with understanding, sometimes with confusion. He never hears me, but it no longer matters.

Before. Second year in law school was filled with pressures posed by the material and the competition. The study group I joined was non-productive. One of the boys began sharing his paranoia about professors who were purposefully trying to fail him. At first we didn't get it, just thought he was over-the-top in his anxiety. Then he came to study group one night wearing a parka over his pajamas and showed up in Contracts class the next day in the same garb. He was "counselled out" (an act we each feared could happen to us) and quickly disappeared. That left five of us, myself and four boys, two of whom did not want to share notes. I was basically on my own except for one boy who proved to be a good partner. It was the two of us against the world. We shared notes, shared ideas, shared fears and almost shared more until I learned that his girlfriend "from home" was coming down for the weekend.

My grades were better than good. I attribute that success to my love of reading. I could read fast and remember almost verbatim what I had read. Thank you, public library of my youth.

I was living in the third-floor walkup, barely surviving as I had to count pennies, quarters, and the more elusive dollar bills that I had saved from my summer job. Hooray that I could type. I suppose a young woman today in my circumstance would have to know how to do everything I did on the typewriter, but now somehow on the computer. Or maybe Ph.D. dissertations are just compiled somehow by the candidate herself. I don't really know. Technology has passed me by. For me, using a typewriter, typing fast and accurately earned me a life.

No way could I hold down a job, even part-time during term, but I had stashed away what I had earned between first and second year.

In addition to this poverty and nose-to-the-grindstone school work, was the necessity of performance in class. My anxiety was always an issue, and during second year I began utilizing some techniques I read about in popular magazines and journals, like *Psychology Today* and *Scientific American.* The relaxation helped as did desensitization. Repeatedly I would imagine myself in the classroom, called on to recite case law or to make some argument for or against the motion. In the imagining I would feel the anxiety, then slowly breathe through it until eventually it would dissipate. By end of term, I had all but conquered my anxiety. Psychologists have undoubtedly developed other more advanced ways of helping people cope with anxiety, but the technique I used worked for me, and I am grateful that it did.

I had one rule about socializing. Accept all invitations that involve a meal. I did manage to date during the year but no one had time for heavy romance. Dating was either sport or brief release of tension. The same could be said for sex.

With all of these changes taking place in my life, the old life kept interfering. Maybe interfering is a harsh word when it is your mother calling. Call she did. Frequently. She would be in tears. Always she had a story of her own victimization. She telephoned late at night or early in the morning. She telephoned on weekdays and on weekends. She always said she wanted me to come home or she wished she could move away like I had done.

These calls were gut-wrenching. My role was to listen, which I did not want to do, did not want to have to do. I wanted to say, "These are not my problems. I cannot solve your problems." I did say, "Why don't you go up to Zona? Your cousins would take care of you." She said she couldn't live in the mountains. "Why don't you visit your mother in Illinois?" She said that Dad would follow her. I never had the answer.

During. Mother called and said Dad had locked her overnight in the gardener's shed in the back yard. She said he had unlocked it when it was time for her to prepare his breakfast. I told Mother to leave. She said she had no place to go. I asked her if she had any money. She said she had a few dollars in her purse, left over from grocery shopping. It was not enough for a motel.

I had an idea. We hung up. I telephoned Argenta Information, then called Mother back. I gave her the phone number for her local Women's Shelter and told her I would meet her there the next day (Saturday, luckily), that we would solve this problem. It occurs to me that had this trauma occurred today, Mother and I would have been in constant communication through our cell phones. Who today has heard of calling "Information?"

I spent every penny I had on an airplane ticket, made my way to Argenta, telephoned the shelter and learned its whereabouts.

Mother was in very bad shape. She had the look of non-stop grief, a combination of red and gray in her face. She kept saying she had to "get the car back" or Dad would find her and kill her or lock her up again.

"I'll drive you back. We will pack up some of your clothes, your jewelry and medicine. I'll take you either up to Zona or you can come to Chicago with me." I remember feeling at that moment that I had to take charge had to be forceful. If I had had the luxury of considered thought, I would not have offered her the possibility of staying with me in Chicago. But it wasn't about me at this point. It was about Mother.

I felt agitation, a battle in my body between wanting to run and wanting to fight. Thinking was the antidote, but thinking in the midst of battle or flight is difficult.

This crisis would happen again, if I didn't stop it. The crises had to stop, for my sanity and peace if for no other reason. But truly there was another reason. My Mother was being mistreated, mistreated with increasing ferocity. She seemed helpless to resolve the problem herself.

Mother accompanied me without a murmur of dissent. We were quite the pair, I desensitizing myself to the possibility of confronting a Kodiak bear with only my two hands, Mother without lipstick, her hair covered with a silk scarf. I remember she smelled of Chanel #5. Even in the worst of times, Mother attended to perfume. I smell Chanel #5 now, and I return to that moment when I stood up and we walked out of that shelter. Mother was slightly behind me, docile, a lamb following her shepherd.

I drove. "The Lord is my shepherd." No, I will not lie down to this pain. "We are marching to Pretoria." More like it. This is battle. This is confrontation. "I am woman."

We entered the house with no problem as Mother had her car and house keys on the same key ring. Breathing deeply, I scanned the living room, dining room, the public rooms as Granny Alexander called them. No Dad. Mother is behind me.

214

Noise from the back yard indicated Dad was mowing the lawn.

"Let's pack your things and leave," I instructed Mother, to no avail as she began walking toward the kitchen door that opened onto the back property. Not listening to my begging her to stop – she perhaps found some strength within herself to face her monster – she sped across the deck, circumnavigated the pool, narrowed the gap between herself and her husband and antagonizer of almost thirty years.

I ran toward the two of them. I don't remember what I was wearing, but I must have had on sandals as I can feel the cool blades of grass on my toes. I would not have been barefoot.

Dad switched off the mower and, facing Mother, began screaming at her, his face and demeanor livid with rage. Mother leaned down and picked up the closest weapon, a gasoline can. She threw it at Dad, then froze in position, shocked at what she had done. I see her now, standing there, her body rigid, her eyes wide, her face emanating surprise. When the gas can hit the ground next to Dad, the top must have come off. Gasoline spilled on his trousers and up his leg, and all over the hot, running lawn mower, the spark plug doused too.

I reached into my purse and pulled out a book of matches. Always be prepared, right, Sam? But my matches did not create the flames. I have to live with the fact that I was tempted, but I did not do the awful deed. If I had struck the match and thrown it toward the gasoline, I don't think I could admit that to myself. I conclude that I did not do the act that changed our family forever. A simple flick of the wrist, an underhand toss, a step backward, those are the behaviors I recall, but I do not feel the match, I do not recall seeing the flame as it traversed the air between us.

I remember the orange, yellow flames, flames all over the lawn mower and the nearby lawn, flames encompassing our abuser. I don't remember placing the book of matches back in my purse. I never thought of them again. I do not know if I threw them on the fire or placed them back in my purse.

Dad had fallen to the ground and was violently struggling to put out the flames. By now he was engulfed. Transfixed and frozen in place, Mother looked at her tormentor and said, "You've killed yourself, you old dog." I reached for her, feeling the heat of the fire, and pulled her away from her the flames.

I desperately looked about for something to knock down the fire. Time was of the essence. I didn't want my father to suffer – in spite of the pain and anguish he had caused us.

"I'm calling 911," I shouted, to whom and why, I am not sure, most likely to myself, to bring me back to some state of reality.

Mother freed herself from my grasp, ran to the gardener's shed calling out, "I put a quilt in here, in case he locked me up again."

Killed himself, Mother had said. Yes, I saw the truth. I told the police the details of the horrid event, how it had happened. Just as Mother had said, he killed himself. He and his alcohol had been doing that for as long as I could remember.

He was no longer my father. He no longer existed for me. A real father never existed for me. I respect the memory of a man who provided food and shelter for Sam and me and who, on his better days, taught us the values of independence and self-reliance. I try not to think of all the values he did not teach us, that we had to struggle to learn on our own.

Occasionally something in my life triggers a memory of that day, and I wonder what I could have done in those moments to improve the situation, to prevent the horror. When I have talked with Sam about that day, he says I should focus on the fact that Mother was not harmed, that my holding her and pulling her away may have saved her life. Sam is good that way. He sees the good in the midst of such evil.

After. These details are less sharp in my mind: Mother gently handing a quilt to me, our frantic attempts at quelling the flames, Mother sinking to the ground, my telling her not to move while I ran to the neighbors. Every action is vivid yet seeming not to be happening. I can see the police, the firemen, the ambulance, sitting with Mother in the hospital waiting room, Sam trying to console us.

That is how I remember it. In rapid-fire shots, each a blurred explosion.

Diana, you are reading this. I have asked my nieces to give these books to you after I die. You ask, why didn't I tell the truth earlier in my diary? Why in all of those years of our friendship didn't I tell you the truth? The answer for me is simple. I didn't want to present myself to the world as "the abused girl." I never wanted to be defined by the abuse of my childhood. I didn't want to place myself in a position where I would have to explain that my own behavior or attitudes in any given situation were not the result of the childhood abuse that I endured. "Oh, yes, you probably feel that way because you were abused." "No," I would have to reply, "my decision to end this relationship has more to do with your behavior than with my past."

I don't feel guilt. I feel satisfied with most of my life, satisfied that I made the most of what presented itself to me. I am satisfied that I did everything I could to protect my mother, and that I loved my brother. I am satisfied that eventually I learned the lessons of love and relationship, that I had so many wonderful people in my life.

Granny Alexander: I don't forgive you. You were raised well and should have honored your father. You should have done more to save him.

Granny, I do not hear you. Your voice is weak. You have left my head. A flower, that is what I am. A Flower of the South is able to do the right thing at the right time. She maintains a sense of calm and control on the outside, no matter how she feels on the inside, and looks stylish and smiles sweetly while she is going through this charade. A flower knows that she lives in a complex world where love exists, where violence and pain are possible, and where her life and the well-being of others can depend on her strength. I may appear fragile, and I may want to lean, but I am bold and unstoppable.

I am not responsible for the life or the death of my father. I cannot honor a person who caused such misery in others. Does that make me a bad person?

I was harassed and stalked by a crazy person. With intent, I told my friends. The stalker disappeared.

Does that make me a bad person?

A blackmailer entered my life. I hired good people who "resolved" the problem.

Does that make me a bad person?

I was brave. I was bold. I helped some people; I did not harm others where there was opportunity. I tried to make sense of life. I loved, and I was loved.

Since I am summing up my life, I am thinking about the influences of the ancestors. They forced me to look backward, but it is my belief that I created my own life, separate from them. My goodness or compassion, or fears, or capabilities were my own. Yes, I listened to their voices, and I considered their points of view, but ultimately I was my own person. I am my own person, good but imperfect.